THE
Game
CHANGER

Katy ♡ xoxo
Archer

KATY ARCHER

ISBN: 978-1-991138-14-9 (Kindle eBook)
ISBN: 978-1-991138-17-0 (paperback)

Archer Street Romance
www.katyarcher.com

CHAPTER 1
CAROLINE

Six weeks ago...

"Stop playing with your hair. It makes you look like you're five years old and walking into your first day of kinder-garten." Leilani gives me a side-eye while taking a delicate sip from her Solo cup.

I scrunch my face at her, then force my fingers to thread together so I'm not tempted to wrap another curl around my pointer finger.

She's right. Playing with my hair makes me look nervous.

Which is exactly what I am, because holy shit, Casey Pierce just walked into this sorority party, and I've never been this close to him before. I didn't even know Nolan U Cougars came to these types of things!

Or maybe I did, because I squished my body into this blue dress that feels more like cling wrap than fabric.

I adjust my boobs and get a quick hand slap from Leilani, who sighs and swivels to block my view of the sexiest man on Earth.

"Okay, stop. You need to take a breath." Her big brown eyes are stern but can't hide that underlying kindness that makes up the vast majority of Leilani Iona's heart.

When I first met my roommate, I was worried that her pristine side of our dorm room and her overly formal handshake greeting were bad omens that spelled out four painful years of college dorm life with an uptight control freak.

But it only took a dinner, a breakfast, one instance of me getting completely lost, and the whole "red-pants, unexpected period" situation for me to realize that Lani's insides are made of cotton candy, rainbows, and mama bear instincts that rival Molly Weasley's. All that stuff is just hidden beneath a well-manicured, perfectly constructed, take-no-shit exterior.

"He's just a guy."

"He's not just a guy, Lani," I huff. "He's Casey Pierce. He's one of the best offensive players in the NCAA. He's scored twenty-one goals so far this season, not to mention all his assists. Do you have any idea how dangerous he is in the slot?"

"No." Lani's expression is drier than the Sahara. "I don't even know what *the slot* is."

"Okay, well it's—"

"And I don't need to know," she mumbles, looking over her shoulder and eyeing up my personal sex dream. "I don't get it. The guy's more ink than skin. I guess his smile's kinda cute, but—"

"*Kinda cute*? Are you kidding me?" I bulge my eyes at her. "Are we looking at the same guy right now?"

She sighs and swivels back to face me. "The tall walking tattoo parlor with the cheesy grin who looks like he's never been introduced to a hairbrush?"

"That's the one." My insides dance as I ignore Lani's sarcasm and peek around her shoulder to drink him in.

He's standing with his hockey bros, scoping out the party.

I love his dirty-blond hair with its wayward, floppy spikes that don't know if they're coming or going. The messy look works for him.

"Seriously, Lani, he's like an orgasm just waiting to happen, you know?" I bite my glossy lip. "And it's not just that he's red hot and I want to lick every tattoo on his body..."

"Ew."

"But he also seems like a really nice guy. He's always smiling and congratulating his team. Laughing and making people around him laugh too. I bet he's sweet as apple pie."

"I've heard he's a total man slut."

"Which means he must be scorching in the bedroom, amiright?" I wiggle my eyebrows at her.

She finally gives in with a snorting giggle. "You have got it so bad."

"So bad." I shift so I can get a better view of him. My pussy is practically weeping knowing how close he is.

And yet how far away.

Usually there are Plexiglass, rows of arena seats, and hundreds of people between us. But right now, there are like ten. Ten bodies I could easily weave my way through.

He's so reachable tonight, my heart is tripping over itself, bouncing around in my chest like it doesn't know what to do.

"Well... tonight could be your chance to find out just how hot he is. I'm sure there are plenty of beds in this house that would happily accommodate your little sexperiment."

"It's not just about sex," I mutter, gulping from my can of Malibu piña colada as nerves skitter through me. "I want to get to know him as well, you know? I've been crushing on him for well over a year now. Ever since the first time I saw him on the ice, I've been a total goner."

"And yet you've never spoken to him." She shakes her head while I practically whine.

"Come on. It's like walking up to your favorite celebrity."

"He's not a celebrity." Lani rolls her eyes.

"He practically is. He's Nolan U royalty, and don't try to say he isn't. The whole team is, and you know it."

She sighs, tucking a lock of wavy black hair behind her ear. "Okay, fine. Everyone thinks these guys are amazing, but they're still human. They poop just like the rest of us, you know. Don't turn him into some god when he's just a guy."

"You're right." I bob my head, trying to agree with her, but deep down knowing she can't possibly be right, because Casey Pierce will never just be *some guy*. He's *the* guy.

"Look, you can't do any of the things you've been dreaming about standing here talking to me." She nudges my shoulder. "So go on. Be bold. Be brave. Get your flirt on."

I down the last of my mixer before handing her the empty can and adjusting my boobs. She smirks at my cleavage, then wiggles her eyebrows at me. She's obviously trying not to laugh at how nervous I am but can't contain her giggles as I fluff my hair, then dip my hip and try to look sexy.

"How's this?"

"You're a ginger siren."

I laugh. She's the only person on the planet who's allowed to call me that.

"He'll be putty in your hands." She adjusts the strap of my blue sequined dress. "Just remember not to talk his ear off—you always get chatty when you're nervous. You've flirted with plenty of guys before. You're good at it, so just... don't lose your mind because it's him, okay?"

I nod, darting my eyes back across the room. Casey's still there, laughing at something Asher Bensen just said.

"But still be you, because *you...* are freaking awesome."

I blink and look across at Lani. She's grinning at me, and I love her like the best friend she is. My heart melts as I give her a goopy smile.

She brushes my unsaid sentiments away with a flick of her hand, but I can tell by the way her cheeks are turning pink that she loves how well I know her and that I think she's the best woman on this planet.

Glancing Casey's way one more time, she turns back to me, her smile fading into a wince.

"What?" I take a quick look to make sure some puck bunny hasn't gotten to him before I can. But no, he's still standing there laughing with Asher.

"Just remember that... this is probably just a onetime thing for him. I've heard he's—"

I raise my hand to cut her off before she can repeat the rumors I don't want to believe. I know I'm playing with fire. If every whisper I've heard is true, he'll probably forget about me after tonight.

My lips pull into a thin line, and I start to wonder if I'm bold enough, brave enough, to play with fire.

"You know you want to." Lani steps behind me, resting her chin on my shoulder as we stare at Casey like he's a movie star. "Just... go in with the right expectations is all I'm saying."

I nod, lifting my shoulder to nudge her off me. I don't want her practicality tonight. I just want to dream and pretend like Casey will see me, talk to me, laugh with me, and fall madly in love after only one night of my company.

I know, I know. I'm the girl in la-la land, right?

But I don't care.

I'll regret it forever if I don't take this chance.

So, I step forward, my heels hitting the hardwood floor as I weave through the crowd and make my approach.

By the time I reach him, I'm so nervous, it's a miracle I don't throw up all over his T-shirt when he glances my way, then looks again, pausing to give me an appreciative smile.

Yes! Blue dress for the win!

I flick a lock of my bright red hair over my shoulder and cross my fingers that he's into girls with orange freckles and hair the color of carrots.

There was no auburn darkening for me when I hit

puberty. My hair has stayed this eye-watering color my entire life, unless we bring up the whole dyeing incident in ninth grade. Which we won't, because it was a complete disaster.

I'm red and I'm loving it.

That's what Mom made me say a million times a day once we finally got it back to its natural color.

"I'm red and I'm loving it," I mutter once more to myself, the words failing to have any kind of empowering impact as I pause by Casey Pierce and hold my breath.

He drinks me in, his lips curling at the corners as he eyes me from head to toe. His gaze lingers over my plunging neckline and squished-up boobs for a beat longer than is probably necessary, but I'll take that as a win too. If he's a boobs man, that works hugely in my favor. Maybe tonight I'll finally be grateful for my double-Ds.

"Hey," he murmurs. The look in his eyes is panty-melting.

My stomach does a little twerk while my chest is going wild with some tap-dancing routine that's making it hard to speak.

Finally, my lips part, and out flows this myriad of hockey-related stats that he probably already knows because the stats are all about him, and did I say hi?

Nope, don't think so.

I'm pretty sure he said, "Hey," and I turned into a human Wikipedia page.

It's like walking up to your favorite celebrity, pointing at them, and saying, "Oh wow, you're Chase Stokes. I loved you in *Outer Banks!*" Like the guy doesn't already know his name, you know?

And that's exactly what I'm doing to Casey right now.

Shit! Shut up, you idiot! Just stop talking!

Eventually the thought registers, and I clamp my lips together midsentence.

He's gonna walk away.

I did exactly what Lani told me not to do, and now he's gonna let out a derisive snort and walk away because I'm a blabbermouth nerd who—

"Wow." He grins. "You know your hockey."

I let out an awkward laugh. "I guess I... am kinda passionate about the game. I've been watching it since before I can remember. My dad's a fanatic."

Casey nods, running a hand through his hair while I resist the urge to swoon and start batting my eyelashes.

Don't you dare, Caroline!

He poops like the rest of us! He poops like the rest of us!

Of all the words Lani said to me, I have no idea why those are the ones I can't get out of my head. This is a nightmare. I should bail.

"Who's his team?"

"Huh? Oh! Avalanche." I grin. "He's a Colorado boy. Born and bred. You?"

"Me too. Montrose."

"Nice." I bob my head. "I'm from Boulder."

"That's not far."

"Yeah, like forty minutes on a good day."

He nods, his eyes tracking past me, his lips curling into a grin that's probably being fired at another woman.

Shit. I'm losing him already.

Because you're talking about drive times!

"Can I get you a drink or something?" As soon as the

words leave my mouth, I spot the Solo cup in his hand and wince.

He laughs, raising it in the air before gulping it down, then licking his lips and grinning. "Sure, let's get a drink."

My laughter comes out as more of a bark, but he doesn't seem to mind as he heads for the kitchen. I glance over my shoulder and spot Lani on the side of the room. She gives me a thumbs-up and I nod, quickly chasing after Casey and what will hopefully be the best night of my life.

CHAPTER 2

CASEY

This chick following me to the kitchen is something else.

I'm surprised I haven't seen her around before, but Nolan U is a big enough school. There are plenty of chicks to be had, and I haven't made my way through all of them yet.

This one, though... not only is she hilarious, but holy hell, she's one hot thing. That red hair was enough to make my dick stand to attention before she even reached me. I've always had a thing for redheads. Don't even know why. I just love how bright their hair always looks. And hers is luscious, man. Big wide curls spilling over her shoulders.

And her tits.

Shit. They are awesome!

If I could personally thank a dress, I would. I'd drop to my knees and praise those blue sequins for gifting me that cleavage. I'm surprised every guy in this place isn't drooling as we walk past them. It kind of makes me want to grab her hand and show them all that she's with me.

But I'm not the claiming kind.

She can be with whoever the fuck she wants.

Because I want to be able to say the same thing.

Tonight, though, she seems to be into me, and I may as well take advantage. I want to see if the curtains match the drapes. I want to run my tongue over those mountainous fun bags and see if they taste as good as they look.

"So, what's your flavor?" I stop at the keg, resting my hand on it.

She wrinkles her nose. "Not beer. I hate beer."

I raise my eyebrows, kinda surprised. How can anyone hate beer?

"I'm more of a mixer girl." She points behind me. "Actually, I bought those Malibus right there. I'll take the last one."

Spinning, I eye up the little cans and take the last one out of its cardboard packaging. I pop the top for her and pass it over before refilling my cup.

As soon as it's full, I raise it in the air. "To fancy-ass drinks and sorority parties."

She laughs and taps her drink against mine.

Shit, I should probably find out her name, right? I won't remember it tomorrow, but it's worth learning it for this party.

I lean in close so she can hear me over the music. "So, what should I call you?"

"Oh, uh... Caroline. I'm Caroline."

"Nice." I step back so I can drink in her lush body again. "I would tell you my name, but I get the feeling you know way more about me than most people do."

"Oh, no." She laughs, her face turning pink. "I'm just a

hockey nut. I know your stats, and I've watched you play every home game. You're such a good skater, and you're fast, man. You always seem to find the gaps. And the way you set up plays, work with your team, you're..." She grins, her words breaking apart with laughter. "I'm fangirling again. I swear I'm not a psycho. I just talk a lot when I'm nervous."

"Nervous?" My head jolts back. "You're nervous of me?"

She tips her head, sinking her teeth into her bottom lip before saying with a blush, "You're like a celebrity crush to me, I guess. And I probably shouldn't admit that, but you caught my eye in that first game I went to, and I haven't been able to stop watching you since." Her pixie nose wrinkles, her big blue eyes disappearing as she shuts those lids and obviously registers everything she just said.

Damn, she's sexy *and* adorable. It's a surprisingly alluring combo.

I usually go for puck bunnies who know exactly how hot they are and want to get down to business ASAP. I tend to gravitate toward the ones who seem to instinctively know this is just about the sex.

This girl, though. She's got personality to spare.

That should be a red flag, because I've made the mistake of getting it on with clingers before, and shaking them off is painful.

But maybe this one's worth the risk, you know?

Maybe she's not a clinger.

Maybe she's just a really big fan who wants to add me to her little black book.

I'm game.

If she knows this much about my hockey career, then she's probably more than aware of my exploits outside the arena. She'll know I'm a onetime guy, and she wouldn't be trying to flirt with me if she was the type of girl who was after more.

I decide my reasoning is good enough and bend down again, getting closer to her ear and telling her a few facts about myself that she probably doesn't know.

"My favorite cereal is Cinnamon Toast Crunch. If I didn't play hockey, I'd spend my life boarding the steepest slopes I could find, and I love watching horror movies." Her lips curl into a cute grin as I lean back and smirk down at her. "Now you go."

"Okay." The tip of her tongue darts out of her mouth, licking the corner, and I nearly miss what she says. "I love boarding too."

Wait. What?

She's a boarder?

Damn, that's cool. I love a girl who can snowboard.

"My favorite breakfast is eggs Benny. And... I was the dodgeball champion at summer camp when I was twelve. Oh, and I also won a prize for being able to fit the most marshmallows into my mouth." She tips her head, looking into the distance with a thoughtful smile. "That was a good year."

I can't help laughing. Seriously, this chick is awesome.

Moving in a little closer, I find an excuse to touch her, resting my hand on her lower back and leaning down to speak into her ear.

"When I was in seventh grade, I was trying to become the next Tony Hawk. I ended up breaking my nose on the concrete, and I'm pretty sure I permanently bruised my balls on a rail slide gone wrong."

Sweet, sticky mixer spurts out of her mouth, and she starts choking on her laughter. I step back, lightly slapping her back as she hacks and giggles, wiping the glistening liquid off her lips and making my cock stir. I want those lips on me. I want to suck that alcohol right off them.

As soon as she catches her breath, I thread my fingers around the back of her neck and pull her forward. She's stopped coughing now, but her lips are still shiny, and before she can even give me her permission, I swipe my tongue across them.

She goes still, her eyes glazing with this fiery kind of hunger when I pull back to check she's into it.

The tip of her tongue darts between her lips again, this time following the line of my lick.

With a guttural groan, I go in for another taste, unable to help myself. The sweetness on her lips is nothing compared to her tongue. It slides against mine, eager and greedy, her tits squishing into my chest when she turns and presses herself against me.

Holy hell. She's smokin'.

Running my hand down her back, I travel the line of her luscious curves, rounding her sweet ass and knowing I've got to have her. All of her. Tonight. Right fucking now.

"Wanna go upstairs?" I mumble between kisses.

"Hell yeah." Her blue eyes are bright and beautiful, the hunger making them sparkle.

It's hard to keep my expression chill as I rest my hand on her lower back and guide her toward the stairs.

I greet people as I ascend, only half paying attention to the shit they're saying to me. I can't think straight. I'm about to have sex with a redhead bombshell whose tongue tastes like pineapple and sin all rolled into one.

Nudging the first door open, I see it's occupied and yell out my apologies for not noticing the sock on the door. Two rooms later, we finally find one that's empty.

By this time, the heat between us is a fucking inferno, and the second the door clicks shut, I pull her against me. Her tongue's back in my mouth, our movements frantic as we wrestle with buttons and zippers.

My pants bunch around my ankles and I trip out of them, flopping onto the bed and bringing her with me. Her little yelp and following laughter ring in my ears.

"You okay?" I check nothing got bruised when we crashed together, a tangle of limbs and half-naked bodies.

"Yeah. I'm good." She sits up, straddling me with an alluring smile that makes Mr. Jones—yes, I named my dick after Tom because the guy's a fucking legend—want to pop on the spot.

My hard ridge settles beneath her wet pussy, begging me to rip those panties right off her and get down to business.

But first things first. Reaching up, I cup her boobs, lightly playing with her nipples as I take my time admiring them. They popped right out of her dress the second I pulled it off her shoulders, and damn, they're as sexy as I thought they'd be.

And how do they taste?

I glide the tip of my tongue between them, rounding the right one and sucking her beaded nipple into my mouth.

She groans, tipping her head back to give me better access.

Fucking delicious.

Pinching her now-glistening nipple, I work my way up her neck, over her chin, and find her tongue again. It's warm and sweet, and fuck, she's fire.

I pull back for some air, loving her soft little pants on my shoulder. Is her heart racing as fast as mine?

Cupping her ass, I grind myself against her, watching her tits jiggle as she lets out a squeak of pleasure.

Fuck, I'm battling the urge to make this the quickest sex I've ever had.

But she's gorgeous, and I want to take my time. Explore.

But holy hell, she's so fucking hot, I want to bury myself inside her and pump like I'm running a sprint at the Olympics.

"We seriously need to get these off." Her fingers curl into the waistband of my boxers, and she gives them a little flick before rising to her knees so I can pull them off.

I've never wanted to be naked more in my life, I swear.

Kicking the annoying fabric off my feet, I can practically hear Jonesy whining when I don't insert him directly into this sexy woman. He wants me to part those beautiful legs and plunge.

But I've just spotted something worth investigating. As she pulls the lacy black fabric down her legs, I see a little red heart on her hip.

"What's this?" I rub my thumb over it with a grin. "You've got a tattoo?"

She laughs. "Not as many as you. This is just a little..." She gazes down at it.

"A little what?"

"It's my Queen of Hearts."

I grin, knowing there's a story behind it but not having the patience to ask. My body won't let me do anything other than roll her onto her back and lean down to kiss the Q beneath the heart. It's fucking sexy, that little splash of color on her hip bone. Sucking it into my mouth, I walk my fingers up her inner thighs and quickly discover that yes, her pussy is a hot, wet oasis.

Her whimpers of pleasure while I stroke her swollen clit, then start sucking on her tits is a sweet kind of torture. I need her. Mr. Jones is fucking begging for release, and I only just hold out.

Clenching my butt cheeks, I quickly get her to orgasm —her writhing body and jiggling tits are the sexiest thing in the whole fucking world. While she rides out the last of her erotic high, I fumble around in my pants pocket for a condom. She continues to pant and moan on the bed, her body shuddering as the last of it travels through her.

It's fucking beautiful.

Ripping the packet open with my teeth, I spit the packaging onto the floor, my hands shaking as I try to wrap my dick in record time.

As soon as the condom is on, I part her legs, lifting the left one up to her tit and leaning over her.

"You want this?" I quickly check, looking into her eyes and grinning when she gives me an emphatic yes that's half groan, half wail.

Her hips are already seeking me out, rising off the mattress as I line up my dick, then slide into her.

It's the best fucking feeling on the planet.

She pulls me in like she's sucking on a straw, her wet heat frying every circuit in my brain.

Plunging deep, I pull out, then thrust back into her— a fast, hard movement that's like taking a hit of cocaine. I'm assuming. I've never done drugs because sex is enough of a fucking high. Why would I need anything else when I've got pussy doing magical things to my dick?

To my entire fucking body.

"Holy shit, you feel good," I murmur against her neck when I lie over her.

She responds with another whimper, and then her teeth are grazing my shoulder, her nails drawing tracks on my back as I thrust and plunge. Then she's grabbing my ass, urging me into her, deeper and faster.

Nudging her hand out of the way, I rise back up, lift her other leg so her knees are on either side of those luscious tits, and I go for it. Her hands curl around the back of my legs as I pump like a piston, our bodies slapping together, reaching a new kind of high. Her feet rest on my shoulders, and I grab her ankle, kissing the tip of her painted big toe before being distracted by whatever the fuck is happening to my body.

I mean, it's happened before.

I come on a regular basis, but this is something—

"Fuck." The word is dragged up my throat, coming out as a raspy croak while my body rejoices.

This addictive feeling floods through me as I reach —*shit*—my—*oh, fuck*—climax.

Coming. I'm coming.

Not coming. I'm exploding.

It's a fucking fireworks display, cum shooting into the condom as I thrust deep and hard.

Her head tips back, her red curls splayed across the mattress, and she lets out a lusty cry. It's the sexiest fucking thing I've ever seen in my life.

CHAPTER 3
CAROLINE

Hands down, best sex I've ever had.

But of course it was going to be, right?

It's Casey Pierce!

He's still inside me. My feet are still perched on his broad, tattooed shoulders.

He's so gorgeous, my insides are melting.

I knew his dick would be wondrous, but it's better than I could have imagined.

Big and long and beautiful.

Can dicks be beautiful?

Whatever. His is.

I don't want him to pull out. I want time to freeze and this moment to last forever.

He's puffing, his heart no doubt thundering the same way mine is. I shift my foot, resting it against his perfect left pec, and there it is—his rapid heartbeat. I'm sure it'll slow down any second now. He's fast and fit and cut—oh, so freaking cut!

But the fact that his heart is racing makes mine soar.

Because I was part of making that happen. My V-jay, my body, made him orgasm, and if that doesn't make me feel like a queen, nothing will.

My personal visit to Orgasm City happened twice throughout that encounter, which I guess makes him my King of Hearts.

Holy shit, that was so good. My insides are shimmering, the odd spasm still glitching my muscles as I float back down from the heavenly stars I've been reveling in.

I'm pretty sure we orbited the sun just now, and no one can convince me otherwise.

That was fucking amazing!

"Wow," Casey finally snickers, leaning back and starting to pull out. "That was hot."

"Yeah." My voice is all breathy, and I can't take my eyes off his back when he turns away to get rid of the condom.

The tattooed dragon swirls from the top of his shoulders to just above his butt. It's a whole Chinese-looking scene, and I can't help running my fingers over the scales of the long, twisting dragon.

"Tatsu," he murmurs.

"What's that?"

"It's a Japanese dragon. I got it designed just after starting at Nolan U. Cost a fuckin' bomb, but it was worth it. I used all of the money I'd earned from my summer jobs." He glances over his shoulder with a grin. "My mom was so pissed."

My lips quirk into a smile as I picture how that conversation went down. *You did what with your money?*

"How long did it take?" My voice is soft as I keep trailing my fingertips across the artwork.

"Thirty-six hours."

"Wow. Did it hurt?"

"Fuck yeah." He turns around with a laugh this time.

"So, why do you get so many, then?" I scan his arm, following the trail of interlinking designs—mostly black ink with splashes of color. The tattoos are a cacophony of pictures, some completely random, like the daisy sitting on top of an arched doorway with this iron handle that has a devil's face on it. And then there's this string of musical notes, floating up from his wrist and curling around an ice cream sundae.

So weird, but it makes me smile.

"I bet each one has a story."

He grins, running his fingers over the various tattoos covering his arms. He lingers on the inner wrist of his left arm for a second, then glances at me, his pale brown eyes warming with a smile. "Pretty much. It's my way of telling the world who I am, what's important to me."

"I like that. Which one was your first?"

He stretches out his right arm, showing me the hockey sticks just below his inner elbow.

"Of course." I laugh.

"I'd just found out I won a full scholarship to Nolan U. I had to celebrate."

"That's the perfect way to do it." I grin up at him, then for some reason feel compelled to kiss those hockey sticks like they mean something to me too.

He cups the back of my head, running his fingers over my curls before lightly fisting the back of them. With a soft tug, he pulls me back so I'm forced to look at him. I love how he's just the right amount of rough. A little playful and a whole lot of thrilling.

His eyes sparkle with amusement before he leans down to kiss my lips. And it's perfect.

It's not the hungry, devouring kiss he owned me with downstairs.

This one is soft, featherlight, and filled with promise.

Maybe I'm gonna prove Leilani wrong.

Maybe I have given this man slut a sizzling encounter he won't be able to forget.

Maybe I'm the girl who's going to make him break his infamous one-time-only habit.

CHAPTER 4

CASEY

She wrote her name and number on my palm.

I let her do it, because I couldn't exactly tell her no.

I think I was still high off that mind-blowing sex, so when she took my hand and pulled the cap off the pen, I wasn't physically able to speak.

"You're gonna call me, right?" She grins down at me, her blue eyes fucking mesmerizing.

Cobalt blue and orangey-red—now I love those colors even more than I used to.

"Yeah, of course," I rasp. The words kinda slip out before I can stop them. But she's standing there in that blue dress again. The one I helped her take off. The one I helped her put back on.

The one that squishes her tits together. Tits I was treating like my personal lollipops only moments ago.

"You better." She giggles, then presses that lush mouth of hers against mine before ducking out of the room.

She's off to clean herself up in the bathroom.

Am I supposed to wait for her?

I don't know.

But the second that door clicks shut, it's like something snaps inside me. An awakening out of my daze.

"Shit," I mumble, scrambling off the bed and grabbing my shirt.

It's on in record time, and I'm out the door, tumbling down the stairs and looking for a quick escape.

Girls don't have this kind of effect on me.

I'm not a one-woman guy. I don't do girlfriends.

Relationships are just nightmares waiting to happen. My mom's love life has given me enough insights to know that romantic bullshit is just that—bullshit.

That's not for me.

Even if the sex was great...

Even if she was funny and entertaining...

Even if I'll never be able to get those blue eyes out of my brain...

I don't do repeats.

So when I spot Ethan and Mick splitting early because of some crisis with Liam's dad, I take the chance to jump in the back of Ethan's truck.

I don't talk on the way home. I just listen to Mikayla worry about Liam and Ethan assuring her that he'll be okay. I kind of want to ask for deets, but I also can't speak. Images keep flashing through my mind—memories of how it felt to be inside that sexy siren. That red vixen had me in her clutches.

Shit, man. It was fucking awesome.

But I can't let it get to me.

Snapping my eyes shut, I lean my head back and start singing pop songs from the nineties. I know I'm desperate when historic numbers like "I Saw the Sign" start running through my brain.

By the time we reach Hockey House, I'm ready to drill a hole into my skull and empty out my memory bank. I need to shake this thing, pronto.

Ethan unlocks the front door, and I murmur my thanks, running up to the bathroom. Thankfully, the two of them are distracted with worries for Liam, which should probably be distracting me, too, but I have something that needs doing before I can focus on anything else.

Pushing the bathroom door open, I race to the sink, staring down at those digits on my palm and knowing what I have to do.

Yeah, it might have been the ultimate hookup, but that's all it can ever be.

One hookup.

Spinning the faucet, I turn it on, letting the water splash onto the porcelain before shaking my head with a wince and washing her ink off my body.

CHAPTER 5
CAROLINE

Five weeks after the ultimate hookup...

So, I went back to the bedroom expecting to find Casey waiting for me, but he'd already gone. I tried not to be disappointed as I searched the sorority party for him. So he didn't say goodbye. Big deal. He had my number. He'd call.

Right?

He was going to call, because he said, "Yeah, of course."

That was five weeks ago.

My eyes flick to my lonely little phone sitting there on my rumpled duvet just waiting to buzz with a text message or sing "Light Switch" by Charlie Puth. I change up my ringtone frequently, and Charlie's my jam right now.

But Charlie hasn't played today.

I work through the five stages in rapid succession.

I've already done this multiple times over the past month or so.

Denial flitters through me with a scoffing laugh. Then comes the anger. I've played with that for a long time. It's made me a grumpy bitch for poor Leilani, but she's handled it like a pro. She even helped me work through my "What if I ask around and find out his schedule?" stage. I swear I would have turned full-blown stalker without her.

"He hasn't called you for a reason, Caroline." She squeezed my shoulders, then slashed the tears off my face. "We knew there was a high chance of this happening."

"But the sex was so good," I blubbered. "We connected, you know? It was otherworldly!"

"I know." She pulled me into a hug while I cried on her shoulder.

Depression.

That sank in like a heavy rain cloud, and I spent a few days in bed, which made me feel pathetic because it was one hookup, you know?

I need to get over myself, but I just... I can't.

Because Casey Pierce was my longtime crush.

And I only got to have him for one night.

Not even a full night.

One mind-blowing, body-sizzling sexual encounter that can never be topped.

Over the past week, I've been working my way to acceptance. Trying to let go and not let that asshole make me cry anymore.

The lying pig was never gonna call me, and he should have fucking said that when I was writing my number on his hand.

But he didn't, and so I held out hope, then turned into a whimpering wreck. And I hate that I've allowed him to do this to me. I will move on. I'm determined to not let that walking dick take up any more of my headspace.

There's just one really big problem.

And no amount of determination is gonna get me out of it.

"Please come to the party with me." Lani walks back past my bed, adjusting her hoop earring and looking so freaking hot. She's gonna score tonight. If that's what she wants.

My eyes travel down her body, taking in that sexy red dress. It fits her like a glove, only just covering her ass. She's a curvy girl with brown skin and an exotic appeal. Her family is originally from Hawaii, but they moved to Colorado when she was like eight.

I think her mother misses the ocean big-time, but they've made a life for themselves in Colorado, and now her dad can't live without the mountains. They live in Silverton, which is miles from here, so Lani only gets home for the longer holidays. When she's really craving a decent home-cooked meal, she comes with me to Boulder, where my parents lavish us with more TLC than I can handle.

I glance at my phone again, willing them not to call. As much as I love my parents, they can never find out about my hookup with Casey... or any of the other guys I've slept with since I've been at college. They'll never understand my desire for sexual exploration. It's not like

I've slept with half the campus or anything, but I've definitely discovered my body since getting here, and it's been fun.

Sure, sometimes I come away feeling kind of empty or icky... but not with Casey.

That was the ultimate hookup.

The only one I ever really wanted.

The one I naively thought I could turn into more.

Shit. Shit. Shit!

"Hello! Earth to Caroline." Lani's bracelets clink together as she waves her hand in my face. "Did you hear me?"

"Uh..."

"Come on. No moping tonight. You have to get up and get yourself back out there. You told me you were moving on, so prove it."

My face bunches, sweat beading the back of my neck as I picture walking into a party and trying to act like I want to be there.

Lani clasps her hands together, looking ready to drop to her knees. "Come on, I'm feeling sexy and hot tonight. I need my wing-woman to help me find the right guy."

"You do look hot." I give her a half-hearted smile. "You're not gonna need me to find a guy. They'll be lining up around the block, believe me." I point at her dress and wiggle my eyebrows. "Your boobs look fantastic, your butt looks incredible, and I will only be deadweight, seriously."

Tell her. You should tell her why you'll be deadweight.

Fear coils in my belly.

I can't! Not until I know for sure.

"You, my gorgeous friend, are never deadweight. You're always in the mood for parties loaded with hot guys. Please. It's at the football house. Their parties rival the hottest fraternities at this school. You know they're always lit. Lots of sexy jocks and good dancing. Some muscly football player can whisk you off your feet and show you a good time. Maybe he'll help you forget about the walking cockhead."

I make a face.

"Or Ben might be there." Her eyes light up. "I know he's Mr. Basketball, but there's crossover at these parties all the time."

My eyes narrow into a glare. "Would you stop? I'm not into Ben. I told you that."

"I don't get it." Her face bunches with confusion. "He's a nice guy, and he's obviously into *you*."

"He's not the guy I'm interested in."

She groans. "Ugh. Would you get over that hockey asshole already? He didn't call you back. He was never going to. And I know he's your longtime crush, but you need to turn what happened that night into a beautiful memory you can cherish. Don't let it ruin your life. Don't let him stop you from going to parties with me and having a good time!"

I swallow, refusing to look at her as I fidget with the chunky ring on my pointer finger.

After a thick beat of awkward silence, Lani lets out a sigh and perches on the edge of my bed beside me.

"I get it." She runs her hand down my back, soft and comforting. "Casey Pierce is the guy you'll always want, but he's a one-hit wonder. Ben's been looking around campus for you. He's a keen jellybean, and I know that if you ever gave him your number, he would call it. A lot."

"I don't want him to call it, okay? He was a drunken mistake, and I just want him to forget he ever met me."

"Highly unlikely. You're gorgeous."

My lips twitch as I attempt to smile. But I can't.

Shit. Will I ever smile again?

Nerves rocket through my body, but Lani is oblivious to the reason why as she gives me a sideways hug and starts begging again.

"Come party with me, pretty girl. Please."

"I just really don't feel like it."

With a huff, she lets me go and stands, her heels clipping on the floor as she paces to her bed. "Well, I do. I wanna go."

"Then go." I flick my hand at her. "We don't always have to do everything together. Fly solo tonight. There's bound to be people there who you know, and I'm sure you'll find some hot guy to shake your booty with. Or you might even score yourself a sexy little hookup." I force my eyebrows to wiggle while my lips try to form a playful smirk.

Thankfully, she blushes and doesn't seem to notice how much effort I'm having to put into this teasing right now. She's obviously in the mood for some loving tonight, and it's helping to distract her.

Lani's not one to sleep around too much. She's not a virgin, but she's very selective about who she lets in between her legs. There was her boyfriend from high school. They dated for like a year but broke up after graduation, not wanting to do the long-distance thing. And then there was Ted from her economics class. He hung around for a few months before she broke it off over political differences. After that came her one and only one-night stand, which she decided she didn't like, and since then, she's been holding out for the right kinda guy. She'll scour this party tonight, hoping to make a connection that will no doubt start with some mild flirting, a date or two so she can test the guy out, then decide if he's allowed to get freaky with her.

Although, by the looks of that dress, she's desperate for a little physical action tonight. Maybe she'll break her "no one-nighters" rule to get through the dry spell she's been having. It's been at least six months, as far as I'm aware.

"You're gonna have an awesome time. Find the hottest guy there, shake that luscious booty of yours on the dance floor, get yourself some sexy action, and tell me all about it when you get back." I try to give her an encouraging smile, but she still looks kinda glum as she snatches her purse, shoving her phone into it before waving at me.

"I guess I'll see you later, then," she mumbles, walking out the door without another glance.

I feel bad.

I should go with her.

But I can't.

Like, I just... I can't.

Standing on shaking legs, I try not to think about the reason why as I grab my wallet and phone, shoving them into the back pockets of my jeans before heading out the door.

I shuffle to the drugstore, walking like I have weights tied around my ankles.

The glass door looms in front of me, the bright lights within making it feel like my own personal torture chamber.

Wandering down to the correct aisle, I spot the stack of pregnancy tests and feel my stomach convulse.

I don't want to do this, but I'm late.

And I'm *never* late.

I wanted to deny it. Pretend it wasn't happening. But it's been nearly three weeks since I was supposed to get my period. I've been firmly planted in denial, trying to convince myself that condoms are bulletproof, that I didn't read somewhere that they're only 98 percent effective when used correctly.

Shit, was it even used correctly that night?

Did it rip and we just didn't notice?

I'm guessing that would drag the "effective" percentage down by a whole lot.

Fuck! Why am I thinking in percentages anyway, when deep down I know my life's about to be over?

My fingers are trembling so much when I reach for the test, I end up dislodging the entire stack. A pile tumbles to the floor with a loud crash, and I drop to my knees, scrambling to collect them back up.

A young guy with a pimply face and too much gel in his hair rounds the corner.

"Are you okay?"

"Oh, yeah. Fine," I mutter, refusing to look up and smile at him like I normally would.

Smile? How the hell will I ever do that again?

He walks over, crouching in front of me. I spot his name badge and realize he works here.

"Don't worry about it." He helps me gather up the tests. "The same thing happened just the other day. A guy came in here and bought a whole bunch. Poor guy looked like he was about ready to pass out—"

"Oh, that's not me," I interrupt him. "I'm taking a, uh, science class, and I need a bunch of these for this experiment we're doing."

"Oh, okay." He doesn't believe me. "So... how many do you need?"

"Um... fifteen?" Does that sound experiment-y enough?

"Cool." He counts them out, and I start wondering how much this is going to cost me.

But do I really care?

Like hell I'm admitting to this pimply teenager that I actually need to pee on these things myself. He's probably already guessed anyway and is too polite to call me on my bullshit.

I sweat it out at the counter while he methodically scans each barcode. Can't he just do one and then hit a few keys on his computer? They do that at the grocery store when you buy multiple items of the same thing.

The door behind me opens, and I glance over my shoulder, relief washing over me when I don't recognize the couple who just walked in.

I have to get out of here.

Swiping my card, I get through the transaction as quickly as possible and bolt out of the store.

"Good luck with your experiment!" the guy calls after me.

I ignore him, my legs working so fast that I end up breaking into a run.

By the time I get back to my dorm, I'm out of breath, my hands still shaking as I dump the tests on my duvet. The boxes clatter together, and I think I might throw up.

"Just do it, Caroline," I order through gritted teeth.

Taking the first box, I tear the package open and struggle to read the instructions.

It's pretty basic, but I read them twice anyway.

Pee on stick.

Wait.

Realize your life is over.

"Got it." I slip into the bathroom, grateful that Huxley's remodel from a couple years ago included private bathrooms instead of the communal ones the other dorms have. Lani and I were lucky to get a spot in this building, and I've never been more thankful.

The last thing I need is to park myself in a public bathroom stall for ten minutes while I wait to find out if this nightmare is in fact my reality.

It takes forever for me to pee. It's like my brain knows what I'm trying to do and my body has frozen in response.

"Come on," I whimper, trying to relax.

Finally a little pee comes out, enough to wet the stick.

I place it on the edge of the sink and bite my bottom lip.

Three minutes.

Why does that feel like an eternity?

Setting my timer, I pace the small bathroom, my sneakers squeaking on the tiles as I will myself not to check too soon. My mind ping-pongs back and forth as I try to pray a negative result into existence.

But it feels like a hopeless whisper.

Which is why I'm not surprised at all when my watch starts buzzing and I pick up the test and spot the big plus sign.

"Shit."

It's the only word out of my mouth for the next five minutes as I try to come to terms with this.

Then I have a moment of hopeful panic, drink like a gallon of water, and pee on fourteen more sticks.

Yes. Fourteen.

I was going out of my mind, desperate for a negative.

But what did I get?

All positives.

ALL positives!

Fifteen crosses staring me in the face, telling me what I don't want to know.

I'm pretty sure I went into a state of catatonic shock after that, because when Lani walks through the door later that night, I'm still sitting on my bed, surrounded by positive pregnancy tests and staring at the wall like my eyes are about to pop out of my head.

She jerks to a stop, her lips parting, her hands shaking as she runs them through her hair.

"Oh my—"

"I know," I whisper, still staring at the wall.

"Are you—"

"It appears so."

She pushes the tests to the side so she can take a seat on the edge of my bed. Resting her hand on my knee, she gives it a little squeeze.

I glance at her face, noticing how shaken up she is.

She gets it.

I knew she would.

And thank God she doesn't say anything.

She just sits there, squeezing my leg and not saying a fucking word.

Because there is nothing to say.

Nothing will take this away or make it better.

CHAPTER 6
CASEY

We had two away games this weekend, and I spent the whole fucking time looking in the stands for a redhead.

At *away* games.

She wasn't even going to fucking be at them, and still I kept an eye out for her.

Because that's what I've been doing for the past five weeks. Looking for her.

I don't want to be, but I can't help myself.

Anyone with red hair is catching my eye these days, and it's fucking painful.

I've tried to get her out of my brain. The week after our ultimate hookup, I was determined. I went on a mission to get myself laid, and I did.

There was the bathroom sex at Offside, the back-seat-of-the-car sex behind the Humanities building—risky as fuck and a total turn-on—and then there was the puck bunny I screwed in her dorm room.

And after each time, as I walked away, my brain was flooded by the redhead.

Yes, I've forgotten her name already. I knew I would.

But I haven't forgotten her.

Which is why I'm lying in my bed on Sunday morning, jacking off to images of her perfect blue eyes rolling back in ecstasy while her luscious fun bags bounced in time with my thrusting.

"Ah." A moan spurts out of me as I start to come.

Fumbling for a tissue, I catch my cum and jerk on the mattress, closing my eyes and riding out the orgasm.

It's good.

But it's not enough.

"Fuck, I need to get her out of my head," I growl.

I have no idea why she's plaguing me this way. It's been five fucking weeks.

This hardly ever happens to me. I've had the odd chick who lingers, and she gets herself a tattoo on my arm.

My eyes pop open and I stare at the ceiling, mentally slapping my forehead.

A tattoo! Of course. That's what it's gonna take.

Scrambling out of bed, I jump through a quick shower, then race downstairs.

"Hey, man. Where's the fire?" Asher laughs at me while I wrestle my Converse on.

"Gotta fly, bro." I snatch my keys.

"To where?"

"I'll show you later," I call over my shoulder, bolting out the door, not even knowing what time it is.

I start the engine of my old Jeep Wrangler—it's a classic from the '90s and is still going strong for me—and check the clock.

"Eleven fourteen," I mumble.

The tattoo parlor in the middle of town should be open by now.

Reversing out of the drive, I'm grateful it didn't snow last night. Digging it out is a bitch of a job, and whoever leaves first has to do it.

The weather hasn't been too bad considering it's mid-February. We'll get another dump of heavy snow before the winter's out. Colorado always delivers, right?

I start wondering if I should try to be squeezing in a boarding weekend at some point, but until hockey season is over, I basically have no life. Between study, tutoring, practices, and game play, I can only just squeeze in the odd party and lunch break.

I'm not complaining. I love hockey, and I'll do whatever it takes to go pro, but the fact that after I get this tattoo, I'm gonna have to go back to Hockey House and spend the afternoon studying is hardly thrilling.

But I've got to keep my grades up. My scholarship demands it.

Pulling onto Main Street, I drive the length of it, then take a left, ducking into a small parking lot. My Jeep shudders as I brake too hard, and I have to remind myself to slow the fuck down.

I'm wiped out after the away games. They were tough, intense. We lost one, won the other, and ended up busing back to campus on a high. But when you're dragging your ass in the door at two in the morning after a few celebratory drinks, then spend your night dreaming about a redhead who just won't leave you alone, the exhaustion is inevitable.

The bell dings above the door, taking me back in time to my first tattoo and the Japanese goddess who gave it to me. She also took my V-card that night, and she has been impossible to forget. The dragon on my back was my attempt to get over her. It kinda worked, plus all the random sex I had when I started college. That helped. It helped a lot. And it's probably what I need to do to get over Lil' Red.

But let's start with a tat.

"Hey, Case." The chick behind the counter smiles at me, her multiple piercings moving as she talks. They always do. She has an expressive face, which pulls the different rings and studs—from her eyebrow to her nose to her lips and tongue—in different directions. "Haven't seen you in a while."

"Yeah, I've been busy." I lean my hands on the counter, tapping my finger. "Don't suppose there's a chance you can fit me in. Just a little quick one on my wrist." I stretch my arm out and point to a clear spot just above my watch strap.

Her lips pull to the side as she checks her computer screen. "You know what? My eleven fifteen is running late, so fuck it. You can take his place. Come on back."

"You're the best."

She smirks at me. "I know."

We walk behind the curtain, and I head to my usual chair, waving to... shit, why am I so useless with names?

"Case, my man!" He grins at me, coming over to slap my hand and give me a quick hug. He pats my shoulder before I step back with a grin.

"Hey." I point at his neck tattoo. "That's looking good."

"Thanks." He cranes his neck so I can get a better view. "We just finished it last week."

"It's awesome."

"What are you in here for?"

"Just a little something on my wrist."

"Ah." The guy starts to laugh. "Who was she?"

He knows me too fucking well.

I answer the question with a little smirk and head to my chair.

Selena—names always come to me eventually—is setting up her gun. Putting it down on the sterilized tray, she pulls on a pair of gloves, then asks me, "What do you want?"

"I was thinking a little red heart. Just here." I point to the same spot I indicated before, and her eyebrow arches.

"A red heart?"

"Yeah, like on a pack of cards. Like a Queen of Hearts."

The side of her mouth lifts into a closed-mouth grin and she nods. "Okay."

I rest my head back, trusting her to give me something good. She's never failed me before, which is why I don't look as she works away on my wrist.

As usual, my eyes water and I have to blink at the sting.

It's not too bad, just a little one like this, but the inside of my wrist is kind of sensitive. Getting a tattoo is like being scratched with a sewing needle. It's bearable, but you're glad when it's over.

Selena works fast, and I'm soon sitting back up and staring down at the little heart on my wrist.

It looks really similar to the one on Lil' Red's hip.

"Awesome," I murmur as she wipes the last of the blood away, then starts covering it up.

"You know all the rules?"

"Yep."

"Need any more of the creams or anything?"

"Nah, I've still got enough left over."

"'Kay." She steps back, whipping off her gloves and shaking her head at me.

"What?"

"I can't decide if a tattoo to commemorate your latest sexcapades is cool or disgusting."

I grin. "It's a reminder of the best ones."

"Mmmm." She's not impressed. She's trying to hide it, but she can't.

"You don't like that I'm a Casanova, huh?"

She sighs. "It's not my place to judge. I should seriously shut my mouth, but..." She shakes her head. "I guess I just want you to fall in love one day."

"Ew." I pull a face. "Why would you say that?"

She laughs, holding out her hand to pull me out of the chair. "Because it's the best sex you'll ever have. It's the best life you'll ever have."

Her cheeks tinge a shade of pink that's so unlike her.

I give her a dry look. "Okay, when did you jump aboard the love train?"

She laughs. "I've been on it for a while, but... this weekend, he asked, and I said yes."

As much as I never want that for myself, I get that she's stoked. So, I do the right thing. I pull her into a hug, lift her off her feet for a quick spin, and tell her, "Congratulations."

"Thank you." She practically skips back out front, and I've never seen her do something so girly before.

"Jeez, love's changed you."

"Get that disgusted look off your face." She frowns at

me. "It's changed me for the better, and one day... oh, one day... I just hope you fall, so you know what this feels like."

"Never gonna happen." I pull out my card and tap it on the machine. "So, where's the big shiny ring?"

"We're getting matching tattoos, dumbass." She rolls her eyes at me. "Like I'd wear a diamond."

I grin at her. "And let me guess, your wedding dress is gonna be black, right?"

She looks at me like I'm stupid. "Of course it is."

Laughter punches out of me, and I lean over the counter to kiss her cheek. "Thanks for the tat. Have fun planning your wedding."

"I will. See you after your next best sex!" she shouts as I'm opening the shop door. It's loud enough for the guy in the waiting area to give me a curious look and the old lady walking past the shop to glance at me with a scowl.

I turn around with a dry glare, which makes Selena laugh, then shake my head and walk to my car.

The air's cold, and I didn't grab my jacket on my way out of Hockey House. Hunching my shoulders, I shove my hands in my jean pockets and immediately regret the decision when my new tat scrapes against my belt loop.

I hiss and pull my hand back, checking that the bandage is still secure.

The new red heart on my skin better fucking work. Because there's no way I'm letting some gorgeous redhead take me down. Love's not gonna change me, because I'm never gonna fall in love.

As far as I can tell, it only ever leads to disaster. Both Ethan and Liam have caved over the past few months, and I've wanted to warn them against it. But they seem so happy, and I don't want to burst their bubbles. I just wish they understood that it's not gonna last.

At least I'll be around to pick up the pieces when it all falls apart.

As much as I love their girlfriends—Mikayla and Rachael—it's inevitable that something will happen to break them apart. It always does.

And then I'll be there. The reliable guy who will never turn his back on his hockey bros. That's about the only thing I can guarantee in this life, my friendship with them. Because even after college, I'm not letting this pack go. I will hound those motherfuckers until they're sick of me, because they're the best family I've ever had, and I don't want to do life without them.

CHAPTER 7
CAROLINE

Why am I doing this?

This is a really bad idea.

But he needs to know.

Does he?

It's a way to connect with him.

That's what drove me to walk out of my dorm and wander the streets. Not aimlessly. I knew exactly where I was going. It's freaking Hockey House! I worked out where it was my freshman year, but I've never had the guts to go there.

I'm still not sure I do.

Except for the fact that I'm currently standing right outside it.

The house looms in front of me while my fingers bunch in and out of fists.

Why do I even want to connect with the asshole who never called me back?

I already know the answer.

Ding. Ding. Ding.

It's because you, Miss Caroline Mason, are a lovestruck idiot who still has a crush on a guy who squished your heart like a grape and will continue to do so.

Leave now.

Leave.

Even as I think it, my legs move toward the door, because my custard brain woke up broken and is functioning on zero common sense. But the conviction I felt about telling him was overwhelming. So I acted on it. And I'm apparently still acting on it, because now the door is right here and I'm knocking.

I'm actually knocking!

This is insane.

Leave!

Run away before someone answers.

The door pops open, and Asher Bensen is standing right there with his neatly styled hair and curious, bright gaze. He's also a winger and is about as fast as Casey on the ice. Whenever they're playing the same line, they're lethal. Watching them is a beautiful thing. Although I'm not sure I'll ever be able to attend another game after this.

He eyes me up and down with a smile while I grip the strap of my bag and try not to pass out.

"Hi." His voice comes out all smooth and charming.

Seriously. I should not be here.

But it's too late now. I can't just spin and run down the street like a crazy woman.

Why not? You ARE a crazy woman!

Swallowing down the impulse to hurl, I clear my throat and say, "H-Hey. I'm looking for Casey. Casey Pierce. He lives here, right?"

"Yeah."

He flicks his hand at me, and I follow him inside. The entryway is crowded with shoes of various sizes—large sneakers and boots piled on top of each other with a small pair of Converse among the mix. They have a girl here.

My chest spasms, then tightens into a tight knot, making it hard to breathe.

I shuffle past the coatrack bulging with winter jackets and quickly shed mine, hanging it over the edge of the stair railing so I can snatch it when it's time to go. Adjusting my checkered shirt—which is probably the wrong choice, because my boobs feel huge today and they're stretching the fabric—I stand just behind Asher in the archway. Tugging at the buttons, I try to rearrange before a wardrobe malfunction happens while also checking out the inner workings of Hockey House.

I have a microsecond of fangirling mania—*I'm standing in Hockey House!*—before shaking my head and willing myself to get a grip.

Asher steps aside once we've walked through the archway, and I can see the open living area with a well-loved couch facing a big-screen TV and a kitchen tucked off to the right. There's more to take in—a glimpse of a dining table with people sitting at it and a room beyond that, which looks as though it has a pool table in it—cool! —but my brain doesn't actually soak any of it in, because...

There he is.

Shirtless.

Just my luck. He still looks fucking amazing.

I licked that skin. I trailed my fingers down those

washboard abs and traced his tattoos. I rested my feet on those broad shoulders.

Oh crap, I can't be here! I can't do this!

You have to! You're here, so make it count.

Don't swoon. Be pissed off, damn it! Make him pay!

Every mushy-brained thought I had when I first woke up shoots out of me as my mission to connect quickly becomes a mission of revenge.

I have no idea why it suddenly switches, but it feels fucking good. So, I settle into my anger and snap, "Hey. You remember me?"

He nods, pointing at me with a smile that makes my heart clench.

Don't you fucking swoon. You're mad, remember?

"I want to say Karen."

Karen? Is he serious? Okay, this is actually helping, because now I'm batshit-crazy pissed off.

He doesn't even remember my name?

I cried over this man. I cradled my phone for days waiting for him to call, and he doesn't even have the decency to remember three little syllables. Ca-ro-line. How hard is that?

I sense movement to my left and spot a short girl wincing and shaking her head at Casey.

Oh shit, it's Mikayla. My hockey buddy.

What is she doing—oh, that's right. She's dating Ethan Galloway, who is also in the room.

This is a nightmare.

Glancing back at Casey, my anger bubbles. This is all his fault. Him and his stupid dick and hot body and... and... his sperm!

"Caroline." I grit out the word. "My name is Caroline."

"Oh yeah." His eyes run down my body, and I can see the lust lighting his gaze.

I guess I've still got it. I'd normally revel in this look, but all I can think is that the second this body changes shape, he's not gonna look at me like that anymore. I still don't know if I'm keeping it or not, but that's not the point right now.

He'll probably never look at me again after I tell him this news anyway.

But damn if I don't want to see that gaping shock on his face when he finds out what he's done to me.

"We hooked up at a party in early January." I lift my chin, trying to look bolder than I feel.

"Yeah, I remember."

Oh, so he remembers *that* but not my name. Charming.

I cross my arms and growl, "You were gonna call me. I gave you my number."

He cringes, running a hand through his hair and making it stand on end. He now looks like a rock star, one of those crazy, wild-eyed drummers with the tattoos and the–

Stop lusting after him!

I look to the floor, waiting for his answer, which comes out as this pathetic kind of rasp.

"Yeah, I'm not..." He hisses, flashing me this apologetic smile when I glance back up. "I don't really do that."

I scoff. Un-fucking-believable. I kind of knew this would be his answer, but it still feels like a slap to the face. "So, what, you just collect girls' phone numbers like little souvenirs? Is that it?"

He looks to the floor, shoving his hands in the pockets

of his baggy jeans like some reprimanded kid. Except now the jeans are sitting real low on his hips, and I can see the top of that sexy triangle leading down to his beautiful dick, and it's seriously not helping.

Shit. Why does he have to be so gorgeous?

And why does he not want me as badly as I want him?

This sucks!

My heart cracks, the heat seeping out of my voice as I resist the urge to cry. "I thought we had a good time together."

"We did." His head shoots up, his eyebrows popping high. It's like he needs me to know I was memorable. Just not memorable enough to call. "I just don't... you know, I'm a onetime guy. Sorry. I thought everyone knew that about me."

I smash my teeth together, hating myself for a brief minute because I did know that about him, but I foolishly thought I could be enough.

Lani warned me, and I wouldn't listen.

You are such an idiot!

"Men can be such assholes. Amiright?" Mikayla steps forward. The pained expression on her face is sympathetic, and I try to smile, show her I appreciate the sentiment.

She gives me a little wave and mouths, "Hey."

I nod to acknowledge her, but that's all I can manage. I'm here for a reason, and if I don't get this over with, I'll regret it.

I think.

Doubts scour my insides as I let out a heavy sigh and tuck a wave of hair behind my ear.

"Look, Casey, we need to talk."

How am I even getting these words out of my mouth?

He smiles and nods. "Sure, what's up?"

I look around the room, noticing how everyone is watching this unfold. They're obviously curious, but like hell I'm doing this with an audience. I raise my eyebrows. "In private."

He gives me an awkward frown, scratching his chest and trying for a smile.

"Truth? Whatever you tell me will get back to these guys anyway, so..." He shrugs.

Seriously?

He tells them *everything*?

Well, that's just fantastic, isn't it?

So fan-fucking-tastic.

I stare at him. Every tendon in my body feels like a string about to snap. I grip my bag strap, trying to decide what to do. Should I bail?

But you're already here. And you can't go through this again.

Just get it out.

"What's said in Hockey House stays in Hockey House," Mick softly tells me. "But we can go upstairs if you want."

"No, that's cool. She doesn't mind, right?" Casey's voice pitches with desperation, like he's afraid of what I'm about to say.

Does he know?

Has this happened to him before?

"I'm gonna tell these guys as soon as you leave anyway."

Yep, he definitely looks scared.

I thought this would feel better.

My jaw works to the side as indecision battles within me.

You're here. Just do it. Do it now!

Maybe it'll be more triumphant once I actually tell him. And maybe it's good that everyone's around to watch this. It's no more than he deserves, right?

"Fuck it," I mutter, unzipping my bag and yanking out one of the tests. I hold it up to him and quickly rush out the words. "I'm pregnant."

He blinks at me like I've lost my mind, so I slap the test down on the counter, making sure he can see the plus sign too. I've had to look at the damn thing for the last week, and it's kind of satisfying watching his eyes bulge this way. It's like he can't believe it. So I ground my metaphorical elbow a little deeper into his ball sack.

"And in case you think that one was a mistake, it's not."

Turning my bag upside down, I give it a shake and the rest of the tests tumble out of it, hitting the counter and the floor, bouncing off the stool. One of them does a flip, then skids across the tiles.

He snatches it up, gaping like he's high on moxy or something.

So I jab a little deeper again. Why not, right? He hurt me. It's only fair.

"It's yours, in case that's not already clear," I snap.

"How do you know?" He's still staring at the test, oblivious to my expression... and obviously his words, because who the fuck says that?

"Excuse me?" I narrow my eyes at him while my heartbeat ratchets up a few thousand notches.

"How do you know it's mine?"

Mikayla hisses and starts shaking her head at him.

I narrow my eyes into a glare. "I know because I met you at a party and thought we had a connection, so I slept with you, and then you said you'd call me."

He cringes.

"And then I stupidly waited for your fucking phone call! So that's how I know it's yours!" My throat starts to swell. My heart is beating so fast right now, I feel like I'm about to pass out.

The urge to flee is overwhelming.

Casey drops the test on the counter, and it clatters against the others. "But we used... we would have used protection. I... I always wrap my dick."

I sigh, struggling to keep myself upright as I mutter, "Those things don't always work. It says so on the box."

"It does?" His voice pitches. "Where? I mean, shouldn't that be in bold or something?"

All the angry energy I was working off earlier is leaving me. It's like the volcano had a quick eruption, and now all that's left is the floating ash—lonely little flakes swirling through the sky, lost and hoping for something to cling to.

But nothing's going to cling here. He doesn't want me. He looks about ready to go into cardiac arrest.

I have to go.

I have to leave. Now.

"I know you don't want this to be your problem," I mumble. "But *Karen* thought you should know."

I can't help that last sarcastic quip. I need it to get me out the door.

Spinning on my heel, I bolt from the room and finally

flee. Like I probably should have done when I first got to the house.

My brain is buzzing as I stumble out the front door, pulling on my coat and trying to run. But I can't.

I settle for a brisk walk, although I probably look like a tortoise because my body seems to be functioning in slow motion right now.

I've done it.

I've told him.

I'm just not sure that I should have.

CHAPTER 8
CASEY

"What are you doing?" Mikayla snaps at me.

The pregnancy tests are piled on the counter, mocking me. I can't take my eyes off them and only barely register Mick's question.

"Reeling," I mutter. "I think the word is reeling."

"Get your ass out that door and chase her down! You might be a whole lot of things, Casey Pierce, but you are not going to let the woman carrying your kid walk away without at least offering to help her out."

Her harsh tone snaps me to attention, and I blink, staring at her while images of my mom flash through me. When she told my dad she was pregnant, he just left her to it. That's one of the reasons I never wanted to become a father. My dad was a shithead. I've never even met the guy, but the way he treated Mom was...

He abandoned her. Us.

And if I stay here right now, I'll be doing exactly the same thing.

My insides clench into a knot so tight, I think I might throw up.

Shit. This can't be happening.

Pregnant. She's pregnant.

With my kid.

Mine.

"Fuck," I shout, slapping the counter and then running for the front door.

Grabbing a coat off the rack, I shove it on, plunging my feet into the first pair of boots I can find. They don't fit right. My big toes are being squished, which means these must be Asher's. I don't bother lacing them up, and he'll be pissed as his laces drag through the dirty slush leftover from last week's snowfall.

"Caroline!" I shout, hobbling after her.

She's shuffling down the road, her shoulders slumped, her arms crossed over those luscious boobs. Red curls bounce against her shoulders as she picks up her pace to get away from me.

"Come on, stop. Please!"

She doesn't listen, and I end up running in these shit-ass boots that are killing my feet. I finally reach her and give her arm a quick tug. She wrenches out of my grasp and spins to face me, her blue eyes flashing.

Shit, she's been crying. Or fighting tears, at least.

Her eyes are so blue, they look like the sky on a cloud-less day when you're boarding on a mountain and you feel like anything is possible.

And now my life is over.

Fuck, she's pregnant.

And I can't turn my back and walk away.

My stomach churns, and I don't know what the fuck

to say to her right now, so I just stand there, probably looking like a desperate douche. The urge to ask her if she's 100 percent sure is overwhelming.

But there are a bunch of positive tests on the kitchen counter right now that tell me it's not a joke.

"I..." That's all I can fucking manage before a sigh steals the rest of my words.

Caroline huffs and shakes her head, looking across the street and clenching her jaw. "I don't even know why I came here today. I just felt like I should tell you."

"Yeah, of course." I nod.

"And I'm not trying to put you on some big guilt trip, although you are an asshole for telling me you'd call and then not calling." Her eyes narrow into a glare that I think is supposed to be angry, but all I can see is injured disappointment.

Fuck! Why did I say I'd call her?

Because you'd just had some of the best sex of your life, and you were still high off it. She caught you in a weak moment. Tell her that.

No fucking way!

I smash my teeth together and stay silent.

"I don't even know why I thought you should know." She scrapes her fingers through her hair, the beads on her bracelets clicking together. A white cloud puff pops out of her mouth when she huffs again. "It's not like I expect you to do anything. You can't even pick up a phone, so why would you suddenly step up for this?"

I wince, hating how shitty this is making me feel.

"I guess I just... thought you had a right to know." The last few words leave her in a rushed mumble, and she sniffs, her chin bunching like she's about to start bawling.

Was this what it was like for Mom?

Did she look this stressed and on the verge of throwing up? Did my dad just stand there like some asshole, not saying anything?

"What are you going to do?" The words stumble out of me, my voice gravelly and low.

Her blue gaze hits me with a look of pure terror before she crosses her arms and looks to the pavement. Her voice is thin and wispy when she finally speaks. "I don't know. I don't know what to do." Her breath catches, like she's holding in a sob, and fuck, I can't do this.

I hate it when girls cry.

I'm not good with that shit.

Mom used to lose it sometimes, and I'd hold her, pat her shoulder, try to make her feel better. But I don't know if it ever really worked.

I'm not the guy who says the right thing. I don't know what the hell girls want to hear when it comes to this kind of shit.

"Uh…" I scratch the back of my neck, getting ready to beg her not to cry, but instead, I mumble, "Well, I'll be there. However you need me, okay?"

I don't know where that came from, but it makes her sniff and glance up at me.

She gives me a skeptical frown, which is great because that's not crying, right?

Damn, she's pretty. Even cynical looks good on her.

My lips twitch like I want to smile. I have no idea why. I guess I just like looking at her. Or I like surprising her, maybe.

"I'm serious. I'm not gonna leave you hanging." I go a

step further, pulling the phone out of my pants pocket. "Here, give me your number."

"I've already done that," she snips.

I cringe, briefly reliving that moment where I washed it off in the bathroom. "Yeah, I, uh…"

"It's a waste of time giving you my number." Her nostrils flare. "You're never gonna call it."

"I will." My eyebrows rise. "I mean, I…" Then they drop as I let out a sigh. "Look, fine, just let me give you mine, then."

Her eyes narrow. "What's the point? Will you answer if I call?"

"Of course I will." I give her an emphatic look and realize just how much I mean what I'm about to say. "If you need me, I'll be there. This is my responsibility, too, okay? I'm not just gonna turn my back. You don't have to deal with this on your own."

She's obviously still not sure whether to believe me or not. Her eyebrows form a wonky line as her lips pull into a frown.

But I hold out my hand, flicking my fingers. "Come on. Gimme your phone. I'll put my number in there."

She makes me wait it out, eyeing me up like I'm the most untrustworthy guy on the planet.

But I stand my ground, and eventually she rummages in her bag, then slaps her phone into the palm of my hand.

"Thank you," I mutter, programming my number in.

She snatches it back, still looking doubtful as her thumbs fly over the screen. My phone buzzes, and I snicker at her text before spinning the screen to show her.

"Yes, this is really my number."

A soft snort comes out her nose before she starts texting again.

Her second message makes me cringe.

It's Caroline here. Not Karen. Not Catherine. Not Kelly. Caroline!

Ca-ro-line.

You might want to remember that.

"Yeah, I will. I swear." I force out a laugh, trying to lighten the moment, but she just rolls her eyes and spins away from me.

"Can I give you a ride home?"

"Nope, I can walk."

"How far is it?"

"I don't know. Half an hour?" She throws her hands up, like the question is annoying.

"That's a long way in this cold. Come on, let me drive you."

"No, thanks." She's still walking away from me, and it's frustrating as hell.

"But what about the baby?" I shout. "Are you supposed to overexert yourself?"

She jerks to a stop, then whips around to face me. Her eyes are bulging, her cheeks going red as she storms back, closing the space between us in record time. It's like staring down a high-speed train as she thunders toward me, then stops just inches from my face. "Are you fucking kidding me?" She jabs her finger into my chest. "For one, it's a half-hour walk, which is hardly overexerting myself."

"It's still kinda cold," I try to argue, but she talks over me.

"And two... and probably way more importantly!" Her voice pitches before she leans in close and starts whisper-barking in my face. "I may have announced this nightmare in your house because Mikayla promised me it wouldn't leave those walls, but that doesn't mean I want the world knowing! So don't start yelling shit about babies in the street, okay?"

I glance up and look around. The sidewalks are empty, but... "Sorry," I mutter.

"Just keep your mouth shut about this. And make sure your friends do too!" She closes her eyes, her hand shaking as she pinches the bridge of her nose. "Shit, I never should have told you."

I take her hand, pulling it away from her face. Her eyes glance over me, and I try to hold her gaze as I squeeze her icy fingers. "You did the right thing. I don't want you dealing with this alone."

She snatches her hand back, shoving it into her coat pocket. "What do you care?"

"I do."

With a skeptical headshake, she gives me a sad frown, then turns and starts walking again. "Just keep your mouth shut." She throws the warning over her shoulder one last time before picking up her pace.

I stand there, watching those red curls bounce around her shoulders and trying not to remember how good they felt twisted through my fingers.

Shit.

How can one perfect moment be turned into such a big fucking mess?

Scuffing my feet along the pavement, I slowly walk back inside the house, kicking off the torture boots with a growl and throwing my coat on the floor.

My friends are all waiting for me in the dining room. As soon as I step through the archway, they all spin to eye me up. Mikayla looks a mix of worried and pissed off, Ethan is cringing, and Asher's got this "no fucking way" look on his face that actually makes me feel understood.

But it doesn't change anything, does it?

She's pregnant.

With my kid.

"Fuck." I slump against the wall, running a hand though my hair and feeling like total shit.

CHAPTER 9
CAROLINE

By the time I get back to my dorm, my nose is an ice cube, and my cheeks are so cold they sting. But I don't care. I needed that walk. Everything Casey said to me ran on repeat in my brain.

I'm still not sure if I can believe him.

The fact that he chased me outside and gave me his number was kind of surprising, but I'm seriously not sure if he'll answer the phone. I kind of want to test it, but then I definitely don't!

Like I need my fears and doubts confirmed.

Swiping my card, I enter Huxley Hall and give a half-hearted wave to the girls who are leaving. They're freshmen—young and giggly, the way I used to be.

Now I'm just a knocked-up sophomore, rocketing my way into adult life at a speed I'm not sure I can handle.

Shit, am I ever going to laugh again?

I can't even imagine it right now.

This past week has been a nightmare, and today

didn't make it any better. Was that what I was looking for? Some kind of relief?

My brain must be zapped. As if I was going to find relief telling Nolan U's man slut that he'd knocked me up. The snake in my stomach squirms and writhes. I stomp up the stairs, willing myself out of this nausea.

Unlocking my door, I walk in and spot Leilani on her bed. She's gazing out the window with this lost, desolate look on her face. Has she been crying?

That can't be right. Lani *never* cries.

Not even when Jack died in *Titanic*. Not when Jojo discovered his mom hanging in the square. Not when Black Widow forced Hawkeye to let her go in *End Game*.

The woman has stunted tear ducts, I swear.

But right now, she looks—

The door clicks shut behind me and she jolts, her head whipping around to spot me.

"Hey." She frowns. "Where have you been?"

I sigh, not sure I even want to tell her. She hasn't been the same since the night I discovered I was pregnant. This whole fiasco has put this weird distance between us, and I'm not sure what to do about it.

Maybe she doesn't either.

How are you supposed to react when you find out your best friend is pregnant? No words will ever make it better, right?

She probably feels as awkward as I do.

Is that why she was crying? Or is it something else?

I should ask, but I'm so emotionally spent right now, all I can do is slump onto my bed.

Studying her face for a beat, I conclude that she actually might not have been crying. Her cheeks are dry, and her eyes aren't rimmed red or anything. She was obviously just lost in thought over something, and I hope to God it wasn't me.

Most likely it's an assignment she's struggling with. The girl likes to get top marks in everything, and she stresses big-time, overthinking shit in her relentless bid for A-pluses and 100 percents. Nothing makes her happier than being top of the class.

"Hey, I asked you a question, wahine. You're supposed to respond." A smile tugs at her lips and I blink, then let out this barking laugh that doesn't even sound real.

"I just, uh..." Shedding my jacket, I stand to hang it up because she'll tell me off if I don't. My hands are shaking as I hook the coat hanger over the rail. "I went to see Casey."

"What?" She bolts upright, her legs swinging over the edge of the bed. "Why?"

"Because I thought I should."

She closes her eyes, shaking her head with one of those noises that parents make when they don't know what to do with their wayward teenager.

I nearly tell her to shut up, but she starts talking before I can get the words out.

"Caroline, I thought you were going to keep this to yourself until you decided what to do?"

"I know." I flick my arms wide. "But I can't decide what to do, okay? I just wanted to see his face when I told him."

She opens her eyes, her gaze making me feel two feet tall. I squirm and start fidgeting with my bracelets.

"Why him?" she mutters, but I can still hear her. I wince, wanting to argue that she was the one who encouraged me to go for it at the party. She was the one who nudged me toward him when I was too nervous to make a move.

But I don't think that's what she means, and—

"So, how did it go?" Her voice is dry and unimpressed.

I purse my lips, then shrug…

Then I plunk onto the end of my bed with a soft whimper. "Like shit. I think. I don't know."

"What'd he say?"

"He was in shock, obvi." I run two hands down my face, then pinch my chin as I stare at the wall and get the words out. "But then he chased me outside and told me he'd be there for me."

Lani scoffs. "Yeah, right."

"He gave me his number." I yank my phone out of my back pocket and wave it in the air. "Told me to call him if I need him."

Her frown changes from skeptical to curious. "Seriously?"

"Yeah." I unlock my phone and check that it's still there on my screen.

"Are you gonna call?"

"I don't know." Curling my fingers around the device, I clutch it to my chest and tip sideways, shuffling on the bed until my head reaches the pillow and I can curl into a ball. "This is such a shit show. This whole thing is…" I shake my head, tears blurring my vision. "I don't know how to deal with this. What do I do? I know my options, but I just don't know which one to take. Both are awful for different reasons." I sniff, my voice turning high and squeaky. "No matter what I do, I feel like I'm gonna regret it. And maybe I shouldn't have told him."

My body starts to shudder, panic working through me in waves as I look ahead to my future and try to picture how much my life will change if I keep it and how I might feel if I don't.

Lani sits on her bed, watching me cry. I can't look at her face. I don't want to try and work out what she's thinking. I don't like this distance between us. I can tell she's unimpressed with what I've done today. She's probably unimpressed with how loose I've been with guys, too, but doesn't want to say it. She doesn't sleep around, and I fully respect that. Maybe she's the one with all the sense, and I deserve to pay this price for what I've done.

Shit!

I hate this!

I want out!

But there is no easy out.

Why hadn't Casey just called? Why hadn't I been enough?

This would all be so different if he liked me as much as I like him. Maybe if he did, this pregnancy thing wouldn't be quite so scary.

Are you fucking kidding me? Yes, it would! This is terrifying! Life changing!

But maybe it wouldn't be so bad if he loved me, you know?

My stomach continues to jerk and convulse until genuine sobs are punching out of me. This whole thing is a mess, and telling Casey today didn't make it better. It just reminded me how one-sided my feelings are.

Sure, he'll be there for me out of a sense of obligation, but he couldn't even remember my name.

Best sex of my life for me.

Another nameless girl for him.

At some point, Lani moves across the room. I don't know how long it's been, but she eventually perches on the edge of my bed, rubbing my back and making soothing noises.

She's trying to make me feel better, but it's not working.

Because nothing can make this better.

Telling Casey made everything all the more real, and now I feel like I'm drowning in this living nightmare.

CHAPTER 10

CASEY

Yesterday was a fuck-fest. And not the good kind.

I didn't get to stick my ding-dong in anyone's pussy, but I feel totally fucked.

The Queen of Hearts is pregnant. With a baby.

My baby.

The idea makes me want to throw up. I can't be a dad. I've never even had one. How the fuck am I supposed to know what to do?

That's the question that haunted me all of yesterday, all last night, and is still plaguing me as I try to concentrate on this lecture about... I don't even know what fucking class I'm in right now!

Rubbing my eyes, I shake my head and sit up, trying to focus.

Biomechanics. I'm in my Biomechanics class.

Focus, you idiot.

I seriously can't afford to fail anything this year, and I'm only scraping by as it is. Sure, I have my tutor, who helps me stay on top of things when I'm away so much, but I'm not a naturally academic person.

I just want to play hockey.

So sitting in this lecture theater trying to learn about anatomical function, although kinda interesting, is not my jam.

Not when my brain is filled with images of holding a crying baby in my arms.

Shit.

I can't be a dad.

I want to forget this whole fucking thing.

Just like your dad did?

Fuck! I can't turn my back on this. I won't be that asshole. But the thought of seeing this through is like a ball and chain around my ankle. The weight of it is gonna drag me right under.

I can't be a parent.

But I can't leave Caroline high and dry either.

Man, the sex was awesome.

Leaning back in my seat, I let myself relive it for just a minute. My dick twitches, excitement flooding my body as I remember that feeling of sliding right between those luscious legs. Holding her knees and pumping into her while she mewled and panted.

Fuck. It was hot.

Shifting in my seat, I adjust my dick, silently ordering it to calm the hell down.

Why am I even thinking this shit?

Maybe I'm lamenting it.

How can something so good—something that can get me so high—be the reason for my ultimate demise?

She's pregnant.

The condom fucking failed.

Shit, what if that wasn't the only time it did?

I've lost count of how many girls I've banged. Are there other babies out there in the world with Casey Pierce DNA rocking through their veins?

Fuck. No. I can't—

I'm gonna be sick.

Slapping my laptop closed, I snatch my stuff and shuffle to the aisle. People eye me curiously, and I mumble that I'm gonna puke if they don't move out of the way. They make room for me instantly, and I hurtle up the stairs and out the door.

My pounding footsteps echo in the corridor as I dash into the bathroom. The second the stall door is locked, I lean against it, resting my head back and closing my eyes.

I'm not gonna puke.

I just needed to get out of there.

Is this how my dad felt when Mom told him she was pregnant?

She's never given me the deets on how he reacted, just that he bailed. And the look on her face the few times she told me over the years has always been the same. He hurt her so fucking badly when he did that.

I refuse to be like him.

I have to find Caroline. Now.

Flinging the door back, I march out of the bathroom and have no idea where the hell to even start looking. I should text her. I've still got her number from when she texted me, but does she even want to hear from me?

She looked pretty pissed storming off down the street. I don't want to make things worse, but... shit!

What if she never wants to speak to me again?

What is she never calls?

Then you've got nothing to worry about, right?

Fuck off! Yes, I do. She's carrying my kid!

Maybe it's better if I "accidentally" bump into her. That way, she can't ignore my text and it will seem like this natural coincidence. Like fate is playing a hand and I had nothing to do with it.

Is that lame?

Yes, it's fucking lame! But do it anyway.

This dogged sense of responsibility plagues me as I scour the campus looking for her. I walk up to anyone with eyeballs and ears, asking if they know a girl named Caroline with red hair.

I get a variety of looks, but most of them are curious.

Casey the Man Slut is looking for a particular girl?

This is unheard of, and I'm probably shaking the gossip tree so damn hard it's gonna bite me on the ass, but I have to find her.

Glancing at my watch, I figure I've got at least one more hour to spare before I'll have to bail on this and start again tomorrow. I have to squeeze in a workout before practice. Just something light to get my body warm and make up for my half-assed attempt this morning. Even the guys noticed, though they were nice enough not to call me on it. I'm off in a big way right now, and they get why. Their silence was appreciated. I don't need to be told about the tidal fuck that's hitting me right now. I know!

Flinging open the main library door, I figure this should probably be my last stop before I head to the hockey arena. It'll likely take me an hour to search every corner of this place. It's three floors.

Walking up to the main desk, I rest my hands on the counter and try for a smile, but who knows what the fuck is crossing my face right about now.

The librarian behind the computer glances up at me. "Can I help you with something?"

"Yeah, I'm looking for a student. Her name's Caroline, and she has red hair." How many times have I said that today?

"Um..." She frowns at me the way most people have for the last hour and a half. "There are a lot of people in the library right now."

"I know." I cringe. "I just..." Running a hand through my hair, I let out a heavy sigh, and she must sense how desperate I am.

"I think I may have seen a girl with long red curls walk in here a little while ago." She points over her shoulder. "I don't know where she is right now, but she went that direction."

My insides jump like I'm an eight-year-old kid who's just been given money for the ice cream truck.

"Thank you," I mumble, hustling away from the desk and starting a systematic search of the first floor.

I don't find her until the second. She's at the end of a large table, her face hidden behind a wall of ginger goodness. Shit, I really do love her hair. I've always loved red hair. I don't even know why, but redheads catch my eye every single time. And she's not just any redhead. She's fucking gorgeous.

I watch her for a minute. She scratches behind her ear with the end of her pen, then tucks her hair back, exposing her face to me.

Yep. Fucking gorgeous.

Will our kid be that pretty? Will it have red hair?

Nausea stirs in my gut again.

I can't have a kid. Why am I even thinking this shit?

Taking a step forward, I walk right into the chair at the end of the table. It tips sideways, landing on the floor with a bang. The noise is stupidly loud in this quiet space, and I scramble to pick up the chair and ignore all the eyes on me.

But then I look up and she's gaping at me. Her blue eyes look about ready to pop out of her head as I jog the last few steps over to her.

"Hey."

"What are you doing here?" she whisper-barks.

"Oh, I just, uh... Fancy seeing you here." I wince and sigh, crouching down beside her and resting my arm on the edge of her table. Giving up my lame little lie, I softly admit, "I've been looking for you."

"Why?"

I frown at her confusion. Is she fucking serious?

Rolling her eyes, she huffs and closes the book she was reading. "I don't really want to have these conversations in public, okay? Could you just call me?" She tips her head to the side, her eyes narrowing. "Oh no, wait. That's right. You don't do that."

I glare back at her. "I didn't know if you wanted to hear from me."

"Yeah, right." She shunts her chair back, gathering her things and shoving them into her bag.

"Come on, I've been searching the whole fucking campus for you. I skipped class so I could find you."

"I didn't ask you to do that," she mutters. "You should have just texted me."

"So you could ignore it? I needed to see you."

Her head snaps up, her fiery blue gaze doing its best to make me feel three inches tall. "Why?"

I study her face for a second, refusing to look away even though instinct is telling me to run like the fucking wind.

She's still staring at me. Her hard glare is a laser beam trying to slice me in two, but I take the risk and gently touch her arm. "I wanted to check on you. Make sure you're okay."

Her cheeks turn the color of milk as she flicks my hand off her and glances around. Our quiet discussion is drawing curious gazes. The guy at the end of the table obviously recognizes me, and the girl two across from him is throwing me a dirty look.

Shit, did I sleep with her?

I glance away, focusing back on Caroline. Her blue eyes are bigger and brighter than before. Not with a smile but with this kind of fear that matches the tsunami in my stomach.

"Come on." I nudge her away from the table and down a row of books until we reach a back corner that's completely secluded.

It's dark and hidden away, probably a great place to have sex. You know, the naughty, rushed kind where the thrill of getting caught makes it that much hotter.

Images of lifting Caroline against the wall and plunging into her overpower me for a second, but I clamp them down when she clears her throat.

Crossing her arms, she frames her luscious tits, and it's impossible not to check them out. They seem even bigger and more beautiful than last time.

Fuck, she's hot.

Gritting my teeth, I glance away from her, focusing on the wall and willing my horny-ass body to calm down.

I'm not here for a quickie. I'm here to check that she's okay.

Get your brain out of your dick and talk to her like a human being!

"So, uh... how are you?"

She shrugs. "About as good as yesterday."

I give her a wincing smile. At least I think that's what my face is doing. She gives me a cursory glance before looking to the floor and clearing her throat again.

"Sorry if I handled that badly," I mumble. "I was kind of in shock."

She brushes her hand through the air like it's no big deal. But it was. I hurt her.

Shit, I wonder how many other chicks I've wounded. I hate this feeling. I don't want to be an asshole. I just... don't do relationships.

I thought she understood that. I'm famously slutty. Everyone knows that about me. She shouldn't have flirted with me if she was after something serious.

She's not, you dumb fuck. She wouldn't have even spoken to you again if she wasn't pregnant with your kid.

She was waiting for your phone call!

The battle in my head continues to rage as Caroline stands there, awkwardly shifting from one foot to the other while I try to form words.

"So... uh..." I trip and stumble over each syllable, frustrated with myself. I've just spent nearly two hours looking for her. To what? Just stand here like an idiot not saying anything?

It's like she's thinking the same thing. When she glances back up at me, her eyebrow rises, the look in her eyes so pointed that I feel like she's sticking a sword through my face.

"I, um… I don't…" I huff, resting my hand on the bookshelf and picking at the spine of a thick-ass book while saying the first dumb thing that pops into my head. "I know it's only been a day, but have you had any thoughts on… what you want to do? Like with the… you know." I point at her stomach. "Are you gonna… keep it?" I wince—this conversation is awkward as fuck.

She frowns, dropping her crossed arms to wrap them around her torso. She fists the sides of her sweater, her lips shaking a little when she opens her mouth to speak. "I can't stop thinking about it. It's stressing me out big-time, because I seriously don't know. One second, I'm thinking terminate, and the next, I'm feeling sick and wondering if I can do that. I just… I can't decide." She blinks like maybe she's fighting tears. Swiping a finger under her eye, she looks up at me and sniffs. "What do you think I should do?"

I jolt back like she's slapped me. I wasn't expecting my opinion to even matter. But now's my chance. I could just come out and say it. *Get rid of the thing. Our lives will be ruined if you go through with this. I can't be a dad. Don't put that shit on me!*

But instead, I say, "It's your body. You need to be the one to decide."

She huffs, flicking her hand up with a scowl. "But it's your baby too. You don't even have an opinion?"

"I…"

Say it. Just say it.

With a soft sigh, I try to, but again, words I never planned slip out. "I want you to do what's best for you."

"So, you don't care if you have a kid or not?"

Ouch. It's like she's trying to bait me with her snappy tone and fiery glare. I decide to play it cool, my shoulder hitching as I force out a soft reply. "If you decide to keep it, I will. I'll care."

Somehow I'll show up. The thought sends black splotches scattering across my vision.

"And if I don't?" Her voice is losing its venom, giving way to a mousy squeak that makes my chest hurt.

Reaching for her arm, I brush my fingers down it. "I'll drive you to the clinic. I'll stay with you while they do it."

Her face goes an even whiter shade of pale.

"And if you keep it, I'll drive you to every checkup and ultrasound and whatever other shit this baby needs. I've got your back, okay?"

My voice is sounding way more confident than I feel right now. I don't even know how these words are coming out of me, but I'm fucking resolute over this. I will not abandon her. My sperm, my mess. I'm seeing this thing through. Even if it does send jolts of terrifying panic right through me. I won't be my dad.

Caroline's head starts to bob, almost erratically, and then she shudders, curling in on herself like this is all too much.

I get it.

I just wish I had the right words to make this better. But I've got nothin'.

"I'm scared." Her voice catches. "No matter what I choose, I'm scared of the repercussions."

She looks up at me then, her blue eyes large and glistening.

I want to take this away for her. For us.

But I still can't find the words. Nothing I say will make this better, so I pull her into a hug, cupping the back of her head and nestling her into my shoulder.

She leans against me, her arms still curled around her middle, while I cocoon her in my embrace and rest my cheek against the top of her head.

CHAPTER 11
CAROLINE

Casey's chest is a brick wall of muscle, but somehow I still manage to mold into it. His hand on the back of my head... the way his thumb is gently rubbing just behind my ear... in spite of the serious turmoil I'm facing right now, this is heaven.

But it's also a dream.

He's only giving me a hug because I was about ready to cry. And hugs don't last forever. I can already feel him shifting away, lightly patting my shoulder—the universal sign for "this hug is timing out."

I need to pull away now, but I can't seem to move.

Maybe because I know this is probably a one-off thing. We're not going to end up together. He's not going to be my boyfriend. He's just being nice to me because I've got his kid brewing in my belly.

Oh shit.

I have a kid brewing in my belly!

A shudder runs through me like it does every time that harrowing thought hits me.

It's freaking terrifying.

"Hey, let's get out of here," Casey murmurs against my forehead. His lips leave a delicate kiss before he pulls back and looks down at me. "Come on, I'll buy you a coffee or something."

My lips curl into a pout as I pull my sleeves down. The sweater I'm wearing is mammoth and swallows my hands easily. "I've already had my quota for the day."

"Your quota?"

"Only allowed one." I point at my belly, my frown deepening to the point that I can actually feel it. Every muscle in my face seems to be straining as my eyebrows plunge into a deep V.

The only reason I know that rule is because my coffee-addicted cousin nearly died during her pregnancy from caffeine withdrawal. Okay, so she didn't nearly die, but she struggled. And I know I'm going to as well. Maybe not the coffee thing so much, but no alcohol? I feel like I need to down three bottles of straight vodka just to cope with this mess.

But I can't do that.

I have to face this shit head-on. There's no escaping the choices in front of me.

I'm lost so deep in this maelstrom that I miss what Casey's saying until he nudges my arm. "What else?"

"Huh?"

"What else can't you have?"

"Um..." I try to remember what else Angela wasn't allowed to eat, but my brain's going fuzzy and—

"Have you seen a doctor yet?"

And now my brain is lighting up with panic, the

neurons, or whatever, all firing at once while I try to answer that question.

It's simple, really. No. That's the answer.

But it's not simple because the no is tied to my big choice.

"Is that a headshake or...?" Casey's voice trails off, and I clear my throat.

My voice still comes out raspy when I finally answer him. "I haven't yet, because... it seemed weird to go if I wasn't keeping it."

"But you might keep it, right?"

I give him a helpless shrug, fisting my sweater in the stomach region and feeling sick.

"I mean, you should go and make sure everything's okay."

Fear pulses through me, a thick beat that's heavy and making my head spin.

I press my fingers into my hairline, rubbing hard lines across my forehead. "But won't that make it real?"

Glancing at his face, I spot the tail end of his pained expression before he gives me a glum smile. "I think that pile of pregnancy tests in my bedroom says it is."

I blink at him. "You haven't thrown them away?"

"I'm going to. I just needed the reminder when I woke up this morning." He points at himself. "Still in shock."

"Yeah, ditto." I let out this brittle laugh that sounds weird. "And I've known for a week longer than you have. Probably more, if I'm honest. It just took me that long to take a test and face this shit."

He sighs and nods like he gets it, his hands going into his hoodie pockets. He's so broad and big. I can't help staring at those wide shoulders and thinking how much I'd love to lean against the right one again.

But it's not like that.

We're not a couple.

We're just two people sharing an egg and a sperm.

"Book an appointment. I'll go with you," Casey says.

My escalating meltdown goes on hold for a second, and I blink at him, shaking my head. "What?"

"What?" His head jolts back. "Why are you looking at me like that?"

"Who are you?"

"What do you mean?"

"I thought you were Casey 'Man Slut' Pierce. Never sleep with a girl more than once. Never call a girl back."

His expression goes blank, and he looks to the ground. I think I've offended him, but I'm only telling the truth, right? I can't believe it would even sting him. I thought he was proud of himself for bagging all those babes.

I roll my eyes, fidgeting with my rings and wondering what to say.

He sniffs, looks at me, then darts his eyes away.

"I just... I don't understand how you can go from that to offering to drive me to an appointment."

He forces a smile. It's tight, and his eyes aren't glimmering with any kind of amusement. "I told you, I'm not being an asshole and bailing on you over this."

"Look, I can tell you don't want to."

"Of course I don't want to!" His arm flicks up in time with his voice. He lets out this disbelieving huff like I've just said the dumbest thing ever. "Neither of us *wants* this, but it's our reality right now, and until you decide what you're going to do, it will continue to be our reality. And I'm not saying that to pressure you, okay? I know this is a big decision and you want to make the right choice for yourself, but..." He sighs, running a hand over the back of his head until the hairs are sticking up all over the place. "I won't leave you hanging. I might sleep with lots of different chicks, but that doesn't make me an asshole. If you need me, I'll be there, okay?"

I swallow, then go back to kind of gaping at him. Not a chin-to-my-collarbone kind of gaping, but my lips are parted, my eyes feel wide, and I don't know what to say.

"Whether you like it or not, you need to check in with a doctor. Just because you don't want to be pregnant doesn't mean you can ignore this."

Pulling out his phone, he starts tapping on the screen, and for some reason, I just stand there letting him boss me around. To be honest, it feels kind of nice having someone take charge like this.

Usually that's Lani. She's great at organizing me and telling me what to do, but she's been off ever since I told her about this pregnancy. I hate it. This gulf has formed between us, and I don't know how to fix it. I shouldn't have told her everything. I should have just kept my mouth shut, because now she's pissed with me for my reckless behavior.

It's weird, actually. Considering she's my best friend, she's being kinda judgy.

Crossing my arms, I frown at Casey when he looks at me.

"The Student Health Center will be the first place to start. I can get you an appointment on Thursday." He shows me the booking form on his phone, and I shudder again. His voice softens. "It's gonna be okay." He starts filling in the form, and I stand there not arguing with him while I quietly lament the shitstorm my life has become.

I should be grateful that he's stepping up.

But for some reason, I just feel hollow, because I know that unless I keep this baby, he's gonna walk on out of my life as soon as it's gone.

And that's not a great reason to keep it, right?

It's not like we're gonna play happy family once the kid pops out. It'll be him visiting every now and again while I deal with night feeds and poopy diapers and a screaming baby.

My heart starts to race, short breaths punching out of me as I picture my future alone, or living with my parents, as I deal with single motherhood.

Squeezing my eyes shut, I force myself to consider the alternative, but the idea of sitting on some sterile bed while a baby is scraped out of my womb is just as horrifying.

I guess I could always give it up for adoption.

My stomach drops, my insides running cold. Do I really want to do that to a kid? Give them away just after they're born so they spend their whole life knowing that the person who should have wanted them the most didn't?

That's harsh. I know it's harsh. People give their babies up with the best of intentions. Logically, I get it.

But when you're the kid who was given up as soon as you popped out, it's sometimes hard to convince yourself that you weren't discarded as an inconvenience.

CHAPTER 12
CASEY

My fingers were shaking so badly when I was trying to fill in that booking form. Caroline didn't seem to notice. Getting answers out of her—like her last name and birth date, so I could fill in the damn form—was a mission. She had this lost, distant look on her face and seemed more and more miserable the longer it went on.

In the end, I had to snap her out of it.

Like literally. I had to snap my fingers in front of her face to get her attention.

She jolted, her eyes popping wide as she mumbled, "I gotta go."

"No, wait." I chased her out of the library, not letting up until she'd acknowledge what time her appointment was.

Shit, she better be here.

I stroll down the corridor, looking at room numbers until I reach the end of the row and stop outside the one she texted to me.

She's on the third floor of Huxley Hall. It's pretty nice.

Way better than the dorm I started out in my freshman year. Thank fuck for Hockey House.

Sucking in a breath, I hold it while I knock, then release it when I hear shuffling behind the door. It cracks open, and I'm met with a brown gaze that's borderline hostile. No, you know what? It's not even borderline. It's just plain hostile.

"Hey." I force a smile, raising my hand in a wave. "Is Caroline here?"

The girl with pale brown skin and a smattering of dark freckles over her nose continues to stare me down until I'm shifting from foot to foot. This is awkward as fuck.

"Lani, would you let him in, please?" Caroline's voice from within the room eases the tightness in my chest.

With a little huff, the woman opens the door. "Come on in, sperm bank."

I give her a little side-eye, and as wide of a berth as I can, while I move sideways through the door and step into a room pristine on one side and a chaotic mess on the other.

My lips twitch with a grin as Caroline comes out of the bathroom and stops by the mountain of clothes on her unmade bed. Her hair is wet but starting to curl, the dark orange becoming the bright, vibrant color that caught my eye the first time I met her.

"Hey." I raise my chin.

"Hi." She gives me a twitchy smile before riffling through her pile. "Where's my blue sweater?"

"The one with the pockets or the turtleneck?" Lani steps forward to help her.

"Either will do."

"Here." Caroline's roommate unearths a blue piece of fabric from beneath the pile.

"Thank you."

"Hmm." The derogatory noise is made while looking at me.

I raise my eyebrows at her, then step forward with my hand extended. "I'm Casey."

"I know who you are." She crosses her arms.

"And you must be Caroline's roommate."

"Mm-hmm."

"Do you have a name, or should I just call you Ice Queen?"

A short laugh bursts out of Caroline, but she quickly clamps her lips together. "Sorry," she mutters to her friend. "But it was a little funny." Caroline's big blue gaze lands on me, and I'm struck by how pretty it is. When her eyes are sparking with a smile, she could take a guy's breath away.

Like right now. She's stealing mine.

"Her name's Leilani, but her friends call her Lani."

"Which means you can call me Leilani," she clips.

"Or Ice Queen." I point at her with a grin and score myself a very unimpressed glare.

With a wincing smile, I tip back on my feet and look to Caroline with a silent SOS. "You ready to go?"

"Yep." She shakes her head.

I can't help a quick grin. I don't think she realized she did that, but I get how she feels. Visiting a doctor sucks at the best of times. And this is so not the best of times.

"Don't forget to ask those questions." Lani steps up to Caroline, her face the picture of genuine concern. It's a pretty strong contrast to the death glares she was firing my way.

"I won't," Caroline murmurs.

Leilani's brown gaze darts to mine. "Take care of her."

"Of course I will."

She rolls her eyes like she doesn't believe me, then takes a seat on her bed, eyeing us up as we walk out of the room. I swear I can still feel her heated gaze on my back after the door's closed.

"Wow, your roommate is…"

"Normally very nice." Caroline sighs. "She's just annoyed that you're taking me to the doctor. She's not your biggest fan and doesn't trust you to take care of me."

"No shit." I raise my eyebrows as we descend the first flight of stairs.

"I think she's just really bummed out for me that I'm in this situation, and it's easier to blame you entirely."

"Yeah, I guess that makes sense."

"But it took two to tango, you know? And it's not like we didn't try to be safe." Her words come out kind of rushed and quiet, her lips clamping together as we pass a couple girls on the stairwell.

"Hey, Casey," some flirty voice greets me.

I raise my hand in a wave, not even bothering to look.

Caroline's gone stiff beside me, and I wince.

Shit, this is awkward.

It's not like we're a couple, so I have every right to flirt and sleep with whoever I want.

But we're heading to a doctor's appointment right now to talk about *our* baby. You don't get more couple-y than that, and… Fuck! I'm hating this.

But I have to do the right thing, right?

Yes. Don't be a dickhead like your old man.

Clenching my jaw, I walk beside Caroline, not saying a word until we reach the Student Health Center and walk up to the counter.

"Hi there." The receptionist smiles up at us, and I glance at Caroline, expecting her to say her name... or something, at least, but she just stands there like a deer in headlights, quick breaths punching out of her chest.

I rest my hand on her lower back, which makes us look like a full-blown couple, but what else am I supposed to do? She's freaking out.

"Hi." I smile at the receptionist. "We're here for an appointment for Caroline Mason."

"Excellent." She pops a tablet on the counter. "Please fill this in. The doctor shouldn't be too long. We're actually running close to on time for a change." Her laughter is merry and bright.

I manage to grin down at her before guiding Caroline to a seat in the corner.

"Just breathe," I murmur. "You're okay."

Her head bobs erratically as I hold out the tablet. Filling it in will hopefully be a brief distraction for her. Maybe it'll stop her spiraling for a little minute.

"Here."

She blinks, taking it off me and biting her lip as I force her index finger to touch the screen.

"You can do this."

"Yeah." The word comes out as a breath as she blinks and finally starts to read and type what she needs to.

I peer over her shoulder as she goes, noting her birthday again and working out her age this time. She's younger than me by a year. Huh, interesting. I thought she was a junior as well, but she must be a sophomore.

My eyes dart to her face, and I can't help frowning.

It feels weird having a kid with someone I don't even know these basic details about.

"What are you majoring in?" I ask.

"Huh?" She glances at me, then back at the form. "Is it asking me that?" She scans the page again.

"No, I'm just... curious."

"Oh." She shifts in her seat, giving me a fleeting smile before starting to tap the column of boxes on the sheet. It's a relief to see her crossing off all the allergies and ailments. She's a healthy chick. "I'm not exactly sure yet, but I'm a numbers geek, so I guess I'm leaning toward statistics. I love data and analysis, that kinda stuff."

"Cool." I nod. "I'm doing sports science."

"Yeah, I figured. My guess is that you want to go pro, though, right?"

"Yeah." It's impossible not to smile at the idea.

She matches my expression. "Yeah, well, I want to be the girl studying your games and doing all the stats analysis on the players and stuff."

"Even cooler." And I mean it. Who knew math nerds could be so sexy? I'm digging it.

She takes in a breath, then signs the form. Her digital signature looks like a five-year-old did it, but no can ever sign a tablet with their finger and make it look half decent.

"I'll take it." Jumping up, I return it to the counter. It's good to move. I'm feeling twitchy, like I've got ants crawling all over my body. What I need is an intense hockey practice. Thank fuck I have one in like an hour. I'm gonna skate like demons are chasing me.

Slumping back into my seat, I check my watch and wince. I should be in a tutoring session right now. I canceled this morning, and he said that was cool, but we'd need to make up the time because the assignments I have piling up are gonna kick my ass if I don't stay on top of them. He's dead set on me passing with flying colors, but if you ask me, "Cs get degrees," and I am totally fine with that.

I've arranged to go see him after practice, which is going to make my night a bit of a suck-fest, but it's better to study with someone than alone, so I just have to lump it. Pros are the number one goal, but they're not a guarantee, and I can't go fucking up my future by being lazy.

My eyes dart to Caroline's stomach.

My future.

Shit. If she keeps this baby, I'm going to have to take that into consideration. It's not like we'll be moving in together, but I'll still have to be around, right? There's no point being there just for the pregnancy. Part of not bailing is showing up for birthday parties and special events too. It's being there after school to throw a ball and play tag. All the things I desperately wanted but didn't get.

Fuck. I can't do this.

I don't know how to be a dad.

For a second, I want to drop to my knees and beg her to abort this thing. It'll hurt, for sure, but then we can move on with our lives and—

"Caroline," A nurse calls into the room. "This way." She smiles at us, flicking her fingers to follow her.

Before we get to the office, Caroline is weighed, her height is checked, plus her blood pressure taken. She then has to pee in a plastic cup, because apparently fifteen positive pregnancy tests aren't proof enough.

Finally, we're walking into a pristine office with posters of skinless bodies on the walls. I immediately start naming the muscles on the closest diagram. It's a force of habit now, and I blame my tutor for that torturous memorization week that nearly did my head in.

"Okay, Caroline Mason?" A doctor walks into the room, closing the door behind her.

We both glance up, and I take in the dark-skinned lady with glasses and a hot bod.

It's impossible not to check out her swaying hips in that fitted pencil skirt as she walks around her desk, but then I feel bad because the mother of my child is right beside me.

Caroline glances at me, then darts her eyes away, crossing her arms over her belly and kind of shrinking in on herself.

My hand takes up an automatic post on her lower back and doesn't seem to want to leave, even after we sit down next to each other opposite the doctor.

"So..." The doctor looks over her iPad, then glances back up with a gentle smile. "Are we excited about this pregnancy, or is it an unplanned thing?"

"Unplanned," Caroline squeaks. "I'm only a sophomore."

"Okay." The woman nods, then starts working through a series of questions.

Her calm, soft demeanor seems to settle Caroline, and I can feel her relax as they talk. I sit there quietly listening in, then tune out for a minute as I gaze at the posters on the wall again, then come back in when I hear the word *options*.

"I don't know." Caroline shakes her head. "I don't know what to do."

"Okay." The doctor nods. "Well, you have a little time. By my calculations, you're about seven weeks along, so it'd be wise to make a decision within the next month, I'd say. The sooner the better, really."

Caroline swallows.

"I know this is tricky. There are a lot of things to consider. Pros and cons to both. But the good thing is that you do have plenty of options in front of you. My job is to make sure you're healthy and safe." She stands, pointing to the curtained area behind us. "Do you mind if I do a quick examination?"

"Uh... no." Caroline stands, and I stay put, shifting awkwardly in my seat as I listen to the curtain swish and murmured conversation.

Finally, the curtain pops back open and I glance over my shoulder, watching Caroline tuck her hair behind her ears and give the doctor a weak smile.

"Everything feels healthy and normal right now. It's great that you're not getting morning sickness. You mentioned mild nausea, which is completely normal. Some women get it far worse, so thank your lucky stars for that."

Caroline's laughter is as weak as her smile as she takes a seat beside me.

"Next time, we'll be able to do an ultrasound and hear the baby's heartbeat."

My stomach drops.

"I know you haven't decided yet, but if you still have the baby in a month, I'd like you to come back for another checkup. In the meantime, I'm going to suggest some prenatal vitamins that you should start taking. Just in case you decide to continue with the pregnancy." Her smile is kind as she scribbles something on a small notepad.

Caroline starts biting her thumbnail, and I gently take her hand, threading my fingers between hers. I'm not even sure why. I don't hold chicks' hands. It feels way too intimate.

Staring down at our intertwined fingers, I'm surprised by how natural it seems.

She squeezes my hand, and I rub my thumb over her knuckles.

"Hey, it's going to be okay." The doctor smiles before ripping off the top sheet of paper and passing it to us. "I know this is overwhelming and scary, but you've got this. You just need to make a choice and then embrace it. The fact that you've got each other for support is huge. Whatever you decide, you're gonna be fine."

"Thanks," I murmur, rising from my chair, suddenly desperate to get out of here.

She thinks we're a couple.

I should correct her, but I don't... and Caroline doesn't either.

Shit. This is bad.

I nudge Caroline out of the room, and we head out of there as fast as we can. I need to hustle or I'm gonna be late for practice. That's the excuse I give her as I unlock the car.

We don't say anything as I drive back to Huxley Hall.

Caroline's biting her thumbnail again, but I don't take her hand this time. I can't. I shouldn't.

We're not a couple, and we can't go acting like one, right? That'll only confuse the situation more. I don't know what the hell that shit was I pulled in the doctor's office, but I can't go crossing that line again.

I punch the brakes, and we jerk to a quick stop outside her building.

"Sorry," I mutter, unable to look at her.

She's staring at me. I can feel her gaze burning my skin.

"Okay, well..." She opens her mouth to say I don't know what, but then she lets out a sigh and leaves my car.

The door shuts, and I finally turn in time to watch her walk away.

"Fuck." I tip my head back, then bang it on the headrest. "Fuck!"

Peeling away from the curb with a squeal, I race toward the arena and pull into a parking spot next to Ethan's truck.

I'm not late yet, but I still run like I am, busting into the locker room and stalking to the bench.

"Where have you been?" Asher looks at me.

"Nowhere," I bark.

Connor and Riley share a confused frown while Baxter looks at me like he's trying to read my mind. I see them out of the corner of my eye, but I refuse to look their way. Guys walk into the locker room pissed off sometimes; that doesn't mean we have to talk about it.

"Okay, man." Asher slaps my shoulder. "See you out there."

He files out of the locker room with the others until

I'm the only one left. At least I think I am. It's not until after I plow my fist into my locker that I notice Liam in the corner. I let out a heavy sigh and rest my forehead against the cold metal.

"Is she keeping it?"

"I don't know," I mumble.

"'Kay. Well, I'm here if you need me, all right?"

"Yeah." I work my jaw to the side and can't even look at him.

If he says some shit like *It's gonna be okay*, I will fucking lose it.

"Get changed. Give it to the ice."

Closing my eyes, I gratefully listen to him leave the locker room and figure that's damn good advice. For the first time ever, I'm tempted to ask Coach for the hardest practice yet. Give me the gauntlet or the iron cross. I'll take it. I'll fucking revel in it.

Anything to stop me from thinking about pregnancy tests and doctor's visits and a redhead with big blues eyes and a baby growing in her belly.

CHAPTER 13
CAROLINE

It's been three days since my doctor's appointment, and in that short time, I've become obsessed with googling things about pregnancy. This is what I do when I'm stressed—I learn. I seriously geek out, figuring the more information the better. I don't think it's actually working in this case, though, because the more I learn, the more freaked out I get.

I've researched pregnancy, focusing mainly on the first trimester, because that's what I'm in. When that got to be too much, I looked into abortion for a while. When I couldn't handle that anymore, I went back to baby stuff and then briefly looked at adoption stuff before coming around to the whole "how much my body's going to change if I go through with this" thing.

What I really should do is throw my laptop out the window.

My search history is a chaotic mess, giving away just how torn I am about this whole thing. Can't I just wish it never happened?

Can't I just go back to being the carefree girl with the uber crush on one of Nolan U's hockey stars?

Everything felt so innocent and fun and light two months ago. Now it's all heavy and intense and... ugh! Casey's face when he dropped me off. I haven't spoken to him or texted him since Thursday, because it was clear he was regretting getting involved. I know he wants to do the right thing, but it's so obvious he doesn't want to, you know?

I don't know what's driving his sense of duty. I mean, I guess I appreciate it, but a little enthusiasm on his part wouldn't hurt.

Enthusiasm? Are you crazy? How can anyone possibly be enthusiastic about this?

Whatever I do, I'm going to have regrets. I just need to figure out which ones I can stand to live with.

"Seriously, would you stop googling shit? Your brain's going to explode." Lani walks into the room, drying her hair after her shower. I turn to watch the steam rolling out of our little bathroom. Her showers are always scorching, and the walls are left with thick layers of condensation, even when she has the fan running the whole time.

Spinning back to face my desk, I slap my laptop closed and plant my elbows on the wood. My head flops into my palms, quickly getting tangled in my thick hair.

"Look, I know this sucks. I get it, okay? But you're only torturing yourself. You just have to make a decision."

"It's not that easy," I grumble.

"I know. No matter what you do, it'll hurt. But the indecision you're warring with is just as much of a killer. I hate seeing you suffer like this."

With a huff, I slap my arms down on the desk and spin back to look at her. She's dressed now, her head tipped to the side as she squeezes the last of the water out of her long black locks. She'll blow-dry it next; she always does.

My head starts to bob as I know exactly what I'll do when she walks back into that bathroom. I'll open up my laptop again, because I am a glutton for punishment.

"Look, maybe we should—"

There's a cheerful knock at the door. Lani flinches, staring at the wood with a cautious frown. "Who is it?"

"Uh, hi, yeah, it's... it's Ben. Caroline and I met at a party a while back."

An ugly feeling spikes through my chest as I whip around to bulge my eyes at Lani.

He lets out an awkward chuckle. "I've been looking for her, and, well, I found out she lives in Huxley Hall. Someone let me in as they were leaving and told me this is her room."

"They're not supposed to do that," Lani softly mutters while my eyes grow even wider.

"I hope you don't mind me showing up unannounced like this. I'm probably..." He sighs, and I can picture his long fingers running through his hair. "I just really want to see her again, and I never got her number."

I cringe, memories of that party coming back to me in fuzzy flashes.

Ugh! I so can't do this right now.

"Don't tell him I'm here," I mouth, dashing into the bathroom.

Squeezing my eyes shut, I hope the sound of Lani

opening our door masks the sound of me clicking the bathroom door shut.

"Ben, hey. How are you? I'm Lani."

"Yeah, I remember. It's nice to see you again." His voice sounds like he's smiling.

"So, you're after Caroline, huh?"

"Yeah. Uh... sorry if I'm crossing a line here." He lets out another awkward laugh. "I swear, I'm not a stalker, I just... can't stop thinking about her, and I'm really keen to reconnect."

My face scrunches as I bite back a whining whimper and rest my head against the wet tiled wall.

"Sorry, she's not here right now. But I'll definitely tell her you stopped by."

"That would be awesome. Thank you."

"Okay."

"Uh, do you want my number? She could call—"

"Why don't you give it to her when you see her?"

"Yeah, all right. I'll, um... I mean, do you know when she'll be back?"

"Today? Probably late. Not sure. But I'll definitely tell her you stopped by."

Great. She's repeating herself. It's so obvious she's lying.

Ben takes a minute to respond, and my stomach tenses as I wait for him to call her on it, but instead he sighs. "Okay, well, thanks. I just... I'd love to see her again, you know?"

"Yeah. I understand." Lani's voice goes soft, like she's smiling, and I scowl at the towels hanging on the back of the bathroom door.

Why is she being so nice to him?

"Well, hopefully I'll see you around." He sounds so disappointed, and now I feel like total shit.

"Yeah." Lani's voice is too tight. "See ya, Ben."

The door clicks shut, and I wait a beat to make sure he's clear of our room before I walk back into it.

"He's gone." Leilani's tone has lost all its sweetness, and I creep open the bathroom door to her unimpressed frown.

"What?" I flick my hand at her.

She crosses her arms with a reprimanding mama look. "You need to tell that guy there's nothing going on between you two."

I roll my eyes. "Has my serious ghosting not been enough for him? The guy just won't quit."

"Because you're not being honest with him! I know you don't want to hurt his feelings or anything, but you're being rude and immature by ignoring him. Just tell him the truth."

"I can't." My voice pitches. "He doesn't want to hear that I'm not interested in him." I let out a groan, fisting the top of my hair. "I never should have flirted with him at that party."

She snorts. "Flirted. Yeah, that's all you were doing."

I narrow my eyes at her. "I was drunk off my ass, okay?"

Lani narrows her eyes and shakes her head. "You can't keep using that excuse. It's not fair to leave him hanging. The guy likes you. He deserves an explanation."

"And what am I supposed to say?"

"The truth might be good." She bulges her eyes at me.

"Like you said, I don't want to hurt his feelings, and it's not like I can tell him I'm pregnant!"

"Why not?"

I whip around to gape at her. Has she lost her mind?

But that look she's firing at me is making my insides squirm. Turning my back with a huff, I start tidying my desk, picking up scrunched gum wrappers and used tissues. "It's not like you haven't flirted with guys at parties before. It doesn't take much to send out what you think is a light, playful message and for them to get the wrong idea."

"I think you sticking your tongue down his throat and practically dragging him into a bedroom was more than a light, playful message. You do realize you're treating him exactly the same way Casey treated you."

My insides bristle, and it takes serious effort not to snap at her to shut up. Working my jaw to the side, I take a calming breath and mutter, "I never once said I'd call him. I didn't give him my number, and he didn't give me his either!"

"Because you bailed on him before he could get his pants back on."

"We tell each other too much," I mutter, throwing away my trash with a growl. Half of it lands on the floor. Dropping to my knees with a string of curses, I snap over my shoulder, "Stop being so judgy. You can't tell me you haven't kissed a random guy at a party before! You've had a one-night stand. You know how they go. A couple weeks ago, you went to that football party with every intention of getting laid. I haven't seen *you* calling anyone back!"

My friend goes stiff, the muscles in her neck straining as she tries to counter my insults. "Stop changing the subject. You're the one in the wrong here, not me."

"I just don't need some guilt trip right now. I have

enough on my plate, in case you haven't noticed. And you standing there being all Miss Perfect and judging my every move is making me feel like shit!"

Lani's lips form a thin, straight line across her face, her nostrils flaring as she looks out the window. I watch those muscles in her neck ping tight, and my shoulders slump.

Am I seriously yelling at my only ally? She may not agree with my decisions, but she's my best friend and I need her.

"Look, I'm sorry." I close my eyes, my voice thick with remorse. "This pregnancy crisis is turning me into a full-blown bitch. I'm not trying to take it out on you. I just wish Ben would leave me alone. And I wish... you weren't so unimpressed by me."

Lani shakes her head. "I'm not unimpressed by you. You're my favorite person on the whole damn planet. I just want what's best for you, that's all."

I swallow, too afraid to ask her what she thinks is best for me. Her answer might be different from mine, and I can't hear that right now.

Dropping the scattered tissues into the trash can, I stand up and straighten my shirt. The vibe in the room is tense and somber. I'm seriously hating it.

"So, anyway... how was that party?" I put on a bright smile, trying to turn this thing around. "I forgot to ask. You flew solo, but did you actually have a good time? Did you meet someone? Did you hook up and have hot, wild sex the way you wanted?"

She clenches her jaw and grits out, "I wasn't looking for hot, wild sex."

"Sorry." I wince at her indignant glare. "I didn't

mean..." I sigh, hating how much I'm sucking at this. I'm trying to make things right between us, dammit. "So, you didn't meet anyone?"

Lani licks her lips, shaking her head as she keeps staring out the window. "Nope. No one worth mentioning."

Aw man. She looks so sad right now.

I close the space between us and glide my arm around her shoulders. "Don't worry, babe. You'll find your man one day."

"I don't need one." She shrugs me off, lifting her chin. "I kinda like being on my own."

My nose wrinkles. "Really?"

Why would anyone choose to be on their own?

Everybody needs someone, right? And being in love, that's like the ultimate goal.

Well, I think it is, anyway.

Leilani's always been a little tougher than me, but I thought even she'd want to find herself a partner one day. Someone she can share her life with.

We've talked about this before, dreamed into the future and painted visions of flying high in our chosen fields and meeting up for lunch dates, then attending parties and going away on island vacations with our hunky husbands.

With a heavy sigh, she walks to her bed, snatching her purse and lifting the strap over her shoulder. "I'm just gonna..." She points to the door.

"Where are you going?"

"I just need a walk."

"Do you want me to come with?"

Shoving a beanie over her wet hair, she glances my

way and gives me a sad smile. "No, I'm good. I think I'll just go to the library."

The door clicks shut behind her, and I stare at the wood, totally confused.

She didn't even dry her hair. I've never seen her walk out the door totally makeup free with wet hair. She doesn't do that.

I have no idea what is up with that girl at the moment. But the idea of having to try and find out feels like too much.

Yes, it probably makes me selfish, but I'm dealing with my own crap right now and I just... I want...

"Shit," I mutter, marching for the door and grabbing my own beanie and jacket.

Maybe I need a walk too.

CHAPTER 14
CASEY

Tapping the controller with my thumbs, I try to navigate the next level of *Devil's Doorway*, but I'm struggling to get into it. I kind of need Mick here spurring me on, but now that she's moved out, she's not around as much anymore.

Right now, Ethan's over at her place. They're probably getting it on. We all need to burn off steam after an intense weekend away. I mean, it was awesome, because we made the fucking playoffs! But both games were brutal, and we had to party hard afterward, right?

We got home at like three this morning, and I should be feeling way fucking better than I am. I should be riding high after the victory.

But I'm sitting here on the couch playing a video game when I should be celebrating balls deep in some wet pussy like Ethan is no doubt doing.

I couldn't even do it at the bar last night. Girls were clinging to us the second we got off the bus, but none of them had red hair, and even though I got pretty hot and heavy with a leggy Latina, we didn't go all the way. I don't even know what stopped me.

Yes, you do.

I tell the voice in my head to fuck off. There's no way I'm going to deny myself sex just because I'm going through this thing with Caroline.

It just stopped me doing it last night at the bar is all.

I'm tempted to go back to Offside right now and find myself some afternoon booty. I kind of need to prove that I haven't lost my mojo.

I end the game and am just standing up to head out the door when it pops open.

"Hey. Anyone home?"

"'Sup, Ashman. I'm just heading out." I grab my keys off the side table, ready to ask him if he wants to play wingman, when I jerk to a stop and blink at the person standing behind him.

"Look who I found walking down our street." He grins at me.

"Uh... hi." Caroline gives me an awkward wave. "He invited me. I hope you don't mind. He wouldn't stop asking. He's kinda bossy." She points her thumb at him and bulges her eyes at me.

I nod. "He can be a very bossy bitch."

This gets an instant laugh out of her, and damn if it doesn't make me feel like a fucking king.

"You wanted to come in," Asher argues, then turns to me. "I could tell she wanted to." Shedding his coat, he offers to take hers as well.

She mumbles her thanks while he hangs up her jacket and steals the beanie off her head.

"Oh." She reaches up to smooth down those vibrant locks, and I can't help grinning at her.

The urge to find me some booty at Offside has disappeared for some reason.

That should be a fucking red flag right there, but I ignore it and head into the kitchen. "You want a drink or something?"

"Yeah, I guess."

"Have you had your coffee for the day?" I smirk at her.

"Yes." She tips her head back with a groan, and I stare at the smooth skin on her neck, wanting to run the tip of my tongue from her collarbone to her chin.

My insides sizzle, and I force Mr. Jones to behave himself, turning away and practically croaking out my next question. "How about a hot chocolate, then?"

"Sounds good."

I glance back in time to see her lips curl into a smile, but something is definitely off. She's looking tired and unsettled.

I want to make her feel better, but I'm not really sure how. What can I say to make her laugh again?

Or maybe I should ask her "Is something wrong?" But will that just open a big-ass can of worms that I won't know how to deal with?

I spin and focus on the boiling water in the kettle while she inches into the kitchen and starts studying the photos on the fridge.

"Oh, that's from last year." I stand behind her and point to a picture of all the guys lifting their beers in celebration. Fuck, she smells good. I want to bury my nose in her hair and inhale like she's a line of cocaine.

She swivels her head, catching my eye as she taps her

finger on the photo. "Look at your face." She laughs at my crazy expression.

"Hey, we'd just won an important game. I have a right to look batshit crazy. I was insanely happy."

She laughs again, the sound cheerful and bright. But then the sound fizzles out and I'm suddenly aware that I'm still standing right behind her, close enough to feel her heat. Her gaze darts away from my eyes, landing on my mouth as a wispy breath rushes out of her. She swallows and shuffles back from me, tucking her hair behind her ear with a twitchy smile.

"So, I heard you won this weekend too. Congratulations. The playoffs. That's big."

Good. Yeah, space. We need space. Because whatever is happening between us right now is fucking electrifying.

I inch back toward the kettle, my brain cells coming back online with a little distance. Spinning around, I face her with a wide grin.

"It's huge, baby." I lift my hands in the air and whoop so loud that she actually jumps.

But it makes her smile come back full force, and fuck, she's so beautiful.

And making her smile that way feels like the biggest win.

As soon as the hot chocolates are done, I pass one to her and then Asher. He takes a seat on the armchair adjacent to me, and we talk about the away games. Caroline asks all the right questions and shows off how much she loves and understands hockey. It makes it easy to talk, not having to explain hockey speak. She gets it. She gets us, and reliving the games with her is triumphant.

She's stoked too. Whatever was pulling her down when she first arrived seems to have lifted, and I like watching her relax.

Once game talk's done, there's a weird lull in the conversation. I should start asking her some things about herself. You know, the whole "she's carrying my kid" thing, so I should probably know her favorite color, but then she points at the controllers on the coffee table.

"Who plays?" She glances between Asher and me.

"We all do, but Casey's the only addicted one." Asher stands, slapping my shoulder before collecting the dirty mugs and walking back into the kitchen.

"I'm not addicted." I shake my head.

"Yeah, he is!" Asher calls.

I throw a glare over my shoulder, then glance back with a winning smile. "I'm really not."

"Sure." She laughs, taking the controller. "What's your favorite game?"

Well, if she's gonna go asking that...

Picking up the other controller, I flick on the TV and walk her through *Devil's Doorway,* acting like a teenager and finding any excuse I can to bump our knees together or mansplain how to use a gaming controller.

I'm not trying to be a douche, I'm just looking for any excuse I can to touch her. I need to get the fuck over myself and pull it together, but she's right next to me on the couch, and the buzz between us is impossible to ignore.

She plays a little, firing looks my way and sending all the blood rushing to Mr. Jones every time she bites her lip or catches my eye.

How we aren't playing tonsil hockey and stripping

each other's clothes off right now is beyond compre-hension.

I do my best to focus on the game, and eventually she sits back and lets me do most of the work.

I can see her starting to get bored, her eyes glazing over, her head tipping to the side. I don't understand, because it's *Devil's Doorway*, the best game ever invented. It's hard not to be offended by her lack of enthusiasm.

"Are you dozing off?" I nudge her with my foot.

She jolts upright, sniffing as she comes out of her daze. "No." Her mouth stretches wide with a yawn.

"Need yourself a nap time, do ya?"

She gives me a side-eye. "Growing a baby is tiring work."

As soon as the words pop out of her mouth, the relaxed vibe in the room gets sucked into oblivion. My fingers go stiff around the remote, the reminder like a slap in the face.

"I didn't mean to say that," she mutters, then closes her eyes with a sigh. "Just forget I said that."

"I can't." I drop the controller, and it clatters onto the coffee table. "It's the truth."

"Yeah," she murmurs. "I'm tired all the time." Her nod is minimal, and the black cloud that's just shifted over us is fucking oppressive.

We both feel it and obviously have no idea how to go back to the chill vibe we were coasting on before.

"I hate this." She jolts off the couch. "I didn't come here to depress you, okay? I just had to get out of my room for a while and away from my computer and all of..." She points at her stomach. "This!" She makes a face. "You were the perfect distraction until I ruined it."

"You didn't ruin it. Here, let's just play something else. Find something good to distract you again. What games are you into?"

She spins to look at the TV, her lower lip sticking out. "*Just Dance*?"

"*Just... Dance*?"

"Yeah, you've heard of it, right?"

I want to say *"Hell no,"* but I have heard of it.

Fuck it, I can still say *"Hell no."*

"We don't have that one."

Her eyes narrow at me. "We can always watch some YouTube clips. Dance along to those. Come on, hockey man." She playfully slaps my knee, and I start shaking my head. "Can the big boy not dance?" Her eyes start to sparkle. "You're so smooth on the ice. It doesn't transfer to anything else?"

"I'm smooth," I argue, grabbing her wrist when she goes for my knee again.

With a light tug, I pull her down onto me. She falls with a gasp, and then her tits are squishing into my chest, her breath mingling with mine as I hold her against me.

"See what I mean?" I whisper, because that's all I can manage. "Smooth."

You're playing with fire, man. Stop this.

But I can't. Because her hair smells so good, and her lips are right there. Those big blue eyes are drinking me in like I'm hot, and who says we can't distract ourselves with something both our bodies obviously want?

My lips part, an invitation to my bedroom right on the tip of my tongue, when Asher strolls back in.

"No doing it on the living room couch. That's public domain, dude." He throws his baseball cap at us.

I catch it just before it hits Caroline's face and drop it on the floor with a growl.

"I was actually about to invite—" A phone starts ringing, cutting me off. "Whose is that?"

"Mine." Caroline scrambles to get off my knee but catches her heel on the coffee table, tipping sideways.

I lunge forward, snatching her arm before she hits the floor and pulling her back to her feet. Her shoulder hits my chest and I wrap my arm around her waist, making sure she's steady before I'm willing to let her go.

She glances up at me, and there's that look in her eyes again.

Fuck, she wants me.

My tongue darts out of my mouth, wetting my lower lip as my gaze drops to her lips.

"You gonna answer that or what?" Asher stalks into the entryway, obviously digging Caroline's phone out of her coat pocket. "Hello, you've reached Caroline's phone."

"Who's this?" a sharp voice says through the speaker, and Caroline winces, sucking in a soft hiss.

"This is Asher. How may I help you?" His smile is all charm, the way it always is when he's speaking to women. It's surprising that his teeth don't sparkle like they do in cartoon movies. Apparently he has a sexy voice, but I don't hear it.

"Why do you have Caroline's phone?" the woman snaps. "Is she there? Wherever the hell *there* is?"

"Calm down, sweet thing. She's right here."

"'Sweet thing'? You did *not* just call me that."

Asher's eyebrows form a quick roller coaster across his forehead. "What's your name, then?"

"Who the hell do you think you are? And what have

you done with my friend? You give her this phone *right now*."

Asher frowns at the device, shooting a surprised look at Caroline before lifting it closer to his mouth. "Well, Miss Pleasant, maybe if you told me your name, I could call you that, because I'm quickly realizing that sweet and you aren't simpatico."

"You don't even know me."

"This short conversation is telling me enough."

"Oh really? And what have you figured out, genius?"

Asher's eyebrows dip into a sharp V. "That I'm currently speaking to an uptight shrutebag who needs to calm her tits and chill."

Caroline slaps a hand over her mouth, dipping her chin and... Is she laughing?

I can't decide what her shoulder shake means, but Asher is getting totally riled by this chick—I think it's Leilani—and he needs to calm his own fucking tits.

Flicking my fingers at him, I hold my palm out for the phone.

"Is Caroline there?" the woman yells. "Put her on *now*, you lumpatious asshole!"

"Happily, if it means I get to stop talking to you!" He shoves the phone at me and stalks out of the room, muttering under his breath.

"Uh... hi, Leilani. It's me, Casey."

"Oh, she's with you."

I cringe and share an awkward look with Caroline. She rolls her eyes, and I hand her the phone. She turns it off speaker and presses it to her ear.

"Hey. Everything cool?" Her face turns a bright pink as her roommate talks to her in staccato. I can hear the snappy beat from here. "Yeah, I'm sorry. My phone was in my coat pocket, so I didn't hear any of your texts... No! We were playing video games..." Her gaze darts to me, her cheeks going redder than her hair. "Yes, that's all we were doing... I'm safe, okay? You don't need to freak out. You're not my mother." She closes her eyes with a sigh. "And I appreciate that. I really do. I'll come back now, okay? We can have dinner together." After a few more nods and a mumbled goodbye, Caroline hangs up. "Well, I'm gonna go."

"Do you need a ride?"

"Actually, I might walk. I need the exercise, and it'll give Lani a chance to cool down." She winces.

"She seemed really riled." I mirror her expression.

She brushers her fingers through the air as she tries to downplay it. "She was just worried. She's really a great person once you get to know her. She can just come across as a little prickly sometimes, but I swear she's really cool."

"Okay." I nod, then point my thumb at the doorway Asher disappeared through. "He can be an uptight prick as well, but he's one of my best friends, so... you put up with shit, right?"

"Yeah." She smiles at me, then dips her chin. "Hey, uh... thanks for a fun afternoon."

"Anytime." I stay where I am behind the couch, because I'm pretty sure if I go anywhere near her right now, I'm gonna want to bury my tongue inside her mouth while running my hands all over her curvaceous body, and then she'll never get back to her stressed-out roommate.

Images of our one night together flash through me,

and I have to spin away, slump onto the couch, and let her leave Hockey House without a proper goodbye.

Fuck.

I run my hands through my hair with a groan and flop back against the cushions.

I've heard that expression "sweet torture" before. I think this is exactly what it feels like.

CHAPTER 15
CAROLINE

I was right about the walk being good for me and Lani.

By the time I get back, she's sitting on her bed smiling. We talk about my afternoon and hers. She checked out a large stack of books at the library. Half of them are for me, because Lani's like that, you know? She never just thinks about herself, which is why I'm now surrounded by fantasy novels, a fluffy rom-com, and a heavy-looking historical fiction. There's no way I'll get through them all, so I just have to decide which one I'll go with.

I blink my heavy eyelids.

Dinner was great, and I'm so stuffed right now. But I can never resist Huxley Hall's spaghetti and meatballs. I gorged myself on that pasta, and now I've got a little food baby going on. I run my hand over the bump in my stomach and have an internal freakout that soon this could be an actual baby bump.

How long does it take before I start showing?

My brain scrambles for that tidbit, then quickly does the calculations as I work out that I've got a good month or so before my pants start getting too tight, and even then, I can probably hide it for a few months after that if I select my clothes carefully.

That's if I keep the baby.

My chest spasms for a second, like someone is fisting my heart.

I can't think about that right now.

I'll never get to sleep if I have this shit running through my brain just before I lie down.

Lani shuffles in her bed, rolling to the side as she gets absorbed in one of her thriller novels. Her long black hair lies against the pillow, draping over the side of the bed.

I stare at it for a moment, then force my eyes back to these books. But I can't even decide which one to read. This is hopeless!

"I'm gonna take a quick shower." I jump off the bed, needing to do something with my body. Movement is good. Maybe I can do shower aerobics or something.

Yeah, and break your tailbone when you slip.

Shutting the bathroom door a little too hard, I turn on the spray and start to undress. As the air hits my exposed skin, my brain starts taunting me with images of Casey. He was so close to me this afternoon, I could smell his deodorant. It was this intoxicating scent that had my lady parts dancing. My insides quiver as I feel myself on his knee again. His lips were close enough to kiss, and I'm sure he wanted to.

He wants to kiss anyone with boobs and a V-jay.

The reminder makes me frown, but then my mind jumps back to January, when he was so close. Inside-me close, his fingers gripping my ankles, his lips nibbling my toes.

I circle my erect nipples, then give them a light pinch. My body zings with pleasure, and I can't help an indulgent smile as I step under the hot spray. The water droplets soon become Casey's kisses, peppering my skin.

Leaning back against the glass, I lift my foot, resting it on the tiles as I picture Casey kneeling before me. His hot tongue would do dirty things to me, and as my fingers circle my swollen clit, I close my eyes and take myself back to that sorority house bed.

Casey teasing my clit. Casey lifting my legs and thrusting into me. Casey's fingers squeezing my breasts, his mouth devouring mine, his teeth lightly scraping my skin.

Quick gasps punch out of me as I build to a climax, my hormones on overdrive as I move my fingers faster and faster—a rush to the pleasure line. It takes mere seconds for the orgasm to hit me, and I splinter apart in the shower, shoving my fingers inside myself and clamping my lips together against a loud wail that will no doubt capture Lani's attention.

My body is heaving as I stand there and let the vibrations work through me. What I wouldn't give for Casey's dick to spear me right now. How I wouldn't love to take it from him—hard, fast thrusts or slow, long ones. Whatever, I'm seriously up for anything, because touching myself doesn't feel like enough.

I want more.

I *need* more.

Actually, I kind of do. Like seriously. I read in my research this week that due to increased blood flow in the area, my V-jay is wetter and more sensitive than usual. I have an increased libido. It even said that I should take advantage of this time with my partner.

Problem is... I don't have a partner.

You have Casey. He said he'd be there for whatever you need.

"Oh, that's so tempting," I whisper into the shower spray before plunging my face beneath the water and trying to be logical about this.

By the time I'm done washing and soaking, I think I've managed to talk myself out of the idea. It'd be a huge mistake, turning Casey into my on-call fuck buddy. Our relationship is complicated enough as it is.

Disappointment sears me as I dry off and slip back into bed. Lani's already turned her light off, and I pull the covers up to my chin and try not to think about how great having sex with Casey again would be.

But it's a bad idea.

Totally.

The worst.

Biting my bottom lip, I try to stop my smile from growing, but I can't.

It might be the worst idea, but oh, it would so be the best experience.

CHAPTER 16
CASEY

I wipe my face down after my morning workout. I pushed hard today, needing to expel whatever this energy is inside me. Ever since Sunday, I've been restless. My brain is a constant tornado, and it's driving me fucking insane.

But there's nothing I can do about any of this shit.

I can't force Caroline into a quick decision over such a massive issue.

The thought that I'm gonna be a dad haunts me. I'm not ready. I don't know what the fuck I'm doing. It kept me awake for hours last night, panic sizzling through me as I tried to imagine what life will be like if she keeps it.

How the hell is she supposed to finish college with a baby hanging off her hip?

How am I?

During hockey season, I'm away so much, and when I am here, expectations are huge. I've got workouts, training, tutoring, classes, assignments, studying... How am I supposed to juggle all of that and a baby?

And then there's Caroline.

Sweet Caroline with her luscious lips and hair and smell and smile and... Fuck.

Dipping my head, I plow my fingers through my hair, wondering if I can squeeze out my brain so I don't have to think about this shit anymore. She tortures me—in the best kind of way—but I seriously don't need this right now.

I'd give anything to go back to the way things were before she threw those pregnancy tests at me.

But then, if she hadn't, she wouldn't have spent the afternoon with me on Sunday, and I'm scared to admit how much I enjoyed it.

"Let's go, Pierce!" Asher shouts at me as he wanders out of the locker room.

I raise my hand to acknowledge that I heard him but still move like a snail as I get ready for the day.

I have classes all morning, then a study break this afternoon where I seriously have to get shit done. I have two assignments due next week, plus a test that I should probably start studying for. And I have hockey practice this afternoon, and the assistant coach already warned me that it's going to be intense.

If we win this game, we'll have a shot at competing in the quarter finals for the Frozen Faceoff. We're ranking top of the table with two games to go. Puck yeah! We're gonna be NCAA champions this year. I can feel it.

Slapping my locker closed, I pull on my jacket and snatch my bag off the floor. Racing after Asher, I make it to his truck just before he starts pulling out of his parking spot. The asshole was gonna leave without me.

"I can't be late again because of your slow ass," he grumbles, peeling away from the arena.

I don't make him late that often. The guy is just anal about being on time.

We walk to the sciences building together, then go our separate ways, and I go to each of my morning classes, taking notes and listening like the good boy I am.

My head is pounding by the time I'm finally free for lunch, and I swear I'd give anything to go home for a nap. But I should probably head to the library and...

Any thoughts of studying disintegrate the second I spot a curvy redhead down the adjacent path to me.

"Caroline!" I call her name without even thinking about it and score some curious looks from the group loitering next to me. "'Sup." I raise my chin at them before picking up my pace and jogging over to a girl who is looking kind of nervous.

I have no idea what's up, but I'm frowning when I reach her. "You okay?"

"Uh... yeah." She grips her bag strap and swallows, her gaze darting away. "I just wasn't expecting to see you." Forcing a smile, she finally glances up at me, but she can only hold my gaze for a second.

"What's going on?" I pry for more. It might not be my place, but she looks jittery as hell, and I don't like it. "Has something happened?" I lean forward, whispering near her ear, "With the baby?"

"No." She jolts back from me. "Everything's fine. It's fine. I'm fine." Clearing her throat, she swallows and goes to turn away from me, but I snatch her arm before she can retreat.

"You are not fine. You're acting weird."

"I'm not trying to be weird. I'm just—" She clamps her lips together.

"You're just what?"

Closing her eyes with a sigh, she tips her head back, then glances around us like she's about to tell me some great secret.

I lean a little closer, but her eyebrows are puckering, and I barely hear her when she murmurs, "It's just hard to be around you."

"What?"

"It's hard," she grits out. "To be around you."

Okay, ouch.

"Why? What'd I do?" It's an effort not to snap out the words.

"Nothing." She tuts and shakes her head. "Just forget it. I'm fine. Everything's fine." She takes a quick step away from me and scuttles left, like being too close to me is physically painful.

What the actual fuck?

When she spins and starts this weird kind of walk-jog thing down the path, I have to chase her. I barely need to run to reach her, and then her hurried steps are about equal to one of my decent strides. As soon as I'm beside her, she rolls her eyes.

"Why are you following me?"

"Why are you acting weird?"

"Because I'm a weirdo!"

"No, you're not." I take her arm, forcing her to stop. "I can tell you want to say something to me, but maybe you also don't. Whatever it is, just spit it out. I said I'd be here for you, and if I've done something shitty, I need to know so I won't do it again."

"It's not..." She sighs. "You haven't done anything shitty. It's me, okay? I'm... the problem." She cringes, her fingers shaking as she rubs her forehead, then huffs. "I have... My body is..." Her cheeks flush red as she looks around her, going quiet as a guy walks past us. He's wearing headphones and probably can't hear what she's saying, but she's obviously embarrassed.

"Do you want to go somewhere private to talk?"

She bites her lip, clearly worried, but I have to get to the bottom of this. Like I can concentrate on anything if I'm worried about her.

"Come on. Your dorm's like a two-minute walk, right?"

"Ye-ah. Y-You... wanna go to my dorm?"

"It'll be private, right? You can say whatever you need to without worrying that someone will hear you."

Her shoulders slump, the wind picking up a red curl and blowing it across her face. Chasing it with her fingers, she tucks it behind her ear and flashes me a desperate frown. "You're really not going to let this go, are you?"

"No." I give her an emphatic look. "You obviously need to get something off your chest, and I said I'd be here for you. Whatever you need. So let's go."

"Whatever I need." She mumbles the words as if she's talking to herself and then doesn't say another damn thing until her dorm door clicks shut behind us.

I slip my bag off my shoulder. It lands on the floor with a thump that feels stupidly loud in this quiet space.

"Okay, Mason. We're alone. No one's watching us. No one can hear you. What gives?"

Wringing her hands, she stands in the middle of the room, her cheeks turning the darkest shade of pink I've ever seen.

Seriously. This is killing me. She'd better spill in the next few seconds or my brain's going to explode.

"So, pregnancy is a funny thing." Her blue eyes dart to the floor as she starts playing with one of the metal buttons of her denim jacket. "And my body is going through a lot of changes."

"Okay."

"And it's weird, you know?"

"Not really, but I can imagine." Would it be rude to say, *"Please get to the fucking point"*?

"And one of those weird oddities is that..." She huffs, running her fingers into her hair and fisting those luscious locks.

"Is that...?" I prompt her.

"There's a lot of pressure, and..." She shakes her head, going still as she finally looks me in the eye. I raise my eyebrows at her, and she bites her lip. "You said you had my back, right? No matter what I needed?"

My insides rattle with a warning. Where the hell is this going?

But I did say that, so I'd better fucking nod.

"So, as the baby daddy, it's kind of your responsibility to ease some of this pressure for me."

I don't know what the hell this pressure is, but... "Sure. What do you need?"

Crossing her arms, she squeezes her elbow, her cheeks going even redder as we finally get to the truth. "I'm horny as hell. It's a first trimester thing, apparently, and I need—" She huffs again. "There's only so much that touching myself will satisfy."

My insides ping, this weird, giddy feeling jumping in my belly. My brain is exploding with images of her touching herself, so much that they nearly distract me from the main point.

Holy shit! Is she asking for me to...?

I can't help a grin. "And what do you need exactly?"

She scowls. Her angry look is adorable, and I am having way too much fun right now. "You're really gonna make me say it?"

I nod, my grin playful as I slowly close the distance between us. "You need..."

"I need... dick. I need *your* dick." She flicks her fingers toward my crotch, and I swear it takes everything in me not to punch the air with a whoop.

I've always made a point to never sleep with the same girl twice, but I'm not even hesitating over breaking the rules for her.

It's my responsibility, right?

She just said it.

Before I can waste one more second thinking about that, I scoop my arm around her waist and pull her against me.

Duty fucking calls!

CHAPTER 17
CAROLINE

His lips are hot and demanding, his tongue a fiery poker in my mouth. I take the burn. I welcome it. My already raging hormones are starting a party right now, and I can feel an orgasm building.

With greedy hands, I push the hoodie off his shoulders and yank his shirt up. It's a chaotic, frantic dance as I desperately try to get to his skin. I want my hands on him. I need to feel the hard ridges of his abs and pecs. I want to skim my fingers down the hairline from his belly button to that mound protecting the one thing I need the most.

His tongue and lips are still massacring my mouth, popping free to suck and nibble my chin, my jawline, my neck as he slips the jacket off my shoulders. It lands with a thump on the floor as I tip my head back, giving him easier access to my skin.

I let out a groan, my fried nerves on the verge of full explosion.

He hasn't even touched any of my most sensitive spots yet and I'm already splintering. This is insane.

Grabbing my ass, he grinds our hips together, and the second his hard ridge brushes my V-jay, I am gone. I let out a gasp, my body vibrating as an orgasm crashes through me.

"Are you...?" Casey leans back so he can look at my face.

I can't see him—my eyes have rolled to the back of my head while I ride out this quick, powerful moment of pleasure.

"Already? We're not even naked yet." His surprise is comical, and I end up laughing through the last of my heady rush. It's my low, I-have-no-control-over-myself laugh that makes me sound like a Disney villain, but I can't seem to stop the sound.

My embarrassment is the least of my worries.

Reaching for his pants, I frantically unbutton them, yanking down the fly and shoving them off his hips before quickly shimming out of my own pants.

He wants naked, I'll give him naked.

"I need you now," I pant. "Like now!"

My urgency makes him snicker. The smile on his face is beautiful, but I don't have time to appreciate it as I jump on my bed and kick my underwear off my foot. I'm lying on a mound of unfolded clothes, and something is digging into my back. I wrestle the book out from under me and throw it to the end of the bed before spreading my legs wide like the desperate woman I am.

He drinks me in for a second, like he's enjoying the view, and I start to whine in my throat. "Come on, Casey."

"One sec, let me grab a rubber first."

"No, it's fine. just get in here!" I point to my V-jay.

He stops reaching for his bag and gives me a quizzical frown.

"What?" I snap. "Stop looking at me like that and get your dick in here right now." I part my folds to make it blatantly obvious. Surely he can see how wet and needy I am. Even just the thought of him plunging into me is enough to make me want to come again.

Seriously. My body is insane at the moment.

"I always wrap."

I tip my head back with a groan. "Are you clean?"

"Of course I am."

"When were you last tested?"

"Actually, just last week and—" He frowns, scratching his head like he's struggling with whatever thought is going through his brain right now.

I don't have time to figure it out. My eyes are staring at his erect dick, and my buzzing V-jay is demanding instant satisfaction.

"So, we're good, then." I beckon him with my fingers.

His frown deepens as he rests his hands on his hips. I stare at his protruding cock—so tall and big and beautiful. I need it inside me.

"Come on, Casey. You're clean. I'm clean. And it's not like I can get pregnant again." My voice pitches with urgency. "Just... whatever. Wrap. Don't wrap. Whatever you decide, can you just do it fast? My lady parts are vibrating down here, and I need some relief. Please. Please!" Yes, I'm begging. Not super proud of that, but I'm beyond judging myself, because I'm pregnant and I'm allowed to act like a crazy, horny woman if I want to! My body is doing weird shit to me, and if Casey can ease some of that pressure, then bring it the fuck on!

With a hesitant eyebrow curl, he moves back toward my bed.

I spread my legs a little wider, whimpering. "Yes, yes, please. Please."

The second his knee hits the mattress, my insides start up a rave. It's wild and lawless, a cacophony of sensations traveling through me as he grabs my thighs and shifts me on the bed. His gentle roughness has me biting my lip in excited anticipation, and then he's stretching over me.

His expert fingers find my folds, easing them apart.

I jerk, seconds away from another orgasm. Seriously, it's like every blood cell in my body is congregating down there, singing a chorus of praise.

"You're so wet," he murmurs, kissing the edge of my jaw.

I nudge my hips, telling him to get on with it, and the second his tip starts to split me open, I'm coming undone all over again.

"Yeeeeeessss." I draw out the word like a loud war cry, grabbing his perfect ass cheeks and forcing him to move a little faster.

That plunging sensation, his large cock stretching me so suddenly, sends a fire rippling through me. No, not a fire—a freaking explosion.

I start panting and moaning. I'm pretty sure more yeses are shouted, and maybe his name is thrown in there too. I'm not really certain because actual thought has abandoned me. I am riding a wave of pure ecstasy, and there is nothing else.

"This feels fucking amazing." Casey fists my hair, his panting whispers filling my ear as he rides me like the wild stallion he is.

Thank God for wild stallions!

I take his pounding thrusts with pleasure.

"I've never done this before." He's still talking, his words only just registering as I pick up on his awe-filled tone. I think he must be talking about the fact that he's not wrapped, and he's right. I've never had condom-less sex before, and it's off the charts.

Add that to my already hormone-fueled body and I'm touching the edges of heaven.

Not just touching... diving headfirst, dancing through those fluffy white clouds, basking in that warm light, floating like an angel.

Lifting my leg, I dig my heel into his ass and he groans, rising up on his arms and changing the angle. My boobs, still tucked securely into their bra, start jiggling as he picks up his pace, his rapid, forceful thrusts quickly sending me over the edge.

"Ahhh!" Gripping his arms, I dig my fingers into his taut muscles while he consumes every inch of me. I'm not sure how much more of this I can take. It's too good, too—

And then he starts to come apart, his movements turning jerky as he groans and sets off a jet inside me. Splurges of pure pleasure that finally give me some relief.

CHAPTER 18
CASEY

Holy shit.

Holy. Shit.

Holy.

Shit.

That was fucking amazing.

I'm still inside her, riding out the tail end of this mind-blowing orgasm. Her tight little pussy is milking me dry, and I want to stay buried in her for the rest of eternity.

Turns out unwrapped sex is fucking fantastic!

And she's the only one I'll ever be able to do it with. Until this whole pregnancy thing is over.

The word *pregnancy* starts to clang around in my brain, killing my buzz, until I force my wayward thoughts back into line.

Be in the moment. Don't fuck this up.

Be. In. The moment!

I blink, trying to get my vision back in focus as I gaze down at her.

Those red curls are splayed across her pillow, and the look of satisfaction on her face is a thing of beauty.

"Better?" I whisper, brushing my finger down her face and trying to talk myself into leaving her luscious body.

It seems a shame that I didn't get to play with her fun bags, but I'm pretty sure nibbling her tits would have made her explode. Her body is so sensitive, it's almost funny. One little brush of my tongue in just the right place could probably make her come all over again.

She still hasn't answered me, and I drop down to my elbows. "Did that do the trick?"

"Yeah. Good job, champ." She pats my shoulder, still trying to catch her breath.

I laugh, feeling like a king as I kiss her lips, then sit back and start the cleanup process.

I have to say one thing for condoms, they're a lot less messy.

This pile of clothes we just did it on is gonna need a washing.

Reaching over her, I yank out a bunch of tissues and hand them to her while I jump off the bed and disappear into the bathroom.

My body is still vibrating as I wash up and catch my gaze in the mirror. I shake my head, my lips unable to fight that smile. I end up grinning like I just won a million bucks.

This is crazy!

Walking back into the room, I grab my clothes off the floor, pulling them on as I glance at the bed. She's doing up her fly, and I kind of lament the fact that she didn't get fully naked. I'll have to do something about that next time.

Next time?

There's gonna be a next time?

Careful, dude.

I ignore my inner warnings and give her a winning smile.

She grins back.

"So, will that tide you over for a bit?" I do up my pants and grab my shirt off the floor.

"Yeah, should suffice."

"It was good, right?" I wiggle my eyebrows. "That no-condom thing." I shake my head, still reeling over how fucking fantastic it felt.

"Yeah, it was pretty awesome. You were a solid seven out of ten."

My head pops through my T-shirt, my body tensing as I register what the fuck she just said.

"Seven?" I flash her a look that I'm sure can only be described as appalled. "Seven."

She nods, her face bunching like she's confused by my offense.

"Seven." I have to repeat it one more time so I can make sure that's what she said.

She nods again, her eyes rounding like I need to get over it.

But no fucking way.

I click my fingers, then point at the bed. "Okay, that's it. Get naked right now. We're doing it again."

She starts laughing. The sound bubbling out of her is nearly as beautiful as the sparkle in her eye. And it's only then that I realize she's messing with me.

That little—

Lunging at her with a growl, I enjoy her squeal as I

pluck her off the floor and throw her onto her bed. Teasing like that deserves a good tickle, and I make sure she's squirming and begging for mercy before I finally relent.

"Okay, okay! You're an eleven out of ten!" She wails the last few words.

"You better fucking believe it, baby. I'm always an eleven."

She rolls her eyes, but I kiss that look away. Feeling her melt against me is a triumph in itself. Her fingers curl through my hair, lightly fisting the back and keeping me against her when I start to pull away.

I laugh into her mouth, swiping my tongue deep until I hear that sexy moan of hers.

Finally pulling away, I stare down at her glistening lips, and it hits me like a crowbar to the head.

She's the eleven. Not me.

She's a fucking twelve.

CHAPTER 19
CAROLINE

"Yeah, I'm good." I hope my cousin can't hear the strain in my voice as I try to put on an upbeat, happy vibe.

It's actually not too hard. Sex with Casey yesterday has definitely put me in a better mood. It really released this pressure inside me. Although I can already feel it building again. Seriously, these horny hormones are a living beast that are impossible to control!

But when I slipped into bed last night, no amount of reliving my afternoon fun could take away the weight of the reality I'm facing. I'm horny as hell because I'm *pregnant*.

"I can't believe I'm going to be joining you next year."

Jolie says that every time we talk on the phone. She's a senior in high school, and we grew up together. She's my cousin who also happens to be one of my favorite people, and we're more like sisters, in all honesty. We're cuzsters. And I adore her cherub face and her smile that is so big, you can see her gums. She's a skinny thing with a dorky awkwardness about her, but that only adds to her endearing charm.

"So, tell me about your week." I nestle back into my pillows. "You find the guts to talk to Mr. Leather Jacket yet?"

"No." She groans. "Ugh. He's like a modern-day James Dean. And the fact that I'm comparing him to an actor from like the 1950s shows how incredibly uncool I am and how out of my league he is."

"You always fall for the bad boys."

"I know, right? What's up with that? He's just so incredibly sexy with his broody face and cut jaw and mussed-up hair and..." She groans again. "Why do I torture myself? Last I heard, he was hooking up with Jennifer Dubois, who is like a modern-day Audrey Hepburn. Her eyes are so big and beautiful, plus she has a great ass. I've got no chance with my squinty little retinas and pancake butt."

I giggle and roll my eyes. "You are gorgeous. Don't go down that path thinking someone else is better than you. She's a girl in high school, same as you. You're not better or worse, just different."

"Okay, now you're sounding like your mom."

I make a face. "Really? Shutting up now."

She laughs. "Anyway, tell me about you. Any hot hookups?"

"Nope." The lie pops out faster than I can even think it. Like I can admit to her that I'm pregnant. She already thinks the fact that I've slept with more than one guy is scandalous. We've both been raised in homes where good, moral girls save themselves for marriage. There's seriously nothing wrong with that. If anything, I can see the benefit of the whole "never having casual sex" thing. There'd definitely be no regrets, right? Thoughts of Ben and a couple other hookups flash through my mind—but when I got to college, I realized I didn't want to live by that standard anymore.

So, I've experimented.

Had some fun.

Got pregnant.

Shit!

I swallow, willing my voice not to crack as I spin another fast one. "I've been too busy studying. They're always throwing tests at us, and I have a couple big assignments due soon. I haven't been partying as much lately."

"Aw. Sad face."

"No, it's all right. Sometimes you've got to be a little bit good before you can be a little bit bad, right?"

She laughs like she gets it, but I'm sure she's never done a bad thing in her life. I'm pretty sure she leaves that kind of shit up to me and then vicariously lives through my wrongdoings.

I wonder how she'd react if I told her the truth.

Shit. I can't.

She might let it slip in front of my parents, and they'll only find out if I decide to keep it. And even then, I'm pretty sure a third-trimester reveal isn't a bad thing. Maybe I can even go somewhere else over the summer and they'll never need to know.

That only works if you're not keeping it.

I skim my hand over my belly, fisting my shirt as I consider my third option.

How could I do that to someone?

I mean, sure, *I* got lucky and ended up with a great family. But no matter how hard I try, I'll never get over the fact that my birth parents didn't want me. I have no idea what their reasons were to give me away. My biological mother wanted a closed adoption, which means we don't know squat about her or my father. Was she young like me? Was she alone, or did they stick together?

Did either of them have red hair and freckles? The number of times I've asked myself that question is too many to count.

No matter how hard I try, I still find myself thinking about them, especially her.

And the thought of putting someone else through that agonizing mystery seems cruel to me.

So, that leaves only two options.

A cold ball forms in my chest as Jolie's voice becomes an indistinct buzz. I "Hmm" and nod as though I'm listening to her story about... a history assignment, maybe?

But the truth is, I'm racing headlong into a swirling vortex of indecision.

I want to ignore this problem, but I can't.

I know I just need to make a choice and stick with it, but it's not like I'm picking between a hamburger and a pizza here. This is huge! And no matter what I choose, I'm going to have regrets. I'm smart enough to recognize this.

"Well, I hope all your assignments go great and you can get back to having fun." Jolie's singsong voice makes me grin.

"Speaking of fun, how's the prom planning going?"

She sighs. "Being on the committee is a nightmare. I wouldn't have volunteered if I'd known Boss Bitch Bella was taking charge. Seriously, she thinks she's the only person in the room with good ideas, and it's driving me crazy."

"Aw, sweetie. That sucks. Bella has always been bossy."

"Yep. And everyone thinks that. We've started warning each other when BBB is coming. And the other day, we actually had a secret meeting without her to talk about our dresses. I know that's not really a prom committee thing, but we were worried that if she was within earshot of any conversation like that, she'd tell us what we all had to wear."

I let out a soft laugh and try to cut off her complaining with a question I know will excite her. "So, what kind of dress are you thinking?"

"You're gonna love it," she squeals, then starts describing this sequined number with spaghetti straps.

I listen as best I can... until my phone starts beeping with an incoming call.

I pull it away from my ear and check the number.

It's Casey.

That's weird. Why is he calling me?

My stomach pinches uncomfortably and I sit up, tucking my hair behind my ear.

"Hey, Jo-Jo," I interrupt her.

"Yeah?"

"I've got a call coming in. Do you mind if I quickly take it?"

"Oh sure, just call me back whenever. I have to go now anyway. I'm getting the look from Mom, because I'm technically supposed to be writing an essay right now and not talking to you."

"Hey, Cinnamon!" Aunt Camilia calls.

"Say hi to your mom for me," I tell Jolie before sending kisses down the phone and hanging up.

"Hello?" I answer Casey's call before it cuts off.

"Oh, you are there. I thought I was gonna have to leave a message, and I really hate that."

I snicker, shaking my head. "Is everything okay?"

"Yeah, I'm just..."

My eyebrows slowly rise as I wait out his silence. He's not giving me anything, and it's making me nervous, so I go for a prompt. "Just what?"

"Uh... this is me just... calling you." He clears his throat. "I'm calling you."

I frown in confusion, about to ask him to elaborate when suddenly... I get it.

He's calling a girl the next day.

He never does that.

Ever.

Except right now.

A smile breaks across my face as something flutters in my chest.

"And if you ever need me to *help you out* again, just send me the word, okay?"

"Okay." I nod, clamping my lips against the giddy laugh that wants to burst out of me. "Thanks for calling, Case."

"Yeah, uh... no problem."

"How much is it killing you?" I laugh.

"Actually, you know, it's not too bad."

"Great." I giggle out the word. "You're very brave."

He growls in his throat, and that just makes me laugh harder.

"Seriously, though..." I let the last of the giggles ride through me before finding my voice again. "I really appreciate the call. Thank you. It means a lot."

"Yeah, well... good. Okay. I'm gonna go."

"Okay." I can't help laughing again as he gives me a feeble goodbye and hangs up.

No wonder he never calls girls the next day. He's so awkward on the phone!

So adorably awkward.

I brush my thumb over my lock screen, my smile growing all over again as I flop back on my pillow with a giddy sigh.

CHAPTER 20
CASEY

I stare at my phone, then catch a glimpse of myself in the reflective glass.

I'm frowning.

Deep.

What the fuck did I just do?

I called a girl... for no particular reason.

What? Did I just want to hear the sound of her voice or some shit?

I must be losing my damn mind.

Slipping the phone into my back pocket, I scratch the back of my head, then shake it.

I called a girl.

And I sounded like a total moron, yet her laughter is still ringing in the back of my head. I kinda like that sound. I can picture her face as she's doing it. It's probably the same expression she gave me when she was calling me a seven yesterday.

A light laugh pops out of me.

"What's funny?" Asher glances up when I slip in beside him at the dining table. We're in the athlete's hall, and I told him to go ahead because I had to make a quick call before coming inside.

He probably thought I was checking in with my mom... which I should probably do, because who knows what shit she's gotten up to this week.

I usually call her every couple weeks to make sure she hasn't done something crazy, like waking up in an apartment she doesn't recognize and not even knowing where she is, or nearly burning her trailer down by not stubbing out her cigarette properly, or backing into the side of someone's car and then trying to drive off and getting chased down by Mr. Road Rage.

These things have all happened, and I'm very aware that I'm not around to take the heat like I usually do.

I'll call her tonight.

Scrubbing a hand down my face, I tug the tray toward me. Asher picked all my favorite stuff, and I thank him with a little nudge of my elbow.

"No worries." He drops my swipe card on the table, and I pocket it before leaving it behind. "So, what's funny?"

"Nothin'." I shrug, and his eyebrows dip together.

"You never *don't* tell me your stories, dude. Even when they're lame. And you're denying me an actual funny one?"

I snicker and shake my head, not really wanting to get into it.

"Come on, man. Gimme somethin'."

With a sigh, I pick up my fork and start poking at the

green salad and broiled chicken. "I was just thinking about a girl I hooked up with yesterday. She was hassling me for being a seven, and I had to tickle her until she admitted I'm an eleven."

He tips his head, his lips jumping in and out of a smile. "From a seven to an eleven. Nice jump."

"I'm always an eleven."

And she's a twelve.

The thought resurfaces, doing weird shit to my chest. I scratch my rib cage and try to ignore this fizzing sensation inside me.

"I don't actually have any personal experience with that."

"Thank fuck," I mutter, then give him a good-natured wink.

"But I have been in the house at the same time you're getting it on with whichever puck bunny is the flavor of the day, and yeah, by the sounds of things... you could be an eleven."

"Oh, Casey." Connor puts on a woman's voice, then starts moaning. "Do it again, baby."

"Just like that," Riley joins in, going for extra breathy. "Yes! Yes! Yes!"

I shoot a dry look across the table, then grin at the football guys who are frowning at my teammates from the table next to us.

"Just talking about how I'm an eleven," I let them know. "I'm a fucking awesome eleven."

"Good for you, man." The big guy with blond shaggy hair starts laughing and turns back to his buddies.

"Puck yeah," Asher murmurs, shaking his head while

nibbling on a chicken drumstick. "Now, can we please stop talking about your sex life?"

Probably a good thing, considering the redhead who seems to be crowding out my headspace these days.

What am I seriously wanting out of this?

Why did I call her?

It's not like I'm trying to form some kind of bond with her.

She's carrying your kid.

My stomach drops the way it always does when I think about it.

That's why I called.

Because I won't be the asshole who leaves her high and dry. Right?

That's gotta be the only reason I was compelled to do that.

Right?

Shit. Maybe this sleeping with her thing is an insanely stupid idea. But if she needs dick, I want to provide. Be the good guy.

Make sure she doesn't find dick someplace else.

The thought makes my insides jolt.

No. I'm not the possessive, jealous type. Like I'd ever have a right to be that.

But fuck. The idea of some other guy between those sensational legs...

The thought of her moaning someone else's name...

I grip my fork, stabbing it into the lettuce leaves like I'm trying to murder them.

"Dude." Connor catches my attention. "What's got you all pissed?"

"Nothing." I steal a quick glance at Asher, who is looking all curious again, then hunch my shoulders with a scowl. I can feel his gaze on me as he slowly stands with his tray.

"I'll catch you guys later. I'm heading to the library for a study session. Hey, Riley, you want to join, man? I can help you with that econ paper."

"You da man, Bensen. Thank you!" The freshman practically trips over himself getting up from the table.

I stay put, ignoring Connor's gaze as he tries to get a read on me.

In an attempt to distract him, I ask an inane question. "What class do you have next?"

"Anatomy." He lifts his chin. "You?"

"I've got—" My words get cut off by the buzz of my phone. I pull it out of my back pocket and check the screen.

Lil Red: So, I need you again.

"I got... I gotta go." Jumping up, I dump the last of my uneaten meal and stow the tray before practically sprinting out of the hall.

Connor shouts something to my back, but I don't hear him.

For real, if he sat me down and threatened to torture me for information, I don't think I could tell him what classes I have this afternoon.

I'm skipping the next one. I know that for sure.

Yes, it might bite me on the ass later, but there's a

certain redhead who *needs* me right now, and like hell I'm gonna leave her hanging.

Duty calls again.

I whoop as I jump off the last three stairs, scaring the crap out of a girl coming up toward me.

"Sorry!" I shout, waving my hand in apology as I run toward Caroline's dorm room.

CHAPTER 21
CAROLINE

Grabbing the popcorn off the table, I shove a handful in my mouth. My eyes are glued to Mikayla's TV. She's the only person I know with access to the game tonight, so here I am in her little living room getting ready to watch the Cougars play. My heart is in my throat as Casey glides onto the ice. He looks focused and ready to demolish the Ravens.

They have to win this game to keep their position on the table. If they do, their final game will be at the Nolan U arena, and if they win that, they'll be playing in the Frozen Faceoff Quarterfinals.

Holy shit, that would be epic.

"Yay. Good luck, Liam, baby." Rachel claps her hands, grinning at the screen when her boyfriend skates onto the ice. He lifts his stick and grins, Ethan right on his tail.

They're obviously looking for the cameras filming the game, wanting to wave to their girlfriends who they know are watching.

I glance at the two besties who are waving back, even

though no one can see them. I'm grateful that Mick invited me over to watch the Cougars' away game. Asher gave Mikayla his login details so we could sign into his Sling account and watch all the sports we want.

Tonight, we're only interested in hockey.

"Come on, cameraman," Mikayla tuts. "Stop focusing on the Ravens so much!"

"He might zoom out in a second. He's just doing close-ups as the players come onto the ice." Rachel's voice is always so soft and sweet.

"I don't like it." Mikayla frowns, snatching a few popcorn kernels before they skitter off the coffee table.

"Only because Ethan's not in the shot anymore." Rachel snorts.

Mikayla fights a grin, her nose scrunching as she ignores her best friend.

I hamper my laughter. These two are fun. I sit on the far side of the couch with my legs curled beneath me, listening to them hassle each other while the players do a quick warm-up.

"Okay, shh, shh, shh." Mikayla waves her hand to shut us up, even though we're not saying anything. "It's starting."

I hold my breath as the referee drops the puck between Ethan and the forward from the opposing team.

"Get it," I murmur under my breath, my body tensing as Ethan swipes the puck away, passing it to Casey, who's coming up the wing at speed. "Yes!" I punch the air while Mikayla bobs on the couch.

"Can you imagine if they score in like the first minute of play?" Rachel giggles.

"That hardly ever happens." I rush out the words,

following the puck as Casey does a quick one-timer to Asher. I'm stoked that they're playing the same line tonight, because they always work beautifully together. It's like they can read each other's minds or something.

"Go, go, go!" Mick shouts as they close in on the goal, then hisses when Asher is slammed against the boards. "Dammit."

"It's okay." I keep my eyes on the screen as they tussle for the puck, then wince as the Ravens player steals around the back of the goal and starts heading for our end of the arena, the puck safely in his possession.

The D-men work in sync to protect the goal but can't stop the deflection shot fired from the right. Baxter slaps his knees together, saving the goal and making all three of us cheer like they've just won the Frozen Faceoff final.

"Yes! Come on, baby!" Mikayla's standing now, clapping and shouting at the TV. "Let's go!"

Ethan and Casey swarm the puck, forcing the Ravens to take a careless shot that fires straight into Connor's stick. He flicks it off to Casey for a breakaway that takes him all the way to the goal.

"You can do this," I whisper, watching his stickwork like a hawk and jumping to my feet as he nears the goal.

Holding my breath, I make two fists, then punch them in the air when Casey does a sweet deek that sneaks the puck behind the goalie's foot. It hits the back of the net, and all three of us start dancing in front of the coffee table.

"Cou-gars! Cou-gars! Cou-gars!" we chant in unison.

Casey raises his hands, skating right into Ethan, who slaps his back while Asher pounds his helmet a couple times.

"This is the best start." Rachel's smiling so wide, I'm surprised her face doesn't hurt.

Maybe it does.

It's totally worth it.

Watching this game with them, being in their cute apartment, makes me feel like I'm somehow part of this hockey family. Oh man, how I wish it was true.

I guess if I have the baby, I could be connected by association, but will I ever be one of them?

No. Not the same way they are.

Mikayla and Rachel belong to this group. They're chosen, cherished. I'm loitering around because of a mistake Casey and I can't just ignore.

I wonder if they know what we've been up to this week.

The way I've been texting Casey any chance I get— the urge to see and feel him so overpowering I can barely stand it. The way I've been using him to relieve my "pressure."

Aw man, I hope not. What would they think of me if they knew that? If they knew everything?

I swallow, shuffling to the edge of the couch and focusing back on the game. Casey's been bodychecked and is aggressively chasing after the puck he just lost. I can't really see his face, but the way his arms are pumping tells me enough. He's in it to win it tonight.

And that's exactly what they do.

Our Cougars manage to shut out the Ramsburg Ravens with a staggering 6-0 win. At this stage of the competition, it's unheard of.

The boys will be flying high tonight. They've maintained their place at the top of the leaderboard, which means they'll be playing at home.

"Puck yeah!" Mikayla pumps the air, laughing when Rachel teases her that she's not allowed to say that.

"I am when they're not around to hassle me for it. So, fucking puck yeah! Frozen Faceoff, here they come!"

"They still have to win the next game."

"They will, Ray! It's home advantage, and they're on fire right now. Nothing's going to stop these guys from going all the way. Right, Caroline?"

"Right." I grin, then laugh when Mikayla grabs my hands and starts dancing in circles.

She tips her head back and shouts, "All the way, baby!"

I join in with the shouting and the laughter, dancing around the tiny living room while the music blasts, playing this weird card game Mikayla made up, and then watching three episodes of *The Office*. It's not until the girls are suiting up to meet the bus that I finally decide to head back to my dorm.

"You should come with," Mikayla offers.

"Nah, it's really late, and..." *It's not like anyone's expecting me to be there.* I bite my lips together and force a smile. "Have fun, you guys. And thanks again for inviting me over. Your place is awesome, and I loved watching the game with you."

"Anytime." Mikayla grins. "Hopefully we'll bump into each other again soon."

I nod, glad I said yes to the spontaneous invitation. She knows how much I love hockey.

Does she know how much I love Casey too?

Don't love him, you idiot.

Just take this for what it is—hot sex and nothing more.

CHAPTER 22
CASEY

Caroline sinks onto me, her wet pussy frying the circuits in my brain. I wriggle my fingers under her skirt and grab her ass, pumping her hips to make the friction a little faster. Mr. Jones is one happy guy right now. He's about to start singing a fucking hallelujah chorus, and as much as I want this to last forever, I want to give in to this orgasm as well.

She's riding me like a motherfucking queen, straddling my legs in the back of my Jeep. We're parked at an abandoned sawmill. Not the most romantic place, but it's private.

Private enough that I could whip off her shirt and suck those titties. Private enough that I could go down on her in the back seat. Her screams of pleasure were guttural, and as soon as she'd ridden the wave, I pulled her into my lap and practically begged her to sit on me.

It didn't take much.

My rigid cock speared her like a knife through butter.

"You feel good," she pants in my ear, her tits jostling against my chest. "So fucking good."

I slide my hand up her back, anchoring her to me as I give her my final thrust and let myself go. A groan rumbles in my throat as I lightly bite her bare shoulder and let my body shake.

She milks me dry as I tip my head back and moan again.

Fuck. She's magical.

She rests her head on my shoulder, her chest heaving as our bodies slowly start to relax. I rub my hand across her back and do a quick scan to make sure no one else has driven or walked into the parking lot.

It's highly unlikely, but still. I don't want Caroline to get busted half naked by some creepy stranger.

"You good?" I kiss her shoulder.

"Yeah," she puffs into my ear before shifting off me and pulling her bra straps back up, tucking those beautiful fun bags away for later.

I grab some tissues from the box sitting between the front seats and hand her some before taking a bunch and cleaning up.

She soon has them crumpled in her hand and is searching around the floor of the Jeep.

"Here." I grab her panties and hold them out on the end of my finger.

"Why thank you, kind sir." She gives me a playful smirk before reaching for them... and going perfectly still.

Her eyebrows pucker just before she drops the balled-up tissues on the floor and snatches my wrist, yanking it toward her. "What's this?"

"Huh?" I scan my forearm, wondering which tattoo she's talking about, until her thumb skims over it.

Oh shit.

"The red heart." She lifts her skirt to reveal her tattoo. "It's just like mine."

"Oh yeah, I, uh... Queen of Hearts." I try for a laugh, but it comes out rusty.

"Did you have it before?"

"Before when?" I'm trying to play innocent, but I think I'm failing big-time.

"Before our party hookup. I don't remember seeing it."

"Oh, um... no," I admit. It's tempting to lie to her and just say I liked it and wanted the same, but for some reason I can't do it.

I have to go for the truth. Or a portion of it, anyway.

"So, yeah... see, sometimes when I meet a person, they stay with me for a bit, and then I get a tattoo to remember them by." I add a sweet smile to my explanation, hoping for a swooning sigh and maybe even a "You got a tattoo to remember me by?"

But instead, her eyes narrow. "*Meet* someone?"

"Yeah." I brush my hand down her cheek. I like how soft her skin is. I like the shape of her face... except when it bunches into a scowl.

"You mean sleep with someone?"

Oh shit. Well, isn't she just a star at reading between the lines.

Of course she is. She's fucking smart, you dumbass!

I work my jaw to the side while she lets out a scoff and starts pulling her panties on like she's securing Fort Knox. There goes V-jay play for the afternoon. Dammit.

"You know, you should really take it as a compliment," I murmur, trying to salvage this shitshow. "Not every girl gets one of these." I tap my arm, pointing out the other tattoos in the same area and then instantly regretting that decision.

Her right eyebrow arches, and she snatches my wrist again, carefully examining the myriad tattoos I've squished in together. "Is this one? The music notes? And the ice cream? How about that daisy? And the stilettos, that's gotta be from a hot hookup. Did she leave them on? Is that why you chose this image, because you wanted to remember her spread-eagle with those pointy heels doing..." She shakes her head and lets me go with a huff. "I don't even want to know where they were."

I want to tell her it's not like that, but she's spot-on. Those heels were the sexiest damn thing that night, and I asked her to leave them on. They dug into my ass while I took her on a glass dining table.

Fuck, I should not be remembering that right now.

I scramble to distract my sex-driven brain and point to her hip.

"What's the story behind yours?"

"Nuh-uh." She shakes her head, buttoning up her shirt and crossing her arms like she's barricading the door.

"Come on. I marked my skin for you."

And it's not like we're a couple or anything. Why is she being so shitty about this?

She rolls her eyes. "You mark your skin for a lot of girls."

But we're not exclusive.

I should just say that to her, but instinct is telling me that will only make things worse right now.

Instead, I admit with a sigh, "Yeah, but I really couldn't get you out of my head, you know?"

Turning to glare at me, her frown turns skeptical. "You mean *Karen*? You couldn't stop thinking about her, huh?"

She's never gonna let that go, is she?

I shake my head and for some weird reason start to laugh. She's kinda cute when she's mad, her eyes getting all fiery like that, her skin flushing to match her hair.

"Shut up," she grumbles.

"Come on, Queen of Hearts. Don't be mad with me."

"I'm not."

I laugh again. I can't help it.

She tuts and lightly slaps my chest with the back of her hand.

Grabbing her fingers before she can pull away, I suck the tips of two into my mouth, then tell her what she needs to hear. "You're the best sex I've ever had."

"Whatever." She rolls her eyes again.

"It's true." I show her my wrist again, brushing my thumb over the red heart. "Yours is the only one in color."

The edge of her lips twitch as she eyes up my forearm. "You know, if you weren't so good at this sex thing, I'd tell you to kiss my ass and never look back."

And the baby thing, but I don't dare say it. I'm on the cusp of getting a smile out of her.

"I love kissing your ass. You have a very fine ass." I snicker when she frowns at me, then give her my best smile. "Come on, you'd miss the Casey lovin' and you know it."

Her lips quirk again, and this time I can see her fighting a grin.

I grin even wider, and she glances at it quickly before looking away with a tut. Then she snatches my wrist for a third time and studies her heart on my skin. After a moment that feels like an eternity, she finally pulls it to her lips, kissing the heart, then licking it with the tip of her tongue.

With a throaty growl, I grab the back of her neck and pull her toward me, sinking my tongue into her mouth and giving myself over to this Queen of Hearts.

CHAPTER 23
CAROLINE

I had no right to be mad with Casey over those tattoos. They all happened before we met, and so what if he wants to remember a few special women in his life? But I couldn't help that surge of jealousy, that desperate sensation that ripped through me, when I realized I can't claim him as mine.

Because he's not mine.

He's just my fuck buddy.

And the only reason he's that is because I'm pregnant... which we haven't spoken about all week. We've kind of been too busy having sex to talk about anything deep and important.

I text when I get horny, and he comes running.

We've done it all over the place, even sneaking in a quickie before his very important hockey game. It was his idea, which thrilled me beyond belief. I got his text just as I was lining up to walk into the arena and met him around the back. He lifted me against the outside wall and pounded me with an urgency that was electrifying.

The fact that we could have been caught at any second made me hornier than ever, and holy hell was it hot.

The Cougars ended up winning the game. I sat, or more accurately stood, and screamed my lungs out. Watching them win and earn themselves a spot in the Frozen Faceoff Quarterfinals was a freaking triumph. Casey played like a Tasmanian devil. I was so freaking proud of him. It would have been so cool to call him mine in that moment.

But we're not a couple.

Not officially.

We're secret lovers, and I'll take it.

Although, watching Mikayla jump into Ethan's arms and Rachel curl herself into Liam's embrace after the game singed me with that jealous burn again. I wanted to do that too. I wanted to freaking leap against Casey, wrap my legs around him, and give him a kiss to remember.

We sufficed by doing it in the bathroom at Offside. It was still great and exciting and everything. Sucking him off in a stall while he tried to muffle his groans, then riding him until he exploded inside me was epic in its own way.

But then we had to leave separately, and while Liam and Rachel swayed on the dance floor together, I stood at the table with the Hockey House boys watching puck bunnies fall all over them.

Casey got his fair share of attention, and I was almost surprised that he didn't wander off with one of the girls.

What does that say about us?

About me?

That maybe I'm not so special after all. Sure, my tattoo has color, and maybe I swooned just a little when he pointed that out. He marked his skin for me. He made it different to all the others. That *is* a compliment, but... I'm not the only one on his arm, and if I'm realistic, I won't be the last. He's just doing me this big favor while I get through the horny phase of my pregnancy. But after that?

I swallow, not wanting to think about it.

"You good?" Leilani licks her ice cream cone as we wander down Main Street. It's a sunny Sunday afternoon, and what better way to spend it than eating delicious treats with my best friend? "You haven't said anything in like five minutes."

"Yeah, I'm good," I murmur, forcing a smile before licking the dripping ice cream off my fingers.

She gives me a skeptical frown, and I decide that I seriously need to get out of this slump and go for a reframe. I'm getting to have sex with the hottest guy at Nolan U. That is freaking epic. He's gorgeous and funny, and I love the way he takes care of me physically. The man knows what he's doing.

So, what the hell am I complaining about?

A genuine smile starts to stretch my lips wide. "I am good, seriously. Life is pretty peachy right now. I mean, sure... I have *the thing* lurking in the back of my mind, but for now I'm just enjoying the moment. And the sex." I wink at her, expecting a playful grin in return.

Instead, I get a scowl that's borderline bitchy.

I'm about to ask her what the hell her problem is when I glance up and gasp.

"Oh shit." I yank Lani's arm, tugging her sideways into an alley. "Hide," I whisper urgently, forcing her to duck behind a dumpster.

"Are you serious?" She spits out the words, obviously super pissed.

The dumpster stinks, and the brick walls of this alley are filthy. Lani stands there trying not to touch any part of her clothing against any of the grimy surfaces while she hides beside me.

I wince and press my back against the wall. Lani peeks out and watches Ben walk past.

"Do you think he saw us?" My wince is becoming a deep cringe.

Lani's unimpressed glare isn't helping.

"What?" I stand up once I'm sure we're in the clear, tugging down my shirt and frowning right back at her. "What is your problem?"

Seriously, my roommate is getting grumpier by the day.

"You're making a mistake." She gives me a pointed look. "You know you're in the wrong here."

I bristle at her words, flashing my eyes at her.

"You could be with a really nice guy." She points down the alley where Ben walked past only moments ago. "Someone who wants you. Someone who is desperate for your number because he wants to call it—every day, no doubt! He'd support you no matter what you decide." She flicks her finger, pointing at my stomach, then shaking her head. "But no, you go for the Nolan U man slut."

My face scrunches as I turn away from her and throw the rest of my ice cream in the dumpster. "We have a connection," I try to argue, but my tone sounds annoyingly lame right now. "And he does support me."

"Whatever." Lani eyes me up and down, tutting and

shaking her head. "He's like a walking STD. He'll screw any girl on campus who will have him."

"He's clean, okay?" I glare right back at her.

Her expression crumples, her shoulders slumping before she flicks her hands in the air. "Do you honestly want him to be the father of your kid? He's a total man-child, allergic to responsibility, and... and..." She huffs. "I just don't get you!"

I gape at her, wondering how long she's been harboring all these angsty feelings. I mean, I knew she hasn't been impressed by my sex-fest, but she's usually way more supportive than this.

"Well, I don't get you right now," I fire back. "You've been so freaking grumpy since I told you. It's like you're punishing me for this."

Lani sighs and shakes her head again. "I don't understand what you see in him."

"Well, you don't have to, because you're not the one who's dating him."

She turns to look at me, her face etched with sadness as she softly asks, "Are you dating him?"

I clamp my lips together and cross my arms, looking away from her.

"You're not. You're just screwing like rabbits. That's not dating, Caroline." Her voice is going gentle now, filled with that desperation for me to hear her. I stiffen when she touches my arm. "I know you don't want to hear this, but he'll probably be long gone by the time this shit gets real. Don't set yourself up for heartbreak. You don't need a man. You can do this on your own. No matter what you decide, I have faith in you."

I flick her off me. The idea of facing what I'm up against by myself is repellent.

I can tell she's about to launch into some spiel about how she'll be there and my supportive family could help, too, but I don't want those people.

I want Casey!

"Just because you're Miss Independence doesn't mean I want to be." I snap out the words. "Stop pressuring me with all your feminist ideals. There's nothing wrong with being a romantic. There's nothing wrong with wanting to fall in love and be in a relationship with someone."

"But it's not a relationship!" She flings her arms wide. "He's not in love with you, Caroline."

The words sting like a slap to the face. My eyes start to burn, but like hell I'm going to let her see that she made me cry.

Clenching my jaw, I give her my best glare before spinning away and storming back onto Main Street.

I don't need to put up with this shit. As my best friend, she's supposed to support me!

Like I want to have my deepest fears thrown in my face!

Hunching my shoulders, I wrap my arms around my stomach and dip my head, scuttling down the street and heading I don't even know where.

Not back to my dorm, that's for sure!

The tears I'm fighting continue to build. I rub my eyes, willing them not to fall as I try to get away from the one person who I thought had my back in this whole thing.

But she doesn't.

And shit... what if she's right?

CHAPTER 24
CASEY

Like some kind of miracle, I have the house to myself. Mick and Ethan left with Rachel and Liam to do who the fuck knows. It probably involves a lot of handholding, nose rubbing, goopy smiles, and giggling.

I roll my eyes, Caroline's laughter floating through the back of my brain as I try to deny how much I love that sound.

Baxter's buried in the dark corners of the library while he tries to get an assignment done, and Asher has some family thing on. His cousin, Harvey, goes to Lennox College (but we'll forgive him that because he's related to Asher), and they have some celebration thing he wanted the whole family to attend.

I smirk, thinking about our rivals. It's lucky his cousin doesn't play hockey, because I wouldn't care whose family he belongs to out on the ice. Although Harvey is a pretty cool dude. We've partied together before. The guy's a ladies' man like me, and we've had some good laughs together, trying to top each other with the crazy-ass shit we've gotten up to.

I take my sweet time in the bathroom, watching YouTube on my phone while doing my business, before finally wandering back to my room. I'm not really sure what I'll get up to this afternoon. I should probably clean up my room. I can't remember the last time I could see carpet all the way from my door to my closet.

But... boring!

I'm used to the house being a hive of activity, and although I thought I'd love this peace and quiet, it's starting to niggle like an itch I can't scratch. I guess I like me some noise and distractions. Too much time alone makes you think deep, and that only leads to life sucking as you consider all that's currently wrong with it.

Baby daddy.

The words taunt me, ringing in my head like someone's just smashed a gong inside my eardrum.

I wince and rub my forehead, reaching for my grandpa's old record player. He gave it to me when I left for college and made me swear to take good care of it. Flicking through the vinyls that came with it, I pull out my favorite glam rock album, because I'm by myself and no one can hassle me for it. Def Leppard starts blasting, and I sing along to "Pour Some Sugar on Me." Yes, it's weird that I like this old-school shit. Asher doesn't get my obsession with music from four and five decades ago. I don't get it either. It's gotta be because my grandpa used to play it when I was a kid. He's a bit of a metal head, and my grandma was into '80s pop. I really had no hope, especially when he passed it all on to me.

"Carry on the legacy, son."

Mom took us away from them when I was still young, and I only see them very occasionally now, but don't they say that your first few years of life are the most critical? Shit gets embedded that you just can't shake, so let me cling to my weird taste in music.

The thought hits me that if I have a kid, there's a chance they'll grow up with weird-ass tastes in music too. If I'm fully involved. If I help raise it, which I should. I mean, right?

My breaths get punchy as I flirt with a full-blown panic attack. Pressing my fingers into my chest, I bend over, sucking in what air I can find... until a voice distracts me.

"Hello?"

I bolt upright, spinning when I hear Caroline's voice on the stairwell.

"Hey!" I shout, jumping out of my room so I can greet her.

Yes! Distraction!

Sexy times!

This is just what I need.

But the second I see her face, I can tell she's been crying, and my gut pinches with a sensation I don't think I've ever felt before. I don't know what the hell it means, but it makes me want to maim whoever caused those tears, then cradle Caroline against my chest like she's a porcelain doll I must protect.

What the fuck?

I'm losing my damn mind.

Near panic attacks and now some Captain America, "protect my woman from all harm" bullshit?

My woman?

Yep. It's official, I've lost my mind.

"Uh..." I shove my hands in my pockets, giving her a gentle smile. "You okay?"

She sniffs and looks back down the stairwell. "I hope you don't mind that I let myself in. I knocked but no one came. Then I heard music, so I tried the handle, and..." She lets out a breath. "I... I hope it's okay."

"Of course it's okay." I snatch her hand and drag her up the stairs, then down the hallway toward my room.

She can sit on my bed while I clean. She can listen to glam rock with me. She can keep me company and make me feel better.

The thought trips me up like all the other ones I've been having this afternoon.

Caroline makes me feel better. And she doesn't even have to be naked to do it.

Although... naked sounds good.

And way more fun than tidying my room.

It might be a good distraction for her too. She's obviously upset about something. What better way to help someone get over their angst than by giving them an orgasm?

My mind starts running with the ways I can make her come.

"What's that smell?" Caroline faces bunches, and she pinches her nose as we walk past the bathroom.

I point at the door with a grin. "Just been in there."

"That's..." She blinks and looks like she's about to gag. "That's eye-watering."

Laughter punches out of me. I'm used to people hassling me about my smelly shits. I've decided to own it and be proud. Clicking my bedroom door shut, I throw my clothes off the bed and onto the floor so she can take a seat.

"I can still smell it. I... I seriously? Did your butt like explode or something?"

I shrug, pointing to the bed, but she doesn't move. She seems frozen by the door, like maybe she wants to flee back out of the house. After a soft sigh, I admit, "I do smelly dumps. That's part of who I am, okay?" My face buckles at her expression. "What? Is that like a deal-breaker? You won't have sex with me anymore?"

The weight of this disappointment is surprising. Wow. I must really like having sex with her, because the thought of never doing it again kinda kills me.

The thought of never hanging out with her again kills me.

And there go the punchy breaths. I try to hide it by holding my breath, and my stomach does this weird spasm while I wait for her answer.

"N... no. No." She shakes her head, and then her right eyebrow arches as she looks me over. "I'm just struggling to understand how something like that can come out of something like you." Her lips twitch with a grin. "What are you putting into that perfect body of yours?"

My relief at her response is too big, but I don't want to dwell on that right now. I just want to look at her pretty face and picture myself kissing it, then nibbling her neck and—

"I'm more interested in what I'm putting into this gorgeous body of yours." I close the space between us, cinching her around the waist and kissing her lips before trailing a path down to her neck.

"Are you seriously trying to seduce me with that blinding stench just down the hall?"

With a huff, I step back and give her a dry look before throwing her over my shoulder.

She yelps but then starts to giggle as I run past the bathroom and take her all the way into the kitchen. Rachel was here this morning making muffins, so the place still smells like bananas and chocolate chips.

"There." I put her on her feet, giving her an emphatic look. "Can you still smell it?"

"No." Her impish grin is adorable, and I feel something in my chest pop.

Seriously. What the hell is happening to me?

The fact that I've just made her smile makes me feel like I've won the Stanley Cup.

I think my smile is turning goopy as I run my knuckle down her cheek. She looks back at me with her big blue eyes, and my heart starts skipping.

Oh shit. I am in so much fucking trouble.

This woman.

I grin, slowly kissing her, letting my tongue glide along hers like I've got all the time in the world. This kiss is different somehow. There's no frenzied need attached to it. I just want to make her feel better. I might not have the ability to dive deep and find out the cause of her tears, but I can kiss them away, right?

Changing the angle, I enjoy the moan reverberating in her throat. Her fingers thread through the hair at my neckline as we sink further into this kiss, like we're burying ourselves in a beanbag, ready for hours of comfort.

Comfort.

Women don't bring me that.

They bring excitement and pleasure.

Comfort is too intimate, but somehow I can't break out of this. I should be terrified, but my useless brain has gone quiet. Still. Almost like it's at peace.

She pulls away from my lips, her breath tickling my chin as she murmurs, "How do you always feel so damn good?"

Her voice is wispy and light. I smile against her cheek, kissing my way up to her ear and whispering, "Let me stick stuff in you, baby. Let me make you feel even better."

She shows me a new laugh. It's sweet and soft as she sinks her teeth into her bottom lip and starts pulling off my shirt.

I help her, throwing the T-shirt over my shoulder as she runs her hands and eyes over my chest and stomach. She's hungry for it. For me.

So, I do what I do best.

Tucking my hands under her arms, I lift her up onto the kitchen counter.

"Wait. Here?"

"Yeah, baby." I wiggle my eyebrows at her.

"But what if someone walks in?"

"We've got the house to ourselves for a few hours. We can do it on every surface in this place and no one will ever know."

She giggles, wrapping her legs around me, but I lightly bat them back down.

"Soon," I whisper against her mouth and start at the top button of her shirt.

She slaps her hand over mine. "And you're sure we're home alone?"

"We most definitely are," I assure her. "We own this castle right now, which means sexy times in the kitchen are on, baby."

And there's that giggle again. Damn, I love that sound.

I let it sprinkle over me as I get back to my shirt-unbuttoning routine. I'm taking things so slow that it's almost painful, and I can tell by the way her chest is heaving that it's almost torture. Sweet torture.

Kissing each new patch of skin I'm exposing, I work my way down to her belly button, circling it with my tongue before working back up to her bra.

It's one that clasps at that front. God bless the person who came up with that idea. Flicking it open, I expose her luscious tits and take my fill, sucking one nipple into my mouth while rolling the other between my thumb and forefinger. Her moan is music as she fists the back of my hair.

"Yes, baby." Her voice pitches, her pants getting high and punchy.

This sensitive body of hers is off the charts.

I can tell she has an orgasm already building as she rests her hands back on the counter, lifting her hips so I can yank her stretchy jeans off and slide those pink panties down her smooth skin.

Spreading her legs, I glide my fingers through that ginger mound of curls before slipping them into her hot, wet core. She's so fucking soft and delicious as I curl my fingers inside her.

She gasps, her chest heaving even more as I continue to suck and pleasure her tits while my thumb lightly flicks her clit.

Her head tips back and she cries up to the ceiling, "Yes! Holy shit, yes!"

CHAPTER 25
CAROLINE

I come in a blinding rush of pleasure. Stars scatter through my body, making me shudder and jump. Casey gently slides his fingers out of me and sticks them into his mouth. He sucks my juices off his skin, his eyes lighting with that playful fire I love so much.

He's so sexy that it's hard to breathe around him sometimes.

"You want more?" He skims his knuckle over my sensitive nipple again, and I jolt at his touch.

"I want," I pant. "I *need*. Get your dick inside me, baby, please." I'm practically whimpering the words as I dig my fingers into the waistband of his sweats and help him yank them down.

His beautiful penis is standing at attention. I wrap my fingers around it, wiping the bead of sticky goodness off its head, then twirling my thumb over the soft skin. He's rigid and smooth, and my pussy is weeping with anticipation.

"You're so gorgeous," I whisper, fisting his shirt and dragging him toward me.

I kiss him deep, my fingers still curled around his pulsing cock while his tongue destroys my mouth. He's so good at this. So amazing at making me feel better.

The second he appeared at the top of the stairs and asked if I was okay, I knew I was.

Sex or not, just being around him makes my insides jump with joy.

And now he's making my body sing in ways that I know no other person ever could.

"Let me in, sweet Caroline. I've got to feel you wrap around me."

His words get swallowed by my tongue. One more deep kiss before I pull back and slide to the edge of the counter.

The second his head touches my opening, I practically come again. My body's on fire for him. I groan as he palms my ass and thrusts into me. It's a quick, powerful movement, and I swear I'm melting as he fills me to my core. I love the way he stretches me, turns my body boneless.

At first I cling to his shoulders, but then my fingers give out and my hands slap against the counter. My breasts, even bigger than usual thanks to pregnancy hormones, jiggle and bounce as he grabs my hips and picks up the pace.

His face is scrunched in ecstasy, and I watch it for a minute, transfixed by the beauty of him. Even his sex face is gorgeous—his lips parted, his eyes squeezed tight as he pounds me.

The slap of our bodies is the best sound in the world.

I can't help panting as a fresh orgasm builds within me. He groans, his fingers digging into my flesh.

And then I hear him gasp.

Wait. What?

That's not—

My head whips around, and I can't help a strangled cry when I notice four shocked faces gaping at Casey and me.

They're decent enough to turn around, but the damage is already done.

I'm not sure I have ever been this humiliated in my life—and I once gave a speech to my entire sixth grade class with my fly down.

CHAPTER 26
CASEY

The second Caroline's body goes stiff and that weird sound comes out of her, my eyes pop open... and that's when I see Ethan, Mick, Ray, and Liam standing awkwardly in the archway. The little fuckers got home early.

Caroline's face is so bright red, she looks like she's been sunburned. She quickly pulls her shirt closed, resting her head on my shoulder and muttering something under her breath that I can't quite hear.

"Uh... hey, guys," I call to their backs as they try to all squeeze out the archway at once and get jammed together in a pack. "I didn't realize you were gonna be home so soon."

"Yeah, we just, uh..." Mick's words peter out as she glances over her shoulder, then quickly whips back around.

"I'm dying. I'm dying. I'm dying," Caroline rasps.

I rub a hand down her back and hide her face with mine, letting her nestle her forehead right into my neck.

"We'll just give you guys a minute." Ethan raises his hand in a wave as they finally coordinate themselves and file out of the archway in a line.

"Okay, they're gone," I murmur, pulling away from Caroline and yanking up my pants.

My cock's complaining bitterly as I tuck him away. I want to assure him that we'll finish later, but I'm suddenly not sure if there'll ever be a later. Caroline's fingers are shaking as she wrestles with her shirt buttons, lining them up wrong and making a mess of trying to get herself decent again. It's such a shame to hide those beautiful fun bags away, and I nearly tell her that, but...

She won't look at me. And fuck, is she crying again?

My face bunches as I feel that agony ride through me.

"Here," I whisper, reaching for her shirt and taking over. Unbuttoning the ones she got wrong, I start again from the top and quickly help her get dressed. She jumps off the counter, still not looking at me as she tries to wrestle her pants back on. She hops around and tips over in her haste.

I catch her, steadying her against my side so she can get her legs into the right holes.

"It's okay," I murmur.

"Okay?" She springs back from me. "Are you fucking serious?"

I open my mouth to reply, but she doesn't give me a chance.

"Your friends just saw us having sex!" she hisses, her face blooming with color again as her eyes bulge and she rests her hand on her forehead. "They saw my boobs bouncing around and heard my insane moaning and...

ugh!" She covers her face with her hands, and I'm wondering how safe it is for me to approach.

But she's gone still, so I take a chance, quietly stepping into her space and wrapping my arms around her.

"Your boobs are beautiful when they bounce around."

She huffs, shoving me away from her.

Okay, wrong thing to say.

"Sorry," I murmur, but then I can't help laughing. "But they are, and it's kind of funny."

"Funny? You think this is funny?" She looks ready to punch me in the balls. "We have to see these people in a minute. What the hell are you gonna tell them?"

I shrug, trying to bring some semblance of calm into this conversation. "Just that I was... servicing my girlfriend."

"Servicing? Ew!" She slaps my chest, then goes still, her eyes rounding. "Girlfriend? Is that what I am?"

Yeah, I don't actually know how that word popped out of me. It never has before. But I can't exactly tell her that, right? Her expression is a minefield of emotion that I can't interpret, and I feel like I'm standing on ice right now. Very thin ice that's about to crack beneath me.

"I don't know," I croak, scraping my fingers through my hair. "I mean, what else am I supposed to call you? I guess you're kind of a puck bunny, but you're more than that, so maybe I should call you my fuck buddy?"

She tuts, shaking her head and shoving past me.

I snatch her arm before she can bail. "Wait. What'd I say?"

"Nothing. It's fine. I'm going." She tries to shake me off, but I won't let go.

"No." I pull her back, her socks sliding across the

kitchen floor. As soon as her shoulder hits my chest, I lean down so I can catch her eye, but she won't fucking let me. Every time I get within range, she looks the other way.

"Caroline, you're not leaving all pissed like this. I know you're embarrassed, but nothing we do or say will change the fact that they walked in on us. I've obviously said something wrong trying to make this better, and I don't want you huffing out of the house, so talk to me."

"It's…" She squeezes her eyes shut. "Just never call me a puck bunny again, okay?" Her fiery glare hits me with a force I didn't count on.

"I wasn't trying to insult you." I frown, not loving the way her eyes are narrowing right now. I scramble to make this better. "I followed it up by saying you're *not* a puck bunny."

"Oh, because fuck buddy's so much better," she scoffs.

Now it's my turn to narrow my gaze at her. "I'm just trying to figure out what to call you," I grit out.

Her expression folds like my answer has hurt her somehow. And then her head droops forward and she whispers, "I don't have to be your girlfriend. Just… whatever. I don't know what the hell we are." She shakes out of my hold, flicking her hair over her shoulder and crossing her arms. Looking out the window, she continues to dodge my gaze.

Her sad voice and expression are killing me, so I respond without thinking. "Well, what do you want to be? You want me for a boyfriend?"

It's kind of hard to believe that anyone would, but the way her head whips around and her eyes seem to light up like a Christmas tree, I'm thinking I finally said the right thing.

I gape at her, my heart rate spiking.

She can obviously sense my fear, because her eyes dim and she shrugs. "I mean... maybe. Only if you want..." Her voice trails off, and I'm left stammering after her.

"I-I thought I was just helping you out."

"You are, but I mean... I wouldn't have asked you to do that if I didn't like you. Which I do. Like a lot, actually." She's mumbling to the floor, her cheeks turning pink. It's a different blush to the one she was wearing before. It's pretty... and vulnerable... and beautiful.

Something swirls in my chest, maybe a warm affection, I don't know, but it makes my lips twitch with a grin. I nudge her chin up with my finger, forcing her to look at me. Her wide eyes finally stare into mine, but it's like she's afraid to hear what I have to say.

But the words slip out like the most natural thing in the world. "That kind of works out well, I guess."

Her eyebrows bunch in the middle. "What do you mean?"

"I like you too."

She wasn't expecting me to say that, but holy shit... the look on her face right now. My smile grows wide as I lean in, capturing her mouth with my own. It's not a deep kiss. Just a connecting of the lips, like a firm sealing of this agreement... or whatever the hell it is.

When I pull back, she grins at me as if I just handed her a million bucks rather than a label I swore I'd never use. I should be trying to get out of this shit as quickly as possible, but I'm standing here feeling like a fucking champion.

Her smile is stunning. Her eyes are telling me shit that gives me wings. It's a heady rush, and one I'll no doubt freak out about later, but for now... for this moment right here... Caroline Mason is my girlfriend.

I've never had one of those before.

I pull her into a hug, wrapping my arms all the way around her, needing to soak this in. I didn't expect to feel this way. It's weird and—

"You guys decent yet?" Ethan calls from the entryway.

"Yes!" I holler. "Come in."

Caroline pulls away from me, her smile disappearing. "I'm gonna go."

"Wait, I—"

Before I can say anything, she's ducked out of the kitchen and would have gotten to the front door if she wasn't blocked by the group coming back into the living area.

"Hello." Connor smiles down at her.

When the hell did he get here?

He's looking her over like he wants to make her his personal popsicle.

I growl, stepping out of the kitchen and staking my claim pretty damn obviously. My arm goes around her shoulders as I narrow my eyes at Connor.

He raises his eyebrows at me and looks like he's trying not to laugh. "So... who's this?"

I can't help another short growl before loudly telling the room, "This is Caroline, *my girlfriend*."

There's a collective gasp before Ray lets out this little

squeal thing, clapping her hands and jumping up on her tiptoes.

"Girlfriend? Oh my gosh, I can't believe someone actually got Casey to use the g-word!"

Mick starts laughing along with Ethan and Liam while Caroline fights a grin.

"You totally have to stay for dinner now." Ray winks at her before gliding into the kitchen and opening the fridge.

Liam follows her, disinfecting the counter while she goes on about what to make for dinner. I stay with my arm around Caroline, listening to her and Mick start up a conversation. I can't help sharing a look with Ethan, who grins at me, shaking his head before joining in the chat.

Soon all eight of us—Baxter showed up and actually stayed for a change—are sitting around the dining table, talking shit and hassling each other about school and hockey and anything else that comes to mind. As usual, ol' Bax doesn't say much, just sits there with this quiet look that's impossible to read. I think he's drinking it all in. I catch his eye at one point, and he smirks at me, then darts a look at Caroline.

Yes, that's right, Bax. I got myself a girl.

I rest my hand on Caroline's back, enjoying my place by her side while Connor spins his fairytale about the time he won in the last ten seconds of his high school championship with a Datsyuk deke.

We all groan and laugh.

"I swear, it happened!" He voices cracks and we laugh some more.

Caroline shares a look with me and I grin back before pulling her against me and kissing her head.

So this is what it's like having a girlfriend.
I can't help this giddy jump in my belly.
It's not so bad.

CHAPTER 27
CAROLINE

After an evening where I gorged myself on too much delicious food and serious amounts of laughter, I'm feeling both euphoric and sick. I rub my belly with a little whimper as Casey drives me back to my dorm.

He laughs. "Rachel's cooking is too good, right?"

"So good." I sit up a little, swiveling to face him. "And she's so nice too. Like the sweetest person ever."

"I know." He grins.

"No wonder Liam's so protective of her. She's got this..." I wiggle my fingers in the air while I hunt for the right word. "I don't know, like a vulnerability about her. With those big, haunted eyes, you know?"

"Yeah." He nods, his expression going serious. "She's had to deal with some rough stuff in the past, but she's stronger than she looks."

My curiosity is piqued, and I open my mouth to ask for more deets, but he shakes his head.

"You'll have to ask her, sorry. But... I can tell you that Liam has been teaching her how to kickbox, and she whooped Asher's ass a few weeks back. The girl's getting good."

I laugh, picturing Rachel in fighting gear, puffing over Asher as he lies writhing on the floor. That's hilarious! I love it when people can surprise you.

Like the way Casey did today.

Nerves skitter through me as I worry my lip. "Hey, um..." I let out a short breath. "That whole you being my boyfriend thing... you didn't just say that because your friends were there, right? I mean, you actually meant it?"

His eyes dart to me before looking back at the road. I notice his grip on the wheel tighten, and my stomach sinks. Shit, he's gonna back out, and I just gave him the perfect window to jump out of.

Crap, Caroline! Why can't you just keep your mouth shut!

My eyeballs start to burn as instant tears want to take me out. I'm shot back to where I was this afternoon when I ran to Casey's place after my fight with Leilani.

Shit. Why does she always have to be right?

With a heavy sigh, Casey pulls to the curb and turns off the engine. There's my dorm. I eye the door, tracing the path I'll run when I bolt from this car and disappear into my room for, I don't know, the rest of eternity maybe?

"Hey." He takes my hand, giving it a gentle tug. "Look at me."

I shake my head. "I'd rather just keep staring out the window, thanks. It'll hurt less."

He snickers, reaching for my face and forcing me to turn. My stinging eyes take in his smile, and for a second, I want to slap him. Is he getting joy out of breaking my heart? Stupid asshole.

The growl in my throat makes me sound like a puppy,

and it just makes Casey snicker again. I shake my fingers out of his grasp and reach for the door handle, but he grabs my arm before I can bolt.

"I meant it." He rushes out the words. "And yes, it terrifies me, but I want to try this boyfriend thing with you. I do."

Slowly turning back to face him, I give him a skeptical frown. He smooths the creases on my forehead with his thumb and nods.

"I'm not sure if I'll be very good at it. You're my very first girlfriend."

"What?"

"I'm serious. I'm a one-night guy. You're the first girl I've ever slept with more than once, and I've enjoyed it. A lot. It's fun getting to know your body." He skims his eyes down me, drinking me in like I'm his favorite painting.

Talk about the feels.

My chest is bursting with them.

"But I like hanging out with you too. You're fun to be around, so let's try this couple thing and see what happens."

I nod, biting my lips together so I don't accidentally tell him I love him.

Casey's a flight risk, and I don't want to screw anything up by admitting how hard I've fallen. I mean, I was practically in love with him before our first interaction. Getting to know him has just confirmed all of my feelings. But I can't let them come busting out of my mouth right now.

No, I have to take this slowly and carefully... ease him into the whole boyfriend thing.

Boyfriend. I grin. *Casey's my boyfriend!*

"What are you smiling about?" His mouth tips up on the right side.

I shrug, trying to contain the giddy giggle that wants to pop out of me. "I'm just happy."

"Good." He leans in to kiss me. "I like seeing you happy. I didn't know what to do when you turned up with tears in your eyes this afternoon."

"Oh, yeah. Sorry about that. I'd just..." I shake my head. "Gotten into a fight with Lani."

"What about?"

My chest hitches. I'm not going into the whole Ben thing with him. I can't. And it's not like I can share Lani's opinion on the matter either. Instead, I shrug and shake my head. "Just stupid girl stuff. You seriously don't want to know."

"How right you are."

I laugh and grab his chin, pulling him close for another kiss.

We sink into it, our tongues gliding against each other. I love the moan reverberating in his throat just before he deepens the kiss. His hands start wandering, running the path of my curves, from my hips to my breasts, then back down to squeeze my ass.

I hook my leg over his thighs, and he scrambles to push the seat back before hauling me onto him. I can feel him growing hard beneath me, and I nestle my V-jay over his ridge and create a little friction.

"What you do to me, woman," he groans against my lips before cupping the back of my head and sucking the tip of my tongue.

His hands glide up my back, rounding over my breasts and giving them a firm squeeze. It hurts a little—

they're really sensitive at the moment—but it's not the kind of pain that would make me want to stop this.

Casey's hands are—

A sharp tapping on the window makes me jump with a gasp. I rip my mouth off Casey's and spin to find a disgusted-looking Lani glaring at me.

"You know you're in public, right?" Her black eyebrows arch, and I wipe my bottom lip. It's swollen and glistening, still tingling the way the rest of my body is.

Casey pops open his door with a sigh, and I slide off his knee, hitting the hard asphalt with a bit of a jolt.

"You all right?" Casey catches my arm, steadying me against him as he climbs out of the car.

"Yeah." I nod, then force a smile. "You remember Leilani." I point to my best friend, who now has her arms crossed and is doing an impressive impersonation of a grumpy matron, the kind who works in a strict-ass boarding school and still uses the cane.

Seriously, why is she acting like this?

"Hi." Casey waves at her, wisely staying on his side of the car.

"Hello." She nods at him, and then an awkward silence settles between us.

My boyfriend shoots me a look, raising his eyebrows, and I let him off the hook with a quick goodbye kiss.

"See you later."

"I'll call you," he whispers against my cheek.

And this time I know he will. I squeeze his arm in thanks and wander around the front of the hood, standing next to Lani while I wave goodbye to him.

As soon as his car has disappeared down the road, I turn to her with a frown. "Did you have to be so rude?"

"What?" Her eyebrows bunch together. "I said hi."

"Yeah, like an ice queen." I bulge my eyes at her. "I get that you don't like him, but you don't need to make it so freaking obvious! He's my boyfriend."

"Your what?"

"Yeah, that's right. We're a couple, okay? He introduced me as his girlfriend to all his friends today."

"Wow." Lani looks like she doesn't quite believe me, and I can't help but snap at her.

"Why are you being so bitchy about this? I thought you'd be happy for me! Aren't best friends supposed to want that for each other!" My voice has risen to a decent shout, but my shoulders instantly deflate the second I see tears fill Lani's eyes. "I'm sorry." I rush out my apology, hating the look on her face right now.

She shakes her head and swipes at her eyes. "No, you don't have to apologize. I probably deserve to be yelled at."

"I hate yelling at you." Surging forward, I pull her into a fierce hug. "I love you. You're my best friend, and fighting with you sucks."

"I know." She kind of whines the words, gripping my shoulders as she hugs me back with the same ferocity. "I'm sorry. I'm not trying to be bitchy. I just don't want you to get hurt."

"He's not gonna hurt me." He just proved that in the car right now when he told me he wants to try this boyfriend thing with me. Happy bubbles pop in my chest as I pull back so Lani can see my face and know how much I believe what I'm saying. "He really likes me."

She nods and sniffs, her smile kind of weak and watery. "Then I'm happy for you."

The smile stretching my mouth wide is huge, I can feel it. I've been waiting to hear her say this.

"I just don't want to lose you," she admits with a desperate little frown.

"You never could." I squeeze her shoulders, then move in beside her, wrapping my arm around her as we walk toward the dorm. "We're stuck together for life. No matter what."

"No matter what," she whispers, staring ahead of us with this lost look on her face.

It unnerves me a little. Lani's usually so in control and confident. She's a boss bitch —strong and sure of herself. I almost don't know what to do with this new version of her. Me getting serious with a guy has really thrown her. And the fact that I'm pregnant.

I guess it's proving to us both that life can't be predictable the way she wants it to be. You can plan your ass off, but unexpected things still come along and disrupt everything.

But change can be good. I have to make her see this.

"Hey, why don't you come out with me and Casey sometime? Maybe if you get to know him better, you'll start to see what I see. He's really funny and sweet and easy to be around. I swear, you're gonna love him."

She gives me a reluctant smile. I can still see that skepticism underneath it, but at least she's nodding.

"Maybe he can join us for trivia night this week."

"Great idea." I beam, squeezing her closer to me before opening the door to our building.

This is awesome.

Lani's gonna see that Casey's great, and then she'll chill out and things can go back to the way they were between us. Two college girls living it up, working hard, and having fun together.

I mean, yes, I still have the pregnancy thing to deal with, but I don't want to think about that right now.

Let's just play pretend for another week or two and let me enjoy this whole "Casey is my boyfriend" thing!

CHAPTER 28
CASEY

I was supposed to be at Biblio Beans fifteen minutes ago, but practice ran over, and now I'm hauling ass to not be late for my girlfriend.

Yep, still sounds weird.

But kinda makes me smile too.

I bob my knee while Asher races down the street. I convinced him to come with me. He was kinda dubious, but when I said trivia night, his inner nerd came to life, and he couldn't say no. He'll claim to everyone that he was just helping me out, but all the Hockey House bros know the truth. We'll take it to our graves, of course, but smooth Mr. Asher Bensen is a closet dork who loves collecting comic books, watching documentaries, listening to classical music... and he feeds off trivia like it's a narcotic drug. The guy is always telling us inane facts about everything, from the latest scientific discovery to how many teaspoons of sugar is in a can of Coke to some historic thing about some historic person who did something significant.

"Did you know that…"

How many times have I heard that line. The guy's a walking Wiki page.

But he hides it all under a veil of hockey and basketball cool, his true geek not really surfacing unless he's too drunk to stop himself or we're the only ones around to hear him.

"There!" I point to the café sign as we zip past it.

Apparently on Tuesday nights, this bookstore café stays open late to run a trivia night. I got the impression from Caroline that it's pretty damn competitive, which is the only thing exciting me about tonight. Oh yeah, and seeing her, of course. And scoring a few points in her good books too. Not sure why I'm even wanting to score points, but this woman has cast some kind of spell over me, and it's making me do shit I never would before.

I'm trying not to think too hard about it.

Asher finds a parking spot down the block, and we jog back to the café, walking in just as Round One is beginning.

Excellent. Not too late, then.

I spot Caroline on the other side of the room and wave to her, weaving through the tables and parking it so that I don't have to sit right next to Leilani. She's glaring at me and mutters, "You're late," while typing something into an iPad.

"Question number four. How many wives did King Henry VIII have?"

"Six." Asher and Caroline lean in together, both whispering the answer to Leilani.

"I know." She taps the answer into the iPad, then

frowns at Asher, who was forced to sit on the other side of her. "Who are you?" She scowls at him.

"I'm Asher."

"And who invited you?"

Asher shakes his head at the rude woman before pointing to me. Then his eyebrows lift before he flicks a narrow-eyed glare at me. "Wait a second. Is this... the shrutebag?" He whispers it, but he's so fucking loud, she hears him anyway.

I wince and shoot him a pleading look that he misses, because he's just whipped back around to glare at the chick who gave his arm a solid backhand slap.

"I don't like that name," she grits out.

"No shit. That's the fucking point," Asher grumbles.

I kick him under the table, thankfully getting the right leg. He jerks, and now his glare is back on me.

"Play nice," I warn him.

Asher huffs and shuffles in his seat while Caroline gives me the human version of a grimacing face emoji.

Yep. She's right. If those two don't cool it, this night is going to be total shit.

"Question five," the trivia host calls across the room. "Where did the Franks settle after defeating the Romans?"

"Gaul," Asher answers immediately, getting a surprised blink from Leilani, who swivels in her seat to check with Caroline.

"Yeah, I think that's right." She nods while Asher frowns.

"Of course it's right. I *know* that's right." He snaps his fingers at the iPad, and Leilani huffs, writing down the answer and giving him a side-eye that's equal parts suspicion and curiosity.

I slide my hand under the table and rest it on Caroline's knee. This is going to be the longest night in fucking history. But as soon as Caroline's fingers curl around my hand, this sense of... I don't know... peace, maybe, settles inside me. I get to spend the night sitting next to her, touching her, watching her face, listening to her laughter. I guess it won't be so bad after all.

The round comes to an end, and the answers pop up on the large screen on the far side of the room. Leilani starts checking our answers and figuring out our score for that round while the host tells a long-winded story that I'm pretty sure will reveal the theme of the next round... if he ever gets to the end of it. People are laughing and calling out their theories.

"I'll get a round of drinks. What's everyone want?" Asher stands, digging out his phone and taking our orders.

At first, Leilani says she doesn't want anything, but after a nudge from Caroline, she gives in and mutters an order that I can't even hear.

"Pineapple juice? Do you need any liquor in it?"

"No." She gives him a dry glare.

"So, just me needing the happy juice, then. Okay." He spins and walks away from the table.

"Does this café even serve alcohol?" I look around, figuring it's got more of a coffee vibe.

Leilani laughs. "No."

The sound surprises me, and wow, her smile is stunning. Look at that, the dragon's got teeth—straight white pretty ones. Can teeth be pretty? I guess they can, because hers are, and she looks gorgeous right now.

If only Asher could see this.

But of course, by the time he returns with a grumpy-looking frown, her scowl has fallen back into place, and she keeps it there for the rest of the night.

The trivia game goes pretty well. Caroline is fucking amazing. She knows as much shit as Asher does. The two bounce off each other, scoring us nines and tens for every round. Leilani knows her fair share as well, and I sit there like a useless lump until the Entertainment round. Finally, I have something to share, even though they only need my help on two questions.

"Who released an album called Swordfishtrombones in 1983?"

"Tom Waits." I get three surprised blinks at the speed of my answer, but my grandpa loved that album.

Leilani dubiously writes it down, and I whoop in her face when the answers are revealed.

The second question I had to think about for a second, but I got it in the end. "What's the name of the group responsible for the 'Macarena'?"

"Los something," I muttered for a minute. I kept landing on Los Lobos, but that was the band who made "La Bamba" a hit. "Los... Los Del Rio. Yeah, I think that's it." I started pointing at the iPad the way Asher had been doing all night, and Leilani agreed with me, typing the answer in the nick of time.

We won that round, too, and ended up winning the quiz night.

I didn't realize our team name was Brainiac Bandits

until they announced the winner and Caroline and Leilani threw their hands in the air with loud cheers.

"Brainiac Bandits? Seriously?"

"Yes!" Caroline laughs, kissing me before taking our prizes, which are food and drinks vouchers for this place.

Looks like we'll be coming back here again.

I share a quick look with Asher, who is shaking his head and fighting a grin as he watches Leilani kiss the vouchers in triumph. There goes her smile again.

I think he's noticing how pretty it is, but the second she senses him watching her, she snaps back into the Dragon Queen scowl and gets up from the table.

"Let's go, Cinn."

"Sin?" I get up, pulling her chair back for her.

Caroline gives her friend a little side-eye before cringing at me. "My family calls me Cinnamon. It's just a pet name. Lani thought it was cute and adopted it without my say-so."

"Cinnamon." I grin, gliding my hand down the back of her hair. "I like it."

"Don't you dare," she grumbles. "My boyfriend is not calling me the same name as my dad. Seriously. Come up with anything else."

"Lil' Red?"

"She's not a stick of gum." Leilani tuts.

"That's Big Red," Asher corrects her.

"I know that, jackass, but Lil' Red sounds gum-ish."

"It is cinnamon flavored," he continues to argue as he follows her out the door, obviously getting some kind of satisfaction over riling her up.

"Those two." Caroline shakes her head as we follow them.

"I know, right? Leave them unattended and they'll probably kill each other."

"It's such a bummer." Her lips turn down in a pout. "I was really hoping our friends would get along so we could hang out like this more. Tonight was really fun." She beams up at me.

I plant a kiss on her lips, wrapping my arm around her shoulders as we amble out of the bookstore.

It was kinda fun.

Sure, I didn't know hardly any of the answers, but watching Caroline rattle them off was fun. Asher was in his element, and even Miss Grumpy Pants showed off a couple of great smiles.

All in all, a good night.

Do I want to do it again?

I'm not usually into domestic shit like this, but as I wander out to the street and realize I now have to say goodbye to Caroline for the night, I can feel the disappointment simmering.

Shitballs. I'm falling for this girl.

I want to have more nights like this one.

My stomach clenches, but the ugly feeling is decimated when she smiles at me, reaching up with her lips and giving me a sweet kiss—the kind you'd see in a Hallmark movie. I deepen it because I can't do small-town Hallmark. Give me passion. Give me fire.

But when she pulls back and looks up at me with goopy eyes, I find myself touching her face, rubbing my thumb across her cheek, and just drinking her in like she's the only girl on the planet.

Yeah, I really am in trouble.

This woman is becoming more than just a tattoo on my wrist.

And no woman has ever been that before.

CHAPTER 29
CAROLINE

I float back to the dorm. Like seriously, it's a miracle my body stays in Leilani's passenger seat and doesn't fly right out the roof of her car.

She doesn't say much on the drive home. Instead, we listen to music, both singing along because it's Miley, and her "Flowers" song is so damn catchy.

Leilani's belting it out like she's trying to make a point.

This worries me a little. She seriously never used to be this adamant about being alone and taking care of herself no matter what. I thought she wanted love, too, but ever since I told her I was pregnant, it's like she's been put off by the idea.

Maybe she doesn't want to have any kids and is paranoid that a relationship will automatically lead to pregnancy.

But I thought she did want kids.

I don't get what's she going through right now, and I should really ask her, but I don't want to ruin the buzz from tonight. Yes, I'm selfish, but I'll definitely ask her in the next day or two. I'll take her out for a cappuccino catch-up, and we can go deep on what's up with her.

We reach our dorm room and I wander in, shedding my denim jacket as she flicks on the light.

"Okay, you have to admit... that was fun." I throw my jacket on the bed and spin to shine my brightest smile at her.

"Winning was pretty cool." She nods, placing her keys in the bowl while making a face. "I didn't know Casey's jerk friend was gonna be there, though."

"Yeah, I didn't either, but it's lucky he was. The guy answered so many of the questions."

Lani's frown deepens. "I know. It's so annoying that he's smart." Plunking down on her bed, she crosses her arms, and I can't help laughing at her.

"Smart guys are usually your jam, babe."

"Not that one." She bulges her eyes at me. "He's so rude and arrogant and blech!" She pokes out her tongue, so I decide to tease her some more.

"He's kind of hot, though. That chiseled face and dark hair. He could be a cover model."

She bites the edge of her bottom lip, then shakes her head with a growl. "Whatever. The guy's a pompous prick."

"Getting your alliteration on. You really must hate him." I wink at her.

She rolls her eyes while fighting a grin. But then with a firm headshake, she clears her throat. "Casey wasn't so bad."

"Not so bad, huh?" I start unlacing my boots, probing for more with a little eyebrow wiggle.

She snickers. "Okay, fine. He was good. Sweet, even. I like the way he kept looking at you like he was slightly in awe. I don't even know if he was aware of it, but he definitely had mushy eyes at one point. He really likes you."

Giddy bells start dinging in my stomach, and I can't contain my giggle. "I know. I still can't believe he's my boyfriend. I thought he might bail on that after I left his place the other night, but he totally hasn't. We're a legit couple, Lei-Lei." I squeal like I've forgotten I'm twenty and do a little happy dance on the edge of the bed.

Lani laughs along with me for a second before her smile drops away and she kills the happy buzz in the room. "You need to tell him the truth."

"What truth?"

"About Ben."

Guilt swells in my throat, and I refuse to look at her as I try to toe off my boot. I haven't loosened the laces enough, and I end up huffing and grunting.

Seriously, why do I wear these boots?

Because they're cool and comfy and you love them.

"Caroline, he deserves to know. It's kinda criminal that you haven't told him yet."

With a desperate little whine, I bend back down and loosen my laces some more. My movements are practically frantic, my fingers shaking as I yank at the laces.

"Ignoring it won't change anything," she murmurs.

"I know that," I snap. "But I finally got him. I can't go fucking this up with the truth! He'll hate me, and I won't risk losing him."

"But—"

"No!" I shoot her a warning look. "I can't tell him I slept with Ben, okay?"

"But you should." She gives me a pained frown. "It's not like you cheated on him. He never called you back. But he does deserve to know that..." Her voice drops off to a soft whisper, and she mumbles the last part. "The baby might not be his."

I swallow, resisting the urge to vomit all over my fucking boots.

We stare at each other across the room for a minute, saying everything without speaking a word. My chest rises and falls as thick, painful breaths punch out of me.

I don't want her to be right. I need her to forget that I made such a stupid mistake with Ben. It was about a week after my hookup with Casey, and I was hurting big-time that he still hadn't called me. Lani convinced me to go to this party, and I got off-my-ass drunk, then ended up falling all over the first guy to start flirting with me. My memories are a little hazy, but flashes have come back to torture me—enough to know the sex was wild, my angst coming out in growls and bites as I rode Ben, fisting his open shirt and pounding on him like he could hammer away my anger with a good fuck.

We used a condom. I'm positive that we did because he made me stop so he could suit up.

Thing is, Casey and I used a condom, too, so...

So...

Shit, I don't know who the father is!

"I need it to be Casey's." My voice quakes, making the words tremble out of my mouth like an earthquake is moving through me.

Lani shakes her head with a sad sigh. "But what if it's not?"

Flicking off my boots, I throw them against the wall

on my side of the room before disappearing into the bathroom. I take my sweet time brushing my teeth and washing my face. I can't look at my reflection in the mirror... which means my best friend *is* right.

"I can't tell him," I murmur again, my stomach roiling at the very idea of having to admit something I can't even admit to myself.

The truth is inconsequential, isn't it? I mean... it doesn't have to matter, right?

I shake my head, not even wanting to think about how full of shit I am.

Of course it matters!

And I'm a terrible, horrible, awful person for allowing things to go this far with Casey and not even once talking to Ben.

But I've loved my happy bubble, and I don't want it to pop.

Slipping back into the room, I refuse to look Leilani's way as she walks past me into the bathroom.

By the time she's done, I'm tucked up in bed, facing the wall and pretending to sleep.

And that's pretty much how the rest of my night goes, me pretending to sleep but not catching an actual wink as guilt and fear rip my insides to shreds.

CHAPTER 30
CASEY

Hockey practice was brutal tonight, but there's no rest for the wicked, right?

Thanks to an assignment that's due this Friday, I'm hauling my ass to the library. I don't have too much more to go, but I need to nail the conclusion and make sure my statements are backed up by credible research, and our ancient professor insists that the Internet is not reliable enough. He wants book references too.

The glass doors slide open and I wander in, hoping I can punch this out in an hour and grab a late dinner on the way home.

Everyone else has gone to Offside, because apparently I'm the only member of the team who can't seem to keep up with his workload. Thank fuck the season's nearly over. I mean, I'll miss hockey, and competing in the Frozen Faceoff is epic. But once that's over and we walk away with the trophy, I'll have a chance to breathe. The practice schedule will drop off hugely, and I'll only have to keep up with my physical training, which is a walk in the park.

The final months of school can be all about working and hanging out with my bros.

And your girlfriend.

The thought brings me up short as I reach the top step on the second story.

I'm still trying to decide whether that's cool or not, but my lips are twitching with a grin, so some part of me must like it.

Then I see her across the other side of the room, and the jump in my chest tells me I must like it a whole fucking lot.

It's her hair that grabs my attention first—those red curls are looking kind of wild and untamed this evening, and it makes my smile grow even more. She's hunched over the table, a semicircle of open books around her as she scribbles something on a pad.

My insides do another jumpy thing as I change course and make a beeline for her table. Screw my assignment. What fucking assignment?

I can't take my eyes off my redhead, which is probably why I notice how exhausted she looks. Her skin is kind of pale, and she has gray bags under her eyes.

This unfamiliar feeling skitters through my chest, and I pick up my pace, walking around the table so I can crouch beside her.

"Hey, sexy," I whisper.

She jerks and whips around to look at me. Her eyes are wide with surprise until she sees it's me, and then she sags back in her seat.

"Hey." Her tired smile is adorable... and concerning.

"You okay?" I trace the edge of her face with my finger. "You look exhausted."

"I'm okay." She sniffs, her smile half-hearted, her eyes looking sad.

I take a seat beside her, keeping my voice low and gentle. "What are you working on?"

"Just trying to get a head start on this big assignment we got today. Thought I'd knock out an hour or two."

"You look like you should be in bed." I tip my head while she lets out a soft snicker.

"No offense, but I don't actually feel like having sex right now."

"I didn't mean that." I grin, wrapping my fingers around her wrist and rubbing that soft skin with my thumb. "You look like you need some decent sleep... or something. Maybe just cheering up. What's wrong?"

Her gaze darts away from mine, and she stares down at the books on the table. "Nothing, just..." She shakes her head.

I should probably probe and cajole the truth out of her. Is that what a good boyfriend would do?

But that's not my style.

So I deal with this the only way I know how.

Slapping all the books shut, I grab her bag and stand.

"What are you doing?" She looks up at me, and I can't tell if she's annoyed or confused.

I grin down at her to hide my doubts. "We're gonna put a smile on that face of yours."

"What?" She kind of laughs the word as I pull her out of her seat. "Where are we going?"

"I'm not sure yet. Give me a second to come up with something I know you'll like."

It makes me realize how little I know about her. Most of our times together have been of the sexy variety, but we sometimes talk after, and when I reach the sliding glass doors, I remember one thing.

Ugh.

But it'll make her smile, so I'll do it.

As I unlock my car and open the door for her—go me, gentleman of the fucking year—I get hit with the realization that I don't care how much I'm about to embarrass myself. If it makes her laugh and smile... if it makes those sad blue eyes sparkle... then I'll do it a hundred times over.

Seriously, I have no idea what is happening to me.

She must have some kind of super mind power magic going on, because this chick is winning me over. She's making me do shit I've never done before.

Shit like walking her into Hockey House, turning on the TV, and loading up *Just Dance* on my PlayStation.

Yes, I bought it on a whim last week. There was instant regret involved, but I didn't delete it, did I? I didn't ask for any kind of refund... and now I know why.

Because I need to put a smile on my girlfriend's face, and I'm pretty sure this is how I'm gonna do it.

"Let's do this thing, lady." I push up my sleeves and move the coffee table to the edge of the room.

She laughs and shakes her head. I'm still not sure if she really wants to do this, but she steps into the center of the room and takes over the controller, selecting some pop song and then getting ready to start.

"Dynamite" by BTS begins, and her hips move in time with the dancer on the screen. She punches her arms and flicks her feet, and I stop for a second, unable to move as I watch her.

She's so fucking beautiful that it hurts to breathe sometimes.

That smile I love so much is tugging at her lips, her blue eyes starting to sparkle.

"Come on." She tips her head at me. "I'm not putting on a private show for you. You have to dance too."

"A private show sounds good." I wiggle my eyebrows, checking out her luscious tits. The V-neck of her sweater is showing off a bit of cleavage, and I'm suddenly having images of poking my tongue into that crevasse and licking—

"Just get over here." She points to the ground, and I jolt out of my fantasy, doing as I'm told.

Hitching up my jeans, I get into position, and she resets the song so I can play the worst round of *Just Dance* that has ever been played. I am fucking useless.

Caroline is doing her thing, looking molten-lava hot as she sways her hips and moves her feet in time with the music. I'm stumbling all over myself. By the end of our second song, she's in hysterics watching me desecrate this dance floor with my terrible moves.

"More dancing, less laughing," I bark at her.

"I can't help it," she giggles, laughing so hard that she can't even do her own moves anymore.

I'm seconds away from calling it quits when the door bursts open and Asher, Riley, and Connor swan in.

"*Just Dance*?" Riley's face lights up. "When did you get this?"

"Last week." I frown at his excited face. "Please tell me you don't play this game."

"Oh, uh..." Riley pulls his expression into line. "Nah, so lame, right? I don't even know why you own it."

Caroline snickers. "I don't think he does either, but I bet you can dance circles around him."

"Really?" Riley's face lights up again. "Is he bad?"

"He sucks." Caroline tips her head back with a laugh.

"Oh, this I gotta see." Asher crosses his arms, his gleeful smile borderline evil as Caroline lines up another round.

"Come on, hot shot, you can dance too." She waves him over and soon has the four of us lined up and ready to play.

The song begins, and like hell I'm letting these douche nuggets beat me.

I give it my best damn shot, but Riley is a freaking king. Asher's not bad either. Thankfully, Connor looks as much like a gorilla as I do, so that brings me some comfort.

Before the round has ended, Ethan and Liam appear.

Somehow, my girlfriend persuades them to join in too.

See, I told you she was magic.

She went for the competition angle, and guys in this house can't resist. Soon we're all competing in earnest, dancing off like this is the fucking Stanley Cup final.

Ethan moves like a brick building, while Riley's a freaking snake in water. Who knew the guy's limbs were made of rubber?

They're into it, though. The determination on Ethan's face is hilarious, and it only gets better when Mikayla walks in the door and sees him.

She jolts to a stop, her eyes nearly popping out of her

head before she scrambles for her phone and starts recording.

The video's gonna be shit—she's laughing so damn hard her hand is shaking. It's that silent laughter that makes her whole body vibrate, and it quickly turns into a squeal when Ethan spins and notices her.

"What are you doing?" He jerks to a stop, forgetting all about the competition and lunging at her. "Delete that!"

"Nope!" She holds the phone away, laughing as he scrambles to reach it.

He's twice her size, but she's a freaking bullet as she shoots out of the room.

Her raucous laughter can be heard above the music as he chases her upstairs and they continue to tussle for the phone.

I turn to check on Caroline, and she's grinning and laughing, congratulating Riley on his awesome score and challenging him to another dance.

They go for it, and Caroline wins. Raising her hands in the air, she jumps over to me, whooping and leaping into my arms.

I kiss her solid, so everyone in the room knows she's mine, before drinking in her laughter.

Fuck. I want her to stay.

In my room.

All night.

With me.

I've never felt that way about a girl before, and part of me is too scared to ask, but then the words slip free, whispering across her cheek and into her ear.

"Wanna spend the night?"

CHAPTER 31
CAROLINE

I gape at him, because that seems to be all I'm capable of doing right now.

Casey Pierce just asked me to stay over.

This is huge.

He stares back at me, his wide-eyed expression telling me he can barely believe it himself.

"Are you sure?" I don't really want to give him an out, but it'd be worse if I didn't and then he regretted this, right?

"Yeah, come on." He places me on the floor before taking my hand and leading me out of the room. "Night, guys!"

There are a few moans and groans as we leave, and by the sounds of it, the game will wrap up now too.

Diverting past the kitchen counter, Casey flips open the pizza box.

"Anyone want the last three slices? No takers? Okay, it's ours." He didn't even pause to let anyone respond, and I laugh as he grabs the box and leads me upstairs.

As soon as the door clicks shut behind him, he offers me a slice of pizza. I check the topping and notice it's only cheese, so I take a slice and munch it down. After all that dancing, I'm starving. And I'm not the only one. Casey inhales the pizza like it's his first meal all day.

I'm only halfway through my slice by the time he's finished his two, and I let him have the rest of mine.

"Sure?"

"Yeah." I lick the grease off my fingers and look around his room while he finishes eating.

It's about as chaotic and messy as mine, which gives me this sense of comfort that I can't even explain. It feels lived-in and homey. There's a slight smell of sweat, but lingering over that is this musky man-smell and hints of cologne that curl the tendrils of desire in my belly. I may not have felt like sex before, but I can feel the urge building within me again.

I'll put it down to all the laughter and fun. The way Casey took my mood and turned it upside down. After a night of basically no sleep and a day of being haunted by a secret I don't want to share, I was stretched thin. But then he saw me, took me away, and distracted me.

And now he wants me to stay.

The whole night!

Pulling my phone out, I quickly text Leilani, letting her know I won't be coming back to the dorm.

Within seconds she sends me her reply.

Lei-Lei: Have you told him yet?

. . .

I glare at my screen, regret burning my insides to ash. She's right, of course, but if I tell him now I won't be staying the night anymore, and this is too epic. Yes, I need to tell him... but can't I just enjoy this night first? It might be my last.

Dumping my phone on his desk, I try to shut down the doubts rattling through me.

"Everything cool?"

"Yeah." I look away to hide my wince. "I was just letting Lani know I won't be home tonight." I glance over my shoulder at him. "You sure you're sure?"

"Yes." He laughs out the word before shoving the last of my pizza slice in his mouth.

I tap my phone and decide I'll text her back later. I can't let her kill this moment for me. I just want to forget what I did and focus on the fact that I'm standing in Casey's bedroom.

I love this guy.

I've always wanted him.

And now I'll be sharing his bed.

The thought sizzles my insides in all the right ways, and I figure that now is the perfect time for a little private show. It'll be a nice way to thank him, right? And it's a chance for me to put a smile on his face after the way he humiliated himself for my pleasure.

Scanning his room, I start mentally mapping out a dance and the space I'll be working in when I spot a record player next to his bed.

"Nice." I grin, pointing at it.

He smiles like he's the proudest kid in the class. "I know, right? It's a hand-me-down from my grandpa. He gave me all his vinyls too."

I crouch on the floor, looking through the selection of '80s and '90s classics. Everything from Michael Jackson's *Thriller* album to Bon Jovi's *Slippery When Wet*. My parents would love this stuff. With a grin, I pull out the Cyndi Lauper album.

"That one belongs to my grandma."

I grin, carefully setting it on the record player.

He helps me get it spinning, and then I lower the needle, stepping back from the bed and starting to move my hips to the beat.

"Are you serious?" Casey gives me an excited grin. "Is it private show time?"

"You bet your ass it is, baby." I dip to the floor, trying to think like a stripper while keeping time with Cyndi's beats. "Girls Just Wanna Have Fun" is rocking out of the speakers, and I throw my head back, letting my hair dance along with me.

Casey looks like a kid in a candy store, nestling back against the pillows and drinking me in like I'm sex on a stick.

I probably look like a dork, but he's not laughing at me as I strip out of my clothes. My boobs are definitely bigger than they used to be thanks to baby hormones, but Casey seems to like that. At this stage, my pants are only feeling a touch tighter, so thankfully I'm still pretty much the same shape as I fling my shirt at him, then slide my pants down.

He sticks his fingers in his mouth and whistles as I lower my bra strap and run my fingers down my arm.

I can tell he's getting excited, resisting the urge to lunge off the bed and grab me.

It feels hot being this desired. It's making me wet and

needy, but I keep going with my dance, unclasping my bra and playing with my breasts as Cyndi starts wailing "All Through the Night."

"So fucking hot, baby," Casey murmurs, licking his lips as I tease a panty drop.

I make him sweat it out for a little longer, until he whines like he can't stand not touching me. Finally sliding the fabric off my hips, I use my big toe to flick them at him, then do a twirl and play with my hair while my naked body sways and gyrates for him.

I've never felt sexier than in this moment, and as soon as I move close enough to the bed, he jumps up and grabs me with a playful growl.

Dragging me onto the mattress, he straddles me, kissing my neck with his hungry lips before sucking my pulsing nipples into his mouth. He plays fair and gives them both equal attention while I tug at his shirt.

He flicks it off as I glide my fingers down his rigid muscles and enjoy his tattooed skin. He's one sexy beast, and I want to lick every inch of him.

I start with the tats on his shoulder, tracing the ink with my tongue while he pants in my ear and tells me how sexy I am.

"You too," I murmur between licks, figuring this tongue-painting thing is going to take a while. Bring it on.

But then he springs away from me, devouring my body with his eyes, the pads of his fingers gliding over my skin.

Standing up, he pulls me with him, kissing me deeply, his hands on either side of my neck as he drinks me in like I'm his life source, the only thing keeping him hydrated.

The blood in my body pulses a thick beat for him, my V-jay throbbing for his touch.

"Please," I whisper against his mouth. "Touch me. Make me come like only you can."

He smiles, brushing his lips over my cheek as he sits back down on the bed, nestling against the pillows and grabbing my arm. He pulls me down in front of him, spinning me around so my back is against his chest.

"What are you—" My words disappear as he spreads my legs, the air kissing my most sensitive spots as he trails the pads of his fingers down my body. I've gotta say, it makes me feel kind of vulnerable, lying here so openly like this. I'm used to him covering me, keeping me safe. But there's also something kind of thrilling about this exposure too.

I curl my toes into the duvet as he paints a line around each breast before squeezing my nipples. The pinch shoots an arrow of pleasure straight down to my core. I whimper, resting my head back against his shoulder while he plays with my nips and nibbles the side of my neck.

His fingers finally start to travel again, brushing over my tattoo before gliding across my pulsing center.

"Yes," I moan. "Please, baby."

I'm not above begging when my body's this wired, but he makes me wait, teasing my clit only briefly before pulling my folds apart. Dipping his fingertip inside me, he takes my moisture and paints my aching folds. The kiss of air against my sensitive skin and his magic fingers feel so good, I can barely contain myself. And then his thumb finds my swollen clit and starts to dance circles on it.

I buck my hips, high-pitched gasps firing out of me as he forces me back down. Forces me to take this pleasure even though it feels like too much.

"Come for me, my cherry girl." He pushes his fingers inside me, and I nearly bust apart on the spot.

The sensations are blinding, and I grind against his fingers, my heart thundering out of time as he continues to work my clit and yes... yes...

Yes!

I splinter. I fall. I flail.

The orgasm rips through me in waves of pleasure that are so overwhelming, I barely know what to do to them. Reaching over my head, I fist the back of his hair and ride it out.

He's still touching me while I writhe on the bed, barely able to breathe, and then he gently shoves me forward.

"On your knees, woman."

I do what he tells me without a second thought. Scrambling over his bed, I thrust my ass in the air, desperate to feel him spear me from behind.

Grabbing my butt cheeks, he gives them a squeeze.

"So fucking sexy."

The sound of his zipper coming down sends a zing right through me. The anticipation is unbearable. I glance over my shoulder, my body burning as he shoves his pants down and lets his dick spring free.

My belly trembles and I dip my head, smiling at the crumpled duvet cover when he parts my cheeks and teases my weeping entrance with his head.

"Please." I whisper the word under my breath, but it

quickly turns into a lusty scream as he enters me with surprising force and speed.

His cock tears right through me, thrusting deep and hard. The pleasure is mind-blowing, and I fist the duvet as he pulls back and does it again, pounding into me with more force than he ever has before.

It feels fucking amazing, and I let him know with cries and groans that can only be defined as ecstasy. He's taking me over the edge in ways he never has before, and I am so down for this.

Our bodies slap together, my breasts rocking and my butt cheeks wiggling as he takes his fill.

Grabbing my ass again, he digs his fingers into my flesh, a moan coming out of him that's raw and primal.

"Fuck," he rasps. "Oh, fuck."

I can feel him on the cusp of fracturing, and I want to be there with him. The build inside me is starting once more, my chest heaving as I threaten to lose my breath all over again.

"Ahhh," I moan, lifting my chin up.

Winding his fingers through my curls, he lightly fists them and rides me a touch harder. It's an almost painful pleasure that's thrilling and addictive. His cock is taking me over, and I'm happily giving myself to its whims of fancy.

"Yes, baby." The words punch out of me as heady gasps, and then his pace changes to short, urgent thrusts that ripple through me and ignite whatever charge has been lying in wait. "Yes!" I cry out as he drives deep and jerks inside me.

Slapping his hands on my ass, he holds on, groaning

as we orgasm together. Two bodies fused by something so powerful, I can't even find a word for it.

I'm not even sure I'll be able to walk after this.

Or move.

Doesn't matter. The way my body's buzzing right now, I'm pretty sure I could stay on my knees like this for the rest of the night.

CHAPTER 32
CASEY

I'm shaking.

That was intense.

Like fucking intense.

This woman.

As my heart starts to slowly drop back to a rate that doesn't make me feel like I'm about to pass out, I glide my hands around to Caroline's belly, then travel up. Cupping her luscious tits, I pull her upright so she can lean back against me.

We're both still panting, sweat coating our skin as I hold her tight, wrapping my arms all the way around her.

I lightly scrape my teeth over her shoulder before kissing the skin and securing her against my chest. Her hair nestles against my shoulder and under my chin. It tickles but I'm not moving for anything.

"That was..." She's still puffing, struggling to speak.

"I know, right?" I flop back on the bed, bringing her with me.

We're a sweaty, wet mess, but I can clean the sheets

tomorrow. Lying on my back, I rearrange her body until she's curled against my side. Her crazy curls still tickle beneath my chin, and I tuck them away, smoothing back her hair while she drapes her arm over my stomach.

I don't know if I'm ever going to be able to form a coherent sentence after that.

I took her deep and hard, but she seemed to get off on it. My cock feels almost tender after such a wild ride, but Mr. Jones fucking loves me right now. He's gone limp, back into rest mode so he can recover, but I can tell he's grateful.

Playing with the back of her hair, I whisper my fingers over her curls as her breathing finally starts to slow, dropping into an even tempo. Cyndi's still playing for us, softly singing, "Time After Time."

Caroline's gone so still against me, I whisper just in case. "Are you asleep?"

"No, my body is still on fire. I swear, if you touch any of my lady parts right now, I'll jump through the roof."

I go to reach for the spot between her legs, and she slaps my hand away with a laugh. "Don't you dare."

With a laugh of my own, I rest my hand over hers and pull it up to my chest, playing with her fingers while I stare at the ceiling.

The lamp beside my bed casts a soft glow over the room. I should switch it off so we can get some shut eye, but I can't move right now. I just want to soak in this: the weight of her body next to mine, her soft, plump boobs squished against my chest and side. I could get used to this.

Fuck. I could totally get used to this.

I blink and do my best not to freak out.

This is everything I didn't want—intimate cuddles and sleepovers. From what I've seen, it only ever leads to fights and stress and breakups.

I never wanted that for myself, but can you hear me asking Caroline to leave right now?

If anything, I'm holding her tighter.

If anything, I'm wanting to whisper secrets in her ear and find out all of hers.

"Hey, when I saw you today"—the words are popping out of me before I can stop them—"you seemed kind of sad. I wanted to make you feel better."

"And you did."

"But I didn't solve the problem, did I? I just distracted you from it."

She sighs, her warm breath hitting my skin.

"What was up? Is it baby stuff?"

Her stillness tells me I might be onto something.

"Have you decided yet?"

"No." Her voice trembles, and I instinctively brush my lips across her forehead. "I guess I've just been playing pretend since we started sleeping together. My body's changing a little, but I haven't had morning sickness or anything, just the odd queasy stomach, so it's easy to forget that I'm even pregnant. I just want to keep playing pretend and ignoring this whole thing. But soon it's going to be obvious. Soon my belly's gonna get big and... I mean, unless I abort."

I can feel her cheek shifting into what I think must be a cringe.

"You don't seem sold on that idea."

"I guess I'm not, but I don't feel ready to raise a child either."

"You could always look at adoption."

The stiffening of her muscles makes me turn on the bed. I need to look at her for this conversation. Resting my hand on her cheek, I brush the wayward curls off her face and search her expression.

"I'm adopted." Her nose scrunches.

"Oh, I didn't know."

She shrugs. "Not many people do. My parents don't look that different from me. I mean, there's no red hair in the family, and they both have brown eyes, but if you didn't know, you probably wouldn't even think to look for it." She bites her lips together. "I've had a great life with them. They're amazing, and I love them."

"But…" I can sense one coming, so I figure I may as well say it.

"But I've always wondered about my parents. Why didn't they want me? Why couldn't they raise me? Why'd they give me away?" Her eyes fill with tears, and it breaks my heart. Like, my chest actually hurts right now.

I brush my thumb under her eye, catching the first tear to fall.

"I don't want to do that to my kid. But I don't want to short-change them either. So maybe abortion is the kinder option, you know? Because… I can't be a mom."

"You could if you wanted to."

Why the fuck am I saying this stuff?

It's not like *I* want a kid. It's not like I can be a dad! I've never even had one, so how the fuck would I know what to do?

But Caroline would make a great mom. I can tell because she's sweet and funny. She's smart, and she cares about other people. I watch the way she smiles at others, and I know she'd drop anything to be there if Leilani needed her. I'm pretty sure she'd do the same for me.

It's more than I can say for my mom. She didn't even make it to my graduation, and I'm lucky if I hear from her once a semester. It's always up to me to call and check in. If I didn't, I'd probably never hear from her.

I'm still deciding whether I'll even bother going home this summer.

Caroline wouldn't be like that.

"You'd be a good mom," I say, and she gives me a grateful smile, but it doesn't stick.

"Keeping this baby will change my life forever. It's not a three-month trial, you know? I'd be a parent for life."

"Yeah, I know." I wince, the idea sending an ugly vibration through my torso. If she's a parent for life, then I would be too. "I'm just saying that... you not being a good mom isn't a factor to consider. You'd be great. It just comes down to if you want to. If you feel ready to change your life. I mean, our lives."

Shit, that's hard to say.

I can't seem to wrap my brain around a future that has me chasing a toddler around a backyard. It's so fucking foreign to me. I can't change a diaper or hold a baby. I've never done either of those things before.

Panic sizzles as Caroline sniffs, pushing me onto my back so she can nestle against my side again. She tucks her head under my chin and curls into me. "It's the question I can't seem to answer. And every time I really make myself think about abortion, I'm struck with that thought that..." She sniffs again, and I can tell she's about to start crying. "If my birth mom had aborted me, I wouldn't exist right now. And that's a real mindfuck, you know? It makes it impossible to figure out whether aborting is the kind option or the selfish one. But then keeping a baby when you're seriously not ready for one is kind of selfish, too, isn't it? I don't know, Casey. I just don't know." Her words catch in her mouth, stumbling out in bursts that are hard to hear.

All I know is that she's crying against me, and I have to hold her and kiss her head and make her feel like she's not gonna fall apart.

It *is* an impossible choice, but it's one she's going to have to make.

She just needs to decide and then live with the fallout.

But not tonight.

Tonight she needs sleep.

And so I stop talking. I stroke her back and let the music play, and eventually her tears dry up and we both slip into blissful slumber where, just for a few hours, we don't have to answer unbearable questions.

CHAPTER 33
CAROLINE

Spending the night at Casey's changed something between us. It's only been a day and a half, but we've been texting constantly. It's not just about the sex anymore. We're closer somehow.

We haven't talked about the baby again, which is probably why nerves are massacring my stomach as I look for Casey outside the law building. There's a really pretty grassy spot where people will picnic as the weather gets warmer.

Today, the sun is shining, but it's still pretty frickin' cold out. Maybe I can persuade him to join me inside. The law building has a great cafeteria.

I scan the area, wondering again why he asked to meet with me. We don't usually do lunch. Maybe this is the new us. I'm not sure. But what if he's wanting to sit down and have a serious chat? What if this is the moment where I have to decide? Part of me wants him to make me, just so I can stop torturing myself over this decision, but another part of me is terrified.

And I still have to tell him about Ben.

Shit. Shit. Shit!

I so don't want to. Casey will be so pissed. He'll hate me forever. And Ben probably will too.

Do I really have to tell them? Can't I just choose who I want the father to be and leave it at that?

Of course you can't, you idiot! You've dug yourself into this great big, fucking hole.

And soon that hole is going to fill with water and I'll be drowning in it... which is maybe what I deserve.

Guilt lashes me again, followed swiftly by a debilitating fear.

Nibbling my lip, I pull out my phone and try to calm myself. Maybe Casey doesn't want to talk about baby stuff. He has a really important game tonight. It's the quarterfinals for the Frozen Faceoff. If they win this, they'll get to play at the tournament in St. Paul's next weekend!

Winning the trophy will be so triumphant for Nolan U. We've never had it before. We've made it to the semis and the finals in the past, but the Cougars have never won the trophy. I want Casey to be on the team that brings it home.

I can't wait to watch him. It's going to be a tough game, but I believe in the Cougars. I always have. They're an awesome team, and they've had a killer season. Tonight is going to be epic.

Maybe Casey just wants to catch up for lunch and distract himself pregame so he's not too nervous or something.

I call his number, because I still can't see him, and the

tune of "Sweet Caroline" starts playing from behind the large pine tree to my left. I frown, the phone still up against my ear as I walk around the tree and see Casey. He's just answering my call when he spots me.

He grins, speaking into the phone. "Hey, pretty girl."

My frown deepens as I stop in front of him. "Please tell me you didn't change your ringtone to that so you wouldn't forget my name."

He barks out a laugh and hangs up. "I changed it because I happen to like that song and... well, you're my sweet Caroline."

It's the cutest thing ever, and I can feel my heart turning to a puddle of mush as I slip my phone away and take a seat on the ground. He's laid out his jacket, and I nestle between his legs and look up to kiss him.

His smile is sweet and adoring, and everything I've worried about since he texted me seems to vanish on the spot. With his arms wrapped around me, keeping me warm, the chill I was feeling before fades to a memory, and I get caught up just hanging with my boyfriend. I can't go shitting all over this moment with the truth. I can sense he just needs things to be light right now. He tells me about his morning classes and how he stayed up way too late last night in order to get an assignment in.

"I'm kinda smashed, but I'll rally for the game. I always do." His smile has a nervous edge to it, and I spin in his arms, hooking my legs over his so I'm now sideways against him. I want to be able to look at his face for this.

"You're gonna be great."

"I know." He glances away from me, staring out across the grassy lawn.

"Casey." I touch his cheek and force him to look back at me. "You're gonna be amazing. The Cougars are going to win, and we'll party hard tonight, baby."

This makes him laugh, and I'm stoked that I've been able to cut through his tension.

"I'll be in the stands cheering you on. I'll be your loudest supporter, I swear."

He grins, kissing the tip of my nose.

"And after the game... and the party... we'll celebrate all over again. You know, in our own special way." I wink at him and lean up to give him a little preview.

My kiss is deep and alluring; I can tell by the way he stiffens against my hip.

I pull away with an indulgent smile, and he shakes his head. "The things you do to me, woman."

"The things you do to me, *man*." I raise my eyebrows at him.

And then his watch starts beeping. With a groan, he turns off his alarm. "My next class starts in about fifteen minutes. I'm just gonna run to the bathroom and then take my sweet time saying goodbye to my luscious lady."

"Okay." I stand up, biting my lips against a laugh as he adjusts himself and tries to hide his semi before walking off to the bathroom.

Leaning against the tree, I wait for him, smiling to myself as I relive the cuteness of our time together. We must have looked like a legit couple in love to anyone walking past.

You are a legit couple.

In love?

Well, I sure am.

My wistful sigh is cut off when I spot someone coming toward me. He's got the biggest smile on his face as he breaks into a jog and stops in front of me before I've fully registered who it is.

Oh shit!

Ben.

"Hey." He's staring down at me like I'm his favorite flower.

Oh shit.

I forgot how tall he is. Tall and broad. Underneath that sweater he's wearing are long, muscular arms. His hands are huge, and I can remember his fingers curling around my hips.

Fuck! This is so bad!

My eyes dart to the law building as I frantically try to figure out how I'm going to get rid of him before Casey gets back. The last thing my boyfriend needs before his big game is this kind of drama.

"B-Ben." I catch some wayward hairs that blow across my cheek, tucking them behind my ear as a cool breeze races up my spine.

"It's so good to see you." His eyes are dancing with this awe-filled joy as he drinks me in.

"Oh, yeah. Nice... nice to see you too."

"I've been looking for you everywhere, but we've kept missing each other. Did your roommate tell you I stopped by?"

"Um... yep." I nod and force a polite smile, scrambling for a good excuse to get out of this conversation.

I can't tell him right now.

I can't admit anything!

Casey's coming back any second!

"We didn't exchange numbers that night we hooked up, and I've been going into stalker mode trying to find you." He laughs while I look past his arm, praying Casey doesn't come jogging down the steps before I can get rid of Ben.

This is a nightmare! I have to get him out of here. Now.

But he's oblivious to my stress. "Listen, I just wanted to say that I had a really awesome time with you at that party. And I know we were drunk, but I remember enough."

I glance back at his face. Big mistake. His eyes are glowing with memories of us.

"It was hot and primal and..." He laughs. "Oh, man, I'd love a repeat, you know? I felt like we had a great connection, and I..." His voice trails off as he finally starts to pick up on my serious lack of enthusiasm.

My face flushes when he catches my eye. I really don't want to be cruel, but I can't encourage him either. "Yeah, I really was so drunk. I can't remember much. Sorry." My words are a mumbled mess as I look to the ground and feel the shame wash through me. It's a tidal wave of guilt and regret.

"Well, maybe we could get together sometime. I could help you remember." Ben gives me a hopeful grin. Stepping in close, he leans his hand against the tree trunk behind me and bends low, looking ready to kiss me.

I gasp and jerk sideways so he can't reach my mouth.

He frowns, disappointment stark on his face as he mutters, "Or maybe not."

"I'm sorry. I..." My voice evaporates when I spot Casey

closing the distance between us. He's looking kind of confused and hella annoyed as he steps up beside us. He must have seen Ben try to kiss me.

"Who are you?" he practically barks.

Ben's eyebrows rise in surprise, but then his face breaks into a broad grin. "Oh, hey. Casey Pierce, right? You're lightning on that ice, man." He extends his hand to my boyfriend, looking so happy to meet him. "Good luck for the game tonight."

Shit. Why does he have to be so damn nice?

I'm feeling worse by the second.

"Thanks." Casey gives Ben's hand a firm shake and asks again, "Who the fuck are you?"

"Oh. Name's Ben. I'm a Cougar too. Play basketball."

"Figures. You're like a walking Burj Khalifa."

Ben laughs, and I'm pretty sure I want to die right now.

Casey's like a bulldog next to a towering Great Dane, and if there was a fight, I've got a feeling my riled-up boyfriend would kick ass.

"How do you guys know each other?" Casey points between us.

No, no, no! Don't answer that!

"We hooked up at a party a while back." Ben blushes while my insides combust. He glances at me with one of those secret smiles, and all I can do is stare back at him, subtly shaking my head. But not subtle enough. His smile only grows, his voice taking on a slightly boastful edge. "We had a good night. A *really* good night." He gives me a wink that's playful, and my heart starts to slither into the burning acid of my stomach.

Shit!

Casey's eyebrows dip. "Oh yeah? When was that?"

"Back in..."

Fuck. No! Don't say it!

"January?"

Ben looks to me for confirmation—this poor clueless man has no idea the bomb he's about to set off.

And now I can't breathe.

I give him a noncommittal shrug and shake my head, but Casey's working it out already.

"January." He nods, looking painfully thoughtful. "How many weeks ago is that?"

"Don't count," I murmur under my breath. "Please don't count."

He must hear me, because when I glance up, his face has turned to stone, his usually warm gaze now icier than the Arctic Circle. My stomach roils like a hurricane is forming inside it, and oblivious Ben decides that now is the best time to keep talking.

"I was just asking if she wanted to go out with me sometime, but now I'm wondering if I've missed something and you guys are together." Ben looks between us. It's clear he's wrestling with his disappointment as he asks, "Are you a couple?"

Casey doesn't even look at him. His icy glare turns a few degrees colder as he stares me right in the eye and says, "No. We're not."

My heart splinters on the spot, and I stand frozen for a second as Casey stalks away and Ben stares down at me in confusion.

"What am I missing here?" He points after Casey, and I shake my head.

"Nothing," I mumble, then spin on my heel. "I gotta go."

Leaving poor, clueless Ben behind me, I grab my bag strap and sprint after Casey. I can't let it end this way. He needs to let me explain. I have to make him understand why I did what I did.

CHAPTER 34
CASEY

"Casey, wait!" Caroline's calling my name, but like fuck I'm stopping right now.

I'm still reeling, dates running through my mind as I work out that—fuck! I might not even be the father.

"Casey, please!" Her voice pitches with desperation, and I can't help but glance over my shoulder. She's chasing after me, and if she's not careful, she might trip and hurt herself.

Dammit!

I shouldn't fucking care, but my feet are stopping and I'm spinning to face her. She slows down, obviously trying to catch her breath as she dribbles to a stop in front of me.

Her blue eyes are bright with anguish, her red curls wild around her perfect face.

Fuck, I hate that she's so pretty.

"Let me explain." Her voice trembles, but I can't help barking back at her.

"Explain what?" I throw my arms wide. "That you

hooked up with two different guys around the same time?"

She cringes, rubbing her forehead with shaking fingers. "You can't be mad at me for that. You're a famous man slut in this school."

"I'm not mad about the fact that you slept with another guy." I spit out the words, meaning them, although the thought of her bumping uglies with some other dude makes flashes of green spurt across my vision. I clench my jaw for a second and take in a sharp breath through my nose. "I'm mad because you didn't—" I huff and throw my arms up again. "I mean, what the fuck, Caroline! How could you not tell me this?"

"I... I..." Her mouth opens and closes a couple times, but no words are coming out.

I close my eyes and grit out the only question to ask right now. "Who's the father?"

"I..." She looks about ready to throw up. "I don't know."

"You don't know." I run my tongue along my teeth and let out this disbelieving laugh.

"I'm sorry, okay. It was a week apart, and I used protection with both of you. I don't know which condom failed, but I needed..." She kind of whimpers, her face bunching. "I need it to be you. So, I made it you."

"Why?"

"Because I'm in love with you!" she shouts at me like I'm stupid for not knowing this already.

The couple walking past us flinches at her volume and I scowl at them, giving them a mind-your-business warning look that they both quickly adhere to. As they scuttle away, I turn back to Caroline, who's shifted close enough for me to smell her perfume.

Dammit!

"I loved you before I even met you." Her voice has dropped to this feathery, husky sound that makes my chest hurt. "And then I *did* meet you, and you exceeded all of my expectations. So now I'm like full-blown head over heels for you." She fists her sweater over her stomach. "This kid can't belong to anyone else. It has to be yours. Casey, please, it has to be yours." Her words are getting fast, panic obviously riding through her as she tries to sell me on this.

But I can't take it.

She loves me? Yet she's been playing me this whole time?

What the actual fuck am I supposed to do with this right now?

She's a liar! Am I just supposed to shrug and say, "Oh well, no biggie"? If that kid in her belly isn't mine, I don't... I don't know what to do with that.

And what if this Ben guy is the father? What if he's totally into it? Doesn't he deserve a chance?

I'll just fuck it up anyway. Maybe it's better if she goes to him.

The idea curdles my stomach, and I don't want to unravel the reason why.

"Please," she whispers, her eyes glassy with desperation. "I need it to be yours."

"What if it's not?" My voice comes out low and gravelly.

She goes pale, her complexion practically translucent as I let that little nugget sink in.

"I want a test," I grit out. My jaw is clenched so tight, my stiff lips only just moving. "I have to know if it's mine."

"A t-test?"

"Yeah, a paternity test. I deserve the truth."

Her eyes go wide, the first tear slipping free as she swallows.

What? Am I asking too much? Is she fucking kidding me?

I'm about to bark at her that she doesn't have a choice over this, but then she nods. "Um... o-okay. I'll, uh... I'm not sure how to do—"

"Well, figure it out. Google it or some shit. Just get it done." I'm sounding like a harsh asshole, but I can't care about hurting her feelings. She's fucking destroyed mine.

This is why I don't do relationships!

How could I walk into one so easily?

Fuck! Fuuuuck!

Her fingers are shaking as she pulls a red curl away from her mouth. "It means I'll have to tell Ben."

"Something you probably should have already done," I growl, glaring at her.

She knows. She knows I'm right. The shame washing over her face right now is raw and real. She looks to the ground, her chin bunching like she's fighting the urge to ugly cry, and I can't watch that shit. I want to stay mad and indignant. It's my fucking right.

So I do the only thing I can—I spin on my heel and walk away.

It takes everything in me not to look back and check on her.

Instinct is scraping at my neck, my muscles tingling with the urge to run back and comfort her. She's crying. I can't hear her, but any dumb fuck could work out that she is.

I can't watch it.

I can't do this.

I was single for a reason, and this is just the reminder I needed.

Relationships burn and destroy you.

They always do.

CHAPTER 35
CAROLINE

I'm going to throw up.

Haven't felt this nauseous all pregnancy, but watching Casey storm away from me is the worst feeling in the world. I stumble back to my dorm, clenching my jaw against the bile surging up my throat. I don't make it to the toilet in time and end up spurting puke all over the bathroom floor.

I heave the rest into the toilet bowl, then slump against the cold wall, staring at my yellowy-brown vomit and feeling numb. It takes me forever to get my ass off the floor and clean up my mess. By the time I'm done, I'm a sobbing wreck, sitting on the bathroom floor in nothing but my underwear, my vomit-splattered clothes falling out of the hamper.

I crawl—yes, literally crawl—out of the bathroom and climb into bed. Pulling the covers over my head, I bury myself in the darkness and cry until my head is pounding.

Casey wants a paternity test, which means I have to

tell Ben. He's going to hate me. Maybe not as much as Casey hates me right now, but I'm guessing he'll be pissed. Or worse, he'll be stoked and want to get together and make a go of this thing. He'll want to be the perfect baby daddy while the guy who owns my heart will want nothing to do with me.

Shit, even if the baby is Casey's, things will never be the same again.

I lied to him.

Lani said I shouldn't. She warned me. But I was so scared that telling him the truth would ruin everything. And it has.

A fresh sob jerks my belly, and I cry some more. Hating myself like I never have before.

I have no idea how many hours have ticked by, but when my phone rings, I jolt like I've been woken from a dozing slumber. I didn't realize you could sleep when your heart hurt this badly. I must be truly exhausted.

For a moment, I wonder where Lani is and why she hasn't been by to check on me, but then I remember her study group. They have a massive assignment due on Monday, and they're in crunch time right now. She told me she wouldn't be around much this weekend.

Flipping my covers back, I dig my phone out of my bag and see I've just missed a call from my mom. I also see that it's been two hours since Ben outed me in front of Casey. Only two? How is that possible? It feels like a century has dragged by.

As she always does, my mom immediately tries again. She knows the depths of my bag and how useless I am at tidying anything. Calling twice usually does the trick, and like a fool, I swipe my thumb across the screen.

"Hey, Mom."

"Hey, Cinnamon. How's my girl?"

"Oh, uh... you know."

"What's the matter?" Her voice changes instantly, and I can picture her face. She's probably in her chair on the sun porch. She loves to read in the afternoons, and since she only works part-time, she has the luxury of escaping into her romance novels every day.

I wish I could escape into one. Give me a sticky-sweet Hallmark with minimal problems and a perfectly happy ending.

Why can't life be like that?

Why does it have to suck so badly?

"Sweetie?" Mom prompts me, and I'm forced to come up with some kind of answer.

"Nothing."

Nothing? Really? Great answer.

I shake my head, trying to brighten my voice. "I mean, nothing very interesting."

And now the world's biggest lie.

But it's not like I can tell her the truth. Ha! She'd be mortified and disappointed, and then she'd tell Dad, and he'd be shocked and... ugh, I can't picture his face right now. That'll send me over the edge. There's already enough negative emotion circling me. I don't need theirs too.

"Your voice sounds scratchy. Are you sick?"

"Just exhausted," I murmur. "School's kind of intense and... you know."

"Yeah, I remember. It was a long time ago now." She laughs. "But I'll never forget my college years. Going to the game tonight will be a nice break for you."

"Oh, yeah." I scratch my head, the thought of going making me want to puke all over again. "Not sure I'll make it."

"But, baby, it's such an important game. You've gotta go. I mean, if your dad didn't have that wedding on this evening, he'd totally be there with you."

"I... I know, um... okay, truth is, I threw up this afternoon, so maybe I am sick."

"Why didn't you say?" Mom's voice fills with empathy.

"I didn't want you to worry?"

I probably shouldn't be framing my responses as questions, but my brain is barely functioning right now. I'm surprised I'm even managing to hold this conversation.

"Oh, sweetie. Was it something you ate?"

"Most likely, although I can't figure out what."

"You must feel awful."

"I'll survive."

Will you?

Right now, I'm honestly not sure. Tears line my lashes, thickening my voice and making it impossible not to sniff. "Hey, Mom. I gotta go."

"Aw, Cinny. You just take care of yourself, okay? Is Lani there to support you?"

"She's got a huge assignment due. I'll be fine. I just need to rest."

"Okay. Well, keep your fluids up, and if you start running a fever, remember to keep as cool as you can. Even though you'll be shivering, make sure you don't bury yourself under the blankets."

"Yeah, got it."

She spurts off a few more pieces of advice before finally letting me hang up.

I snuggle back down into my bed, tucking the covers under my chin and staring into my empty bedroom.

The game. Casey's big, important game that I was going to be there for.

It's not like I can go now. If I show up, it might throw him completely. I can't be in the stands cheering him on when I've gone and hurt him so badly. Shit! This is why I didn't want him finding out before the game. And now everything is so screwed up!

Closing my eyes, I feel the whimper climbing up my throat. It pops out as a soft cry, then turns into a gasp when Leilani walks in.

"Hey." She blinks in surprise. "What are you doing? Are you okay?"

I roll over, turning my back to her so I don't have to do this all over again.

"Caroline?" Her thick boot heels pock-pock-pock across our linoleum floor until I can feel her standing by my bed, looking down at me. "What happened?"

"He knows. You happy?"

She sighs. "I'm guessing he didn't take the news too well."

"Of course he didn't. He's human." My voice is so cut up with emotion that I don't even recognize it.

Lani's hand lightly squeezes my shoulder, her voice a soft contrast to mine. "Did he dump you?"

"Yeah, I think so." The words shake out of me. "He wants a paternity test."

"Oh shit."

"I know," I squeak. "How could I let this happen?" My voice finally breaks apart, overrun by new sobs.

Leilani takes a seat behind me, gently rubbing my back and murmuring things I can't soak in. It's probably empty promises like "It'll be all right." But that's a lie.

It won't be.

It can't be.

I lost Casey—the only guy I've ever truly wanted.

And it's what I deserve, because I did lie to him. And he has every right to never want to speak to me again.

Lifting my knees to my chest, I curl into a ball and cry myself to sleep.

Just before I drift off, I hear Lani's soft apology. She has to get back to her group, but she'll be by to check on me later.

I can't respond. My throat hurts. My head feels like it's being split in half. So I just stay still on the bed and listen to her creep out the door before finally drifting away for a small reprieve.

CHAPTER 36
CASEY

The arena is packed. We knew it would be. Coach even included a bunch of stuff about focus in his pep talk. This is a big game. The Nolan U Cougars made it to the Frozen Faceoff semifinals four years ago, and we lost. This is our chance to turn things around. This team will go all the way and make a little history for our school.

Expectations are high—like landing-on-the-moon high—and we'd better deliver tonight. A bunch of important people are in the stands, including the university president and several board members. I'm sure the line of suits just behind the box are the bigwig donors who the admin need to treat like royalty.

That must be Jason's dad up there. He's got the same arrogant smirk as our annoying team captain. It should have been Ethan, but money talks. Thank fuck Jason's graduating soon and Ethan can finally take his rightful place.

I don't pay them any attention as I skate onto the ice. I swore to myself I wouldn't do it, but I can't help checking the stands for a crop of red curls. I look three times during my warm-up, but I don't see her once.

She might be there.

Chances are, she might not.

Not after the way I left things with her this afternoon. She looked devastated, and I can't get her expression out of my head. But each time I start to crumble, I'm reminded of the fact that she's a big fat liar and I'm back to that fiery anger, which I need more than ever for this game.

At least I think I do, until we're halfway through the second period and I'm so riled by the aggressive play from the other team that I start throwing some of my own back. They're fighting dirty tonight, and I know I'm above all that shit, but when I get tripped going for the puck and the referee does nothing, I can't hold it in anymore.

It doesn't help that the fucknugget who tripped me is now snorting down at me. The derisive look on his face is punchable, and I have no choice but to act.

With a growl, I jump back onto my skates and charge him, slamming him against the boards and taking a swing at his head. My stick clatters to the ground as I go wild-bear feral on his ass.

The gloves are off in seconds, and we're going for it. Fisting each other's shirts, we skate in circles, growling and taking swings when we can. The second I manage to tip him sideways, the officials skate in and pull us apart. I get pushed toward the Cougars' box, scoring myself a flying insult from our team captain on my way past.

I give him the finger, my heated glare making him back off before I slam against the boards and am facing a very pissed-off Coach.

"You're out." He points his thumb over his shoulder.

I already know this. While fighting might be part of the game in the professional league, it isn't tolerated at the NCAA level. I knew the referee was going to eject me the second I flicked my gloves off, but I didn't give a shit. I'd had enough.

Fuck hockey!

Fuck this whole damn place!

I thump into my seat, swearing up a storm and throwing my drink bottle onto the floor before Coach barks, "Go cool off!" He points to the exit. "And don't even thinking about showing your face again until you can sit here and support your team. You let everyone down!" he roars at me.

The crowd behind us has gone kind of quiet, ignoring the current play as I stalk away from my team and head for the locker room. He sends one of the assistant coaches after me, but I spin around and growl, "Fuck off!" before storming down the tunnel.

Shouldering the locker room door open with a roar, I stalk into the room, pacing for a minute before smashing my elbow into my locker and hitting my funny bone, which isn't fucking funny!

My fingers tingle and burn while I grab at the pain, hissing out a bunch of curse words just as the door swings open.

"I said fuck off!" I shout, then deflate the second I see who's standing there. "Oh."

"Hello, son." Ethan's dad steps into the room.

I don't know how he got permission to be in here, but I also don't give a shit. The second I see his kind face smiling at me, I feel like maybe I can survive this shitstorm.

"Having a bad night?"

I scoff and shake my head, nearly laughing at his mildly spoken question.

He grins and takes a seat beside me when I plunk down in front of my locker.

He lets me wait it out in puffing silence for a few minutes before finally saying, "I've got a feeling that whatever's going on for you right now is a lot more than a blind referee."

A snort comes out my nose and I glance at him. "You saw it too? The fucker tripped me right up."

"Yep." He nods. "You had every right to be pissed."

I deflate, slumping forward and resting my elbows on my knees. "I doubt Coach sees it that way."

"Oh, he will. But then he'll go on to tell you how controlling your emotions is part of being an elite athlete."

My head droops forward.

"The thing that's a big red flag for me is that you're usually pretty good at keeping it cool out there on the ice. You're focused. It's like you enter another dimension when you're playing. But tonight..." He clicks his tongue.

I steal a sideways peek at him.

"I could tell the second you skated out, something was off." He catches my eye. "Wanna talk about it?"

"Not really," I grit out.

"Okay." He nods, then nudges me with his elbow. "Do you *need* to talk about it?"

I sigh. "Probably."

"I'm all ears, kid."

Wincing, I cup the back of my head and spill the truth as quickly as I can. It only takes me about ninety seconds because I'm talking so damn fast, but he gets the gist.

"Wow." He leans back against the lockers, blinking into the empty room and obviously struggling for the right thing to say. "That's kinda big."

"Yeah." I shake my head, scrubbing a hand over my mouth. "Maybe it's for the best anyway. I can't be a father."

"So, she's definitely keeping it, then?"

"Who the fuck knows?" I mutter.

"Well, if she decides yes… what if it's yours?"

I squeeze my eyes shut, hating the question.

"I can't be a dad," I finally rasp. "I don't know anything about raising a kid."

"No one does. You gotta learn on the job."

"Come on." I sit back and glare at him. "I never had a father. How the hell am I supposed to know what to do?"

"There are plenty of men out there who have been raised by a single mother and ended up being amazing dads. What makes you any different from them?"

I open my mouth to argue, but I can't think of a rebuttal fast enough.

"Look, parenting's hard. No matter what background you come from, there's no specific rule book for your specific child. You have to figure it out as you go, and you can think you're as prepared as you wanna be and you'll still get the shit surprised right out of you. And there are a million different books and pieces of advice. All of them contradict one another, and sometimes it's damn near impossible to know what to do, but here's the thing…" He leans forward, his eyes starting to dance with a look that I can only describe as pure joy. "It comes down to two simple rules—love them and show up for them no matter what." He shrugs. "It's that easy."

My forehead bunches into a tight frown. I can feel it. "It's not that easy."

"Yeah, it is, man." He gently slaps my shoulder. "Trust me on this. All your kid wants from you is love and attention. Whether you let them cry themselves to sleep or have them attached to you twenty-four seven. Or whether you feed them homemade solids or the stuff bought from the store. Whether you play them Mozart or Beyoncé. Whether you teach them to skate or hand them a football. None of that shit makes any difference. All you have to be is there. All you have to tell them is that you'll always love them."

Once again, I open my mouth to argue, but nothing comes out.

"You could screw up in a hundred different ways, Casey. But if your kid knows you're gonna love them no matter what and show up when it counts the most, you're acing parenthood. If you're committed to not abandoning this woman and your unborn kid, then you're halfway there."

I give him a weak smile, thinking about how I stormed away from Caroline this afternoon. But the thought of seeing her again makes my stomach revolt. How do I ever look at her and trust her after what she tried to pull?

She should have told me the truth.

What if the kid's not mine?

I don't want to get involved with a mess that fucking big!

Which means she's not your girl anymore.

The thought punches me in the chest, and I slump forward again.

"I know it's tough, but you *are* going to get through this."

I give him a half-hearted smile. "I wish I had a dad like you."

"What are you talking about? You *do* have a dad like me." He points at himself and winks before slapping me on the shoulder and getting up.

"I'm gonna try to catch a bit more of the game, but I'm here if you need me, all right?" He walks to the door and stops to check that I heard him.

I nod and lift my hand in a wave, watching the door until it clicks shut behind him.

His words run through me like liquid honey, thick and viscous, sticking to every part of me.

Could I really be a dad one day?

I never thought I could be, but...

Leaning back with a heavy sigh, I slap my shoulders against the metal locker as images of me skating with a little kid twirl through my brain. Would it be a boy or a girl? Would he have shaggy hair like me, or would she have long red pigtails? I could teach him or her to play video games. Caroline could teach them to dance. Music would ring through our house—songs from every decade. We'd laugh and sing. Our house would be a chaotic, comfy mess with unmade beds and toys strewn across the floor. They'd come to my games, cheering for me and doing cute shit like pressing their faces against the plexiglass so I could "kiss them" before the games. We could be so happy.

It's the weirdest vision I've ever had.

And the thing that's confusing me more than anything is, I'm not freaking out.

Because maybe I could do it, you know?

Maybe I could be a dad. If she was doing it with me, maybe I could.

Except the kid might not be mine.

The kid might belong to a tall basketball player with "golden boy" written all over him.

"Fuck!" I snatch my helmet off the bench and smash it down on the floor.

CHAPTER 37
CAROLINE

The Cougars lost the game by one goal.

Casey got kicked off the ice for fighting, and rumors are already circulating that the loss is his fault. Mean comments were peppered all over my social feeds this morning, and I can't stop reading them and crying, because this is my fault.

I contributed to his behavior last night.

He wouldn't have been in such a foul mood if I hadn't lied to him.

I feel sick. My head is killing me, and although I haven't puked again, my stomach is a ball of nauseous knots.

It's only being made worse by the fact that I have to somehow find the courage to see Casey again and get this paternity test underway. I realized that I don't have to talk to Ben, I can just get a swab from Casey and if he's the dad, then sweet, Ben never needs to know.

But Casey probably hates me even more than he did before.

So, my only other option is to ask Ben, but that feels a million times worse. Sure, he likes me now, but he definitely won't when I tell him I'm pregnant and the baby *might* be his, but it also might not.

"Don't suppose you could give me a swab of your DNA so we can find out."

Ugh! Can you imagine?

That'd go down like a bucket of cold sick.

And I just... I can't.

All I want to do is hide under my bedcovers until this whole thing is over. Even then I might not resurface. The life of a hermit wouldn't be so bad, right?

There's a sharp knock at my door and I tense, curling in on myself and slipping my phone under my pillow. Maybe if I pretend to be asleep, they'll go away.

"Cinnamon," Dad calls through the door. "It's us, baby girl. Are you well enough to open the door?"

I have no idea what they're doing here, but the little girl in me forgets that I don't want to see anyone and flings back my covers. Bolting out of bed, I open the door... and the second I see my dad, tears fill my eyes.

"Baby girl." He gives me a sad smile and wraps his arms around me. He doesn't even know why I'm crying, but he comforts me like the best dad in the world, because he is.

As I'm clinging to his shoulders, it starts to sink in that I'm gonna have to tell him the truth, because I've always told my parents everything. Well, mostly. You know, the really big stuff... it comes out, especially when we're around each other. I can't hide behind a phone call this time, and I start to cry a little harder.

"Oh, Ronnie, she must be feeling so sick." Mom

bustles about the room, tidying up my clothes, sniffing them and either folding them away or throwing them toward the bathroom. She'll do a load of laundry for me while she's here. She always does. "When was the last time you washed anything?" She frowns, then shakes her head. "Doesn't matter, I'll put a load in for you today."

"What are you guys doing here?" I mumble against Dad's chest. I've curled myself against his side, my arm around his waist, as we watch Mom tidy.

"You sounded so sick on the phone yesterday, we had to pop down and make sure you were okay."

"But don't you have that birthday party thing today?"

"We sent our apologies."

"Mom, you shouldn't have done that."

"You always come first, Cinny." Dad kisses my head. "Now, let's get you back into bed."

"Have you had anything to eat this morning? Can your stomach handle it?" Mom's got the laundry basket against her hip. "I'll go down and pop this in, then swing past the dining hall on the way back up."

I wrap my arms around myself when Dad lets me go and stare at my mother. Tears flood my eyes, and soon I can't see her past the blur. She's such a good mom. I can't imagine ever being so kind and thoughtful and organized. She takes such great care of me. She always has. And now I'm carrying a baby and—

My body shakes with a sob, and I can't stop the whine in my throat. I cover my mouth with my hand, but it's obvious I'm about to fall apart.

"Sweetheart." Mom puts the basket on the end of my bed and moves into my space, rubbing my arm. She shares a concerned look with Dad before softly asking me, "What's wrong?"

"I'm pregnant." The words come out before I can stop them, and the temperature in the room drops by a thousand degrees.

Mom's lips part, and she blinks at me like she doesn't know who I am anymore.

Dad takes a step away from me, his crestfallen expression the tipping point. My knees buckle and I drop to the floor, covering my face and sobbing in earnest. I didn't realize I had any tears left, but here they are—ugly, wailing cries. They don't even know the worst of it yet.

Two strong hands curl around my shoulders and help me back up. I shuffle to the bed, Dad's arm around my waist as he helps me get under the covers. Mom smooths them around me. She's still blinking and can't seem to look at me.

Neither of them has said anything, and I'm on the verge of screaming, "Just say it!" when Dad finally sighs.

"How far along?"

"Um..." I curl my fingers into the covers and try to remember. "About ten weeks."

"Okay." Dad nods, rubbing his cheek. His eyes dart over my face, but he can't really look at me. "And the father? Does he know?"

My expression buckles and Mom gasps, reaching for my hand. "It was consensual, right? I mean, this isn't some kind of college date rape thing, is it?"

She looks near panicked, and I quickly reassure her that it's not. "I knew what I was doing. I wanted to do it."

"But you didn't use protection?" Dad shuffles on his feet, crossing his arms, then uncrossing them. I've never seen him this uncomfortable before, and he does couples counseling.

"Of course I did. I always do."

"Wh-What?" Mom's blinking again. "You make it sound like you..." She licks her lips and shares another look with Dad before struggling to ask, "How often do you... do this sort of thing, Caroline?"

I groan and tip my head back, refusing to look at either of them while I rush out the words. "Since getting to college, I've been... discovering... myself."

Their disappointment is thick and oppressive. I know they wanted me to wait until I was married... or at least engaged. They're all about commitment, then sex. They raised me to think that way, but my curious body couldn't wait.

I don't regret it... although, maybe there's some merit in only sleeping with one partner rather than this casual sex thing, which has gotten me into the worst possible situation.

Mom pats my hand. "Well... uh... okay, um..."

"I thought we taught you better than that." Dad's voice has gone low and gruff. He gets quiet when he's super pissed, and I can hear him struggling as he grits out the words, "Sex isn't supposed to be cheap. It's a precious, beautiful gift that you save for the right person."

I nod. "I know that's how you feel, Dad."

"Well...," Mom says hopefully, her smile unconvincing as she desperately looks for a positive in all this. "Have you... found the right person?"

"Yes," I whisper. "But..."

"He doesn't want you," Dad huffs. "Well, he's not the right one, then, is he? Did you tell him you were pregnant, and then he bailed? Where is he? I want to talk to him."

"No, Dad, please." I close my eyes. "It's not like that. He... We were together, and now I'm not sure. It's complicated."

"Why?" Mom tips her head to look at me, her eyes finally focusing on my face. "Is it the pregnancy?"

"Kind of," I murmur, curling in on myself. How am I supposed to tell them this?

They're both looking at me now, their confused frowns making me sick. Their expressions are going to change to shock or disgust soon, and I don't know if I can do this.

Just say it!

Sucking in a breath, I quickly get the words out before I flake. "I slept with two guys only one week apart, and I don't know which one is the father. I told the man I love that it was him, and he just found out yesterday that it might not be him, and he's so mad at me now and wants a paternity test, which means I might have to tell the other guy about all this, and I don't know how he'll react, and this is a nightmare!" I wail the last part and cover my face again so I don't have to see them process all of this.

The silence is painful.

But maybe not as painful as Dad's broken whisper. "Oh, Caroline. What have you done, baby girl?"

I whimper into my hands. "Not that it makes it any better, but the second guy was a total mistake. I was stupidly drunk, and I just slept with him because the guy I've wanted all along didn't call me back."

Mom closes her eyes and swallows, swaying on her feet a little.

Dad steadies her, his hand on her lower back as he tries to absorb everything I just said.

Maybe I should have left out the underage drinking part.

"This man..." Dad clears his throat. "The one you say you love... is he the one who didn't call you back?"

"Yes." My voice is so tiny.

"So, why would you want someone like that?"

"I don't know!" I sit up, burying in my fingers in my hair. "Because I've had a crush on him since the first day I saw him. He's *everything*. I finally found the courage to talk to him, and we hit it off. Since I told him I was pregnant, he's been amazing. I've fallen even harder, and... and... now he'll probably never talk to me again. He doesn't want me anymore."

"If the child you're carrying is his, he'd better!" Dad barks.

I look up at my father then. The frown lines on his face are deep. They make me feel like I've let him down, and I hate this feeling so much.

"I'm sorry," I whisper. "I didn't mean for this to happen."

"Of course you didn't." Mom finally steps back to the edge of my bed and perches on the side of it. Taking my hand, she rubs her thumb over my knuckles. "You've gotten yourself into quite the pickle, young lady." She kind of laughs out the words, like she's trying to break the tension in the room, but it doesn't work. "So, when you said you're throwing up... that's not food poisoning?"

I shake my head.

"How bad's your morning sickness been?"

"Not bad at all." I sniff and suck in a breath. "That's

the first time I've thrown up, and I've had minimal nausea. I felt so sick after my argument with Casey that my body just reacted that way."

"Casey." Dad nods. "What's his last name?"

"Dad," I whine. "You're not talking to him."

"Well, I'll have to eventually. If he's the father," he grumbles. "Who's the other guy?"

"I'm not doing this with you." I shake my head.

He growls in his throat, shoving his hands in his jacket pockets and looking away from me.

"He only wants to protect and help you," Mom murmurs. "You're his baby girl."

"I know." I close my eyes with a heavy sigh. "I'm sorry I've let you down. I know you have very strong views on all this stuff. I understand that you must... hate me right now."

"Caroline." Mom says my name like I've just hurt her feelings. "We could *never* hate you. Ever." She cups my cheeks, gently forcing my head up, and gives me a firm look. "You are our precious gift, and we will love you no matter what. Just because we don't agree with all your choices doesn't mean we won't be there for you when you need us." Her lips pull into a sad smile. "And we're going to be here for you through this. I know you must be terrified."

I nod, my throat swelling up so quickly, I can't speak.

"But you're gonna be fine. We'll be here every step of the way. We'll help you raise our grandchild. We'll get you through the rest of college. This is all going to work out."

I rub my hand over my belly. "So, you think I should keep it?"

They both jolt in surprise, like any other option is ludicrous.

Mom's expression crumples. "I think you'll regret it if you don't. I think your birth mother, wherever she may be, still thinks about you. She still misses you and wonders how you're doing, even if she wishes she didn't. I don't want that for you."

"But I can't raise a baby, Mom. I'm just a kid."

She sighs and starts to nod, then shakes her head. "You're old enough to drink and sleep around, which means you're old enough to live with the consequences of those choices."

"But I used protection," I squeak. "I was responsible."

Dad clears his throat, clenching his jaw against whatever remark he's obviously fighting not to say.

He and Mom share a look that I don't want to decipher before she turns back to me. "You can do this, Caroline. You're kind and loving, and when you hold this baby in your arms, it's..." She shakes her head, a look of wonder filling her expression. "It's instinctual. Everything in you will want to hold and protect that little child and do your very best. You'll love your son or daughter with everything you've got."

I'm not sure I believe her. I mean, sure, I could love a baby, but could I honestly give it the best shot at life? The shot it deserves?

"We'll be with you every step of the way, Cinnamon." Dad steps forward, cupping my cheek. His brown eyes fill with tender affection. "I'm gonna be a grandpa."

I let out a watery laugh. His face is so cute right now. I can't stop the tears as they stream down my face.

"This wasn't the plan." I shake my head.

"Life has a funny way of throwing us the unexpected. But it'll be for a reason. I believe that." He nods. "This child might feel like an inconvenience right now, but it's going to fill your life with so much joy."

"And I know things are complicated with the father issue." Mom blinks, struggling to say the words. "But you're gonna figure that out, too, and whether that person wants to be involved or not, you at least know that your baby's going to have a steady home with us and you. It'll get all the love it needs."

I nod, appreciating her kindness but still feeling the pain ride through me.

I want Casey.

I want him to be there, to be part of this.

I want him to be the dad.

But what if he's not?

I'll never see him again. The thought breaks my heart. I'm so in love with him, and I thought, just for a moment, that maybe he was falling for me too. That maybe I was enough. He wanted me just because I was me. We'd gotten so close.

And then Ben came along and ruined everything.

But it's not his fault.

It's mine.

I could have told the truth so many different times, and I didn't.

Now I've lost Casey.

And I'll probably never get him back. But if I have even a shred of hope that he'll let me talk to him again, I'm going to have to get that paternity test.

CHAPTER 38
CASEY

It's been a week since we lost that quarterfinal game.

Since I lost Caroline.

I can't get her out of my head, and it's driving me crazy.

School's been a pit of rumors and accusations. People are pissed that I lost my temper on the ice, and I'm an easy target. Blame me for the loss. Forget the fact that my entire team was playing too.

I don't give a shit what they think about me, but I've been avoiding all my usual hangouts and coming home as fast as I can each day. The guys are protecting me as best they can, except the team captain. Jason is so fucking pissed at me, and he's telling anyone who will listen what a fuckup I am.

Thank God he's not captaining the team next season.

My hockey bros have been bummed out about the loss. They haven't blamed me, but that doesn't take away the burn of losing. It's hard to be around them all, hard to look them in the eye and answer their questions about what's eating at me.

So my room has become a haven, and I've been keeping to myself, blasting my music, stuffing my face with stale pizza, and missing Caroline with an ache that's fucking painful.

It's pissing me off.

I don't want to think about her. I want to feel nothing when it comes to that beautiful redhead, but she's consuming me, and I'm losing my fucking mind.

"King of Wishful Thinking" is playing on repeat on Spotify.

I'm blasting that shit, thinking about Grandma and how she used to sing it when she danced around the kitchen baking.

I loved staying with them when I was growing up. I didn't get to do it very often, but I had a few sweet summers at their place, and I wanted to live there forever. Grandma showered me with treats and music. Grandpa showed me how to build a birdhouse. We worked in his garage for hours, rocking out to Def Leppard and Bon Jovi while we hammered and sanded.

I want to go back to the simplicity of those days.

Part of me wants to call them, but I'm not sure they'll understand my crisis. They're old-school, and that's partly why their relationship with Mom dissolved. They were so disappointed in her for getting pregnant at such a young age, for sleeping around in the first place. They could never really get over it. Even though they loved me and were nice to me, I was always the mistake they could rub in her face.

Shit, if I call them now and tell them how I might

have knocked up a girl in college, it'll go down like a lead balloon.

I can't tell them.

And I won't tell Mom either.

Nah, I'm just gonna lie here, hugging this pillow to my chest and staring at the ceiling while Go West tells me that one day I'll get over this chick... because I'm the king of wishful thinking.

Fuck!

I thump the bed with my fist, anger coursing through me like it has been all week.

Every time I think about the fact that Ben might be the dad, I want to break something.

Which throws me, because that shit should bring me relief. It would take all the responsibility off me. I'd be a free man.

But I don't want that.

And that thought brings with it a whole new flood of angry confusion, because I never wanted to tie myself down to anyone. Being a free agent is my jam.

Until Caroline.

Until she made me realize how fucking awesome having a person could be. Someone I could call mine. I fucking loved it.

I love her.

I wince, squeezing my eyes shut and not wanting those three little words ringing in my head.

I don't do love.

I won't.

Face it, man. You are! And there's nothing you can do about it!

It's tempting to get up and go to a bar. I'll get shitfaced and start systematically screwing my way through Nolan U.

And every girl will leave me unsatisfied. I know they will.

Because I had red, saucy hotness, and she was perfect.

A perfect little liar.

Snapping my eyes shut, I clench my teeth as the song comes to an end, and that's when I hear the voices outside my door.

"Talk to him!" That's Mikayla.

"He'll talk when he's ready." And Ethan.

"He's listening to pop music from the '90s! Believe me, he's ready!"

"She's right, man," Asher agrees. "Old-school pop? We've got something to be seriously worried about right now."

I roll my eyes, tempted to turn up the music even louder as the song starts up again, but then the door swings open as they break the cardinal rule and don't fucking knock!

"Get out," I growl, throwing my pillow at them.

Liam snatches it before it hits Rachel in the face, giving me a dirty look as he throws it on the floor.

Sweet Rachel gives me a sad smile, and my anger deflates.

She always has that effect on me. She's so gentle, it's impossible to be mad around her.

With a heavy sigh, I roll onto my side so I don't have to look at any of them.

"I can't handle this," Asher mutters, snatching my phone and killing the music. "I get that you're going through some shit right now, but you don't have to torture all of us."

I glare at him, raising my middle finger with a snarl.

He goes to grab it, and I turn my hand into a fist and punch out at him.

"Really? It's like that?" He slaps my fist away.

"I said get out!" I roar and see Rachel flinch out of the corner of my eye. That little move makes me feel like shit, and I slump onto my pillow with a groan. "Please, just go away."

"We're not going anywhere." The bottom of my bed shifts, and Mick takes a seat by my feet. Her little fingers rest on my ankle. "At first we thought it was the hockey game."

"And then we thought it was those assy rumors about it being all your fault." Asher folds his arms, still staring down at me.

"But now all the music is making us think that you're dealing with some kind of romantic thing. Did you and Caroline break up or something?" Ethan takes a seat beside Mick, and I try to kick him off the bed.

The asshole doesn't budge, giving my knee a hard horse bite in retaliation.

I flail, nearly kicking Mick in the face.

"Hey!" Ethan grabs my foot, his look lethal as he moves in to protect his girl. "Watch it."

"I didn't mean to," I mutter.

"You didn't, actually, so I don't have to kick you in the balls," Mick chirps, giving me a playful smile. "However, I might have to slap you in the face if you continue to drown the airwaves with '90s pop songs and mope in your room like a smelly sloth. Seriously, dude, this is so not you. What the hell is going on?"

I sit up, resting back against my pillows and mussing my hair. "You assholes aren't going to leave until I tell you, are you?"

"Nope." Mick smiles cheerfully while Rachel winces and mouths an apology at me.

I roll my eyes, shaking my head and rushing out the truth. I say it so fast, I'm surprised they keep up with me, but once I'm done, I scan their faces and know they must have heard it all.

"Wow." Asher's head jolts back.

Liam cringes, running a hand through his hair. "That's messed up, man."

"What are you gonna do?" Ethan's face is etched with concern.

I shrug. "What *can* I do? I just have to wait and find out if one, she's keeping it, and two..." My face bunches. "If I'm the dad."

"What?" Rachel's face puckers. "But... you're in love with her."

"I never said that," I snap.

Mick snorts. "You didn't have to. It's obvious."

"Which means you being the biological father or not makes zero difference." Rachel moves into my line of sight, forcing me to look at her. I could just shift my head, but her gaze is kind of magnetizing. She looks so full of fucking certainty right now. "This isn't all about the baby. I mean, sure, I'm not saying raising someone else's child would be easy, but if you love her..." She lets the sentence dangle, obviously hoping I'll agree with her. I clench my jaw and look at the wall, but she keeps talking anyway.

"Which you do, by the way, whether you deny it or not. You can't just throw that all aside because of... of DNA."

I glance back in time to see her eyebrows pucker.

"You want to be with Caroline, and you're hurting because she lied to you. But I get why she did it." Her lips curl into a grin. "She wants you. She loves you. And she knew you'd never give her the time of day unless she did something drastic."

"Well, that's true," Mick murmurs, her nose wrinkling. "And you've got to admit, it's kind of cool that she did; otherwise, you never would have known how great and amazing it is to be in love."

I poke out my tongue like I'm going to gag. "Amazingly painful, don't you mean?"

"It doesn't have to be. You're the one sitting here moping and being all angry and sad. All you have to do is call her. Forgive her. Tell her how much she means to you."

"Tell her you don't want to lose her," Rachel continues for Mick. "Tell her that even if the baby's not yours, that doesn't matter, because you love her and this baby is a part of her, so you'll love it too."

"What if it's Ben's?" My stomach roils.

"Then it's Ben's, and you'll co-parent. You'll make it work." Liam shrugs like it's simple. "Besides, she still might decide to abort the pregnancy."

Rachel frowns. "But I want to see Casey be a baby daddy. Can you imagine how cute he'll be with a kid? Talk about adorable." She starts to beam.

With a groan, I scrape my fingers through my hair. "It's not that easy."

"Yeah, it's gonna be really hard." Ethan nods. "But you

just have to make a choice. It really comes down to if you want to be with Caroline or not. If you think you can move on and be happy without her, give that a try, but..." He tips his head. "Speaking from experience, the love thing is kinda cool."

"Only kinda cool?" Mick jumps off the end of the bed with an indignant frown. "Boy, you better talk that shit up right now."

He grins. "Being in love is a solid nine out of ten."

Her lips part like she's insulted, but she's fighting a grin already. Looking at Rachel, she shrugs. "Looks like someone's not having sex for a month again. Thought he would have learned his lesson the first time, but maybe he's just really stupid." She winks at Ethan while Rachel starts to laugh.

"Being in love with you—" Ethan jumps off the bed, grabbing her shirt and pulling her close. "—is a solid eleven out of ten."

Caroline's a twelve.

The thought whistles through me as Mick flicks her fingers, demanding more. "That's better. Keep going."

"It's the best thing that's ever happened to me."

"Because I am..." She waves her hand in the air.

"A pain in the ass?" He scratches his chin.

"Not having sex for month!" She slaps his chest, pushing him away, and heading for the door.

He bolts after her. "Lil' mouse, you couldn't handle not having me for a month."

"Oh, just watch me try, Tall Man!"

As usual, growls and squeals ensue, and we're left to sit here listening to those two idiots. A moment later,

Ethan's door slams shut, and we all know they're getting it on.

"Assholes," I mutter, shaking my head.

Asher gives me a sympathetic pat on the shoulder. "Do you want that or not?"

I sigh, tipping my head back against the wall. "I want it."

"Yay!" Rachel claps her hands. "Go make it happen." Then she sniffs and gives me a kind smile. "But maybe take a shower first."

I give her a dry glare, but that just makes her smile grow. Leaning over the bed, she pecks my cheek. "Love you, Casey."

All I can manage is a soft grunt in response.

That's obviously enough to satisfy them all and they trail out my door, leaving me to stew on my own.

Those fuckers are probably right.

They make it sound so easy, though, and it's not. If I stay with Caroline, if she keeps the baby... it's complicated as hell. And no amount of romantic bullshit will take away the day-to-day reality of this.

It'd be so much easier to just let her go.

I sigh, staring at my phone, tempted to lean over and get it blasting Go West again.

But instead, I punch the pillow behind me and grab my towel, heading for the bathroom and a hot shower.

CHAPTER 39
CAROLINE

Despite my constant headache and roiling stomach, the weekend with my parents turned out to be not so bad. They forced me out of bed, made me shower and change, then took me out to lunch. We ended up driving to a pretty spot in the mountains, and we spontaneously booked a night in a cabin up there. I woke up to birds twittering outside my window and a mountain view that filled my soul.

Dad and I have always found solace in the mountains. Whether they're covered in snow or the summer sun is baking off the rocks, those large formations speak to us.

Man, I can't wait to go boarding again.

But that weekend wasn't about carefree fun in the snow.

We sat by the fireplace, ate indulgent food, and talked our ears off.

Mom and Dad helped me form a bit of a plan. They actually made the whole baby thing sound doable, especially with them offering so much support. It'll mean huge changes for my next academic year, but Dad's offered to come with me and talk to the right people so I won't fall too far behind. The baby is due in October, so I could take half a semester off to deal with all that, then restart my studies in the spring. That wouldn't put me too far behind, and my parents have even offered to rent a place near the university so we can all live together until I graduate. They'll help me raise this little one. So no matter what, I'll be supported.

It would mean them both taking large chunks of time off work or even quitting, and we argued about that for a good hour or so.

"We will always put our family first. That tops everything." They both said that sort of thing in a hundred different ways, and it made me wonder if I'll have the ability to do that too. To be so selfless.

Can I honestly handle this parenthood thing?

At moments I found myself thinking, *Maybe being a mom doesn't have to be so terrifying. Maybe I can do this.*

And then other times, I was caught up in all I'll have to sacrifice, and I felt that panic and mind-numbing reluctance wash through me.

When they dropped me back at Nolan U on Sunday evening, showering me with hugs and words of affirmation, I felt far more centered and settled, though.

I had a plan in place, and I could face this.

That was a week ago, and since then, I've been on a roller coaster—plunging into fear-filled doubt before rising on a brief wave of positivity before the plummeting starts all over again. I've felt off-color and taken two sick days. I'm not actually sick, just exhausted and not wanting to face the world.

But when I woke up this morning, I knew I couldn't keep delaying.

I've googled exactly what I need to do for a prenatal paternity test. My parents have offered to pay for it, and there's nothing stopping me... except myself.

So that's why I'm holding my breath as I open the door of the law building. I'm on the hunt for Ben, and the last time I saw him was outside this place, so I figure it's a good start. It's time to get this paternity test underway. I know I can't contact Casey until I've done my part to start the ball rolling.

I should just be asking for *his* DNA rather than letting Ben in on this whole thing. I now know that I only need to speak to one of the potential fathers—if that test comes out negative, then the answer is clear.

The thing is, as much as Casey seems like the easier option, he's not. Because I think he hates me, and having to talk to him again terrifies the shit out of me. What I did to him was awful. He has every right to never want to speak to me again. I screwed up so badly. I had gold in the palm of my hand and rather than taking care of it, I... I shat all over it with my lies and deceit. I didn't mean for it to unfold that way. Things just went better with Casey than I expected. He said he'd be there for me... then he met my needs and called me his girlfriend and...and I couldn't bring myself to be honest. I was so scared of losing him that I totally disrespected him. It took a raw, ugly conversation with my parents for me to see that... to truly understand where Casey must be coming from and how he must be feeling.

The thought of what I've put him through forms a fresh wave of remorse and shame to roll through my stomach. It aches and burns and reminds me why I can't approach Casey right now.

Once I know the truth, I can finally call him with the world's biggest apology... and the three words I want to say more than anything—"You're the father."

Please let that be true! I silently beg as I shuffle into the building.

I've missed Casey so much this week. The ache inside me is unbearable. As much as I'm scared to face him again, the number of times I've picked up my phone to text or call him has been insane... to the point where Lani actually threatened to confiscate my phone.

She's been good for me, pulling me out of bed and mopping up endless tears as I've tried to process all of this. I don't know how she puts up with me sometimes. She's been really quiet and withdrawn, which tells me I must be getting on her nerves, but she's too good of a friend to turn her back on me.

The fact that I'm thinking of keeping the baby and doing this thing no matter what happens with Casey and Ben made her smile a little, so she must be proud of me for starting to figure out what I want and going for it.

Wiping my mouth with shaking fingers, I then rest my hand on my forehead. The headache I've been battling this week is brutal. I'm really hoping after I tell Ben the truth, it will ease. The tension I've been living with is taking its toll, and I have to get moving on this thing.

Dread bubbles in my belly as I inch my way toward the law building dining hall.

I can hear the rise of conversation as I draw near, and my steps falter. Resting my hand against the wall, I suck in a breath and try to remember what I was going to say to him.

"Ben, hi, yeah... there's a chance you're the father of my kid. Only a chance, though, because I also slept with Casey that week and... I don't suppose you'd mind taking a paternity test, would you?"

I close my eyes, trying to put myself in Ben's shoes for a second and thinking how horrific that news is going to be for him.

Why am I not just going to Casey!

Because you lied to him and he lost the hockey game, and you can't!

I hate this on every level.

I hate myself. I hate alcohol. I hate one-night stands.

Letting out a shaky breath, I hear Dad's voice in my head.

"It's done, Cinny. You can't change the past. You just have to make the best choices from this point on, and whether you like it or not, finding out who the father is has to be done. So just do it."

He told me that on the phone last night when I confessed that I still hadn't talked to Ben. I know he'll be calling me later, following up. I should resent him for that, but I kind of need that motivation.

Pushing myself away from the wall, I shuffle a little closer to the dining hall, the smell of food making my stomach roil as I peek around the archway. The place is full. I scan faces—in-depth conversations, laughter, shouting from one table to the other. There's a loud group of guys near the back, shoving each other and howling like chimpanzees. Whatever they're doing is obviously hilarious. One of the guys is super tall, and I hold my breath, wondering if it's Ben.

"Are you looking for someone?"

"Huh?" I spin around, glancing down at a short girl with a pixie haircut and a curious smile. "Oh, I just... Yeah, I was looking for Ben..." I shake my head, realizing I don't even know the last name of the man who might be my baby's father. "Ben." My voice shakes. "Tall, basketball player, Ben."

"Oh, him. Yeah, he usually has lunch in the athlete's hall. I think he's only got like one class in this building. And it's today, because it's my class too." She grins. "You could wait for him if you wanted."

"That's okay." I flick my hand through the air, grasping at the easy out. "I'll catch him another time."

You are such a coward!

I ignore the taunting voice in my head and burst out of the building, scrambling down the stairs and heading for my next class.

It's not for another hour or so, but I can find a bench and study or something.

Or you could stop being such a chicken and head to the athlete's hall.

I'm probably not allowed in there, but there's bound be someone coming or going from the building. They could get Ben for me, tell him to meet me outside so I can end his carefree life with a few short sentences.

Gritting my teeth, I veer left and amble my way to the sporting side of the school. The closer I get, the more tall, muscly athletic people I pass. Girls with high ponytails and fit-looking bodies. Guys who tower over me, their broad frames looking like brick walls as they wander past. I start playing a game and trying to guess which sports they play. The basketball guys are easy to spot, and I scan for Ben, relieved every time I don't see him.

I'm kind of hoping to not see anyone I know.

My steps slow even more when the thought that I might bump into Casey hits me.

Shit. He has lunch in the athlete's hall sometimes. I must be out of my fucking mind coming over to this side of the school.

Abort mission! This can be done another day.

I'm one second away from turning around when I stutter to a stop and fight the urge to pass out, because holy shit, there he is.

Casey Pierce with his messy hair and tattoos and perfect nose and smile.

I haven't seen him in a week, and he's still gorgeous. My heart seems to leap and split at the same time. I can't move as I watch him talking to a couple girls with high ponytails and perfect asses and a guy with a big, dopey grin.

Casey says something that makes them all laugh, and that ache inside me blooms with an intensity I can't handle. I love how funny he is. I've always loved that about him.

Spinning around, I figure waiting for Ben outside the law building is a much better idea... or just delaying this entire thing until tomorrow.

But then I hear my name.

"Caroline!"

Oh shit, Casey saw me.

I pick up my pace, wondering if I should break into a run.

"Caroline!" he calls again. "Wait up!"

My traitorous feet slow to a stop just before his fingers curl around my arm. He slowly spins me to face him, and I keep my eyes on his tattooed forearm.

"Hey." His voice is soft, the total opposite of the harsh growl he left me with last week. "What are doing here?"

"I'm, uh..." I cringe. "I'm looking for Ben."

"Oh." He lets me go, takes a step back. I stare at his scuffed Converse, so dirty and beat-up, the laces fraying at the ends. I love how mussed-up and disheveled he always is. There's something so carefree about him that speaks to my soul.

Glancing at his face, I drink in his short whiskers and wayward hair. He must have washed it this morning or last night. It has a fluffy, shiny look about it.

And then I get to his eyes. They're gazing at me with this wounded sadness that breaks my heart.

I'm desperate to apologize, but instead I say, "I... I know you want me to do this paternity test thing, so I'm just trying to... get that done. I'm sorry I haven't gotten onto it already. I've just..." I let out a pitiful laugh. "I really don't want to. I know that doesn't matter, but it makes it easier to procrastinate, you know?"

His forehead wrinkles. "Why didn't you just come to me? If it's negative, *then* you can tell him about the baby."

I work my jaw to the side, my voice failing me for a second. After a thick swallow, I manage to say, "I didn't think you'd want to see me again unless you knew you were the father." I shake my head, too ashamed to look at his face anymore. "And even then, I mean, you might never... want to see me again." My voice disappears, making my last few words basically inaudible.

Casey's still looking at me; I can feel his gaze like he's drinking me in or something. But I have no idea how he's feeling. Is he mad I said that? Or relieved? Is he about to go, "You're right," then spin on his heel and walk away?

"I'm sorry," I blubber, the apology tumbling out of me. "What I did to you was so wrong. I should have told you the truth from the start, but I was so afraid you wouldn't want me. And then time passed and we got closer and it just became harder and harder to admit the truth... even to myself. But I never stopped to think about how it would feel for you. I was being selfish, which is the opposite of loving someone." My breath catches, my words starting to wobble and spurt out in short little gasps. "I just can't have someone else's kid when you're the only guy I've ever truly been in love with." I squeak the last part, then cover my mouth with the back of my hand. My stomach is jerking with silent sobs as he stands there staring at me.

He's not saying anything and it's killing me.

What's he thinking? What's he going to say or do or—

He moves. Stepping an inch closer, he settles his hand on my cheek as a girl glides past us. She gives us a curious glance but keeps walking. Casey doesn't seem to notice her as he lifts my chin. His thumb rubs over my skin as his eyes grow a shade darker.

"Fuck it, you don't have to do this."

"What?" My face bunches with confusion.

"The kid's mine. No matter what any test says, it's mine, because..." His lips twitch with a smile that seems hesitant before growing with confidence. "You're mine."

"I'm... yours?" I blink, my slow-ass brain struggling to

wrap my head around what he just said. "You want me? I mean, after everything I did, you still want me?"

His eyes smile before his lips do, and I barely have time to process what the hell is going on before his mouth covers mine. He cups my cheeks as he kisses me with blatant possessiveness.

He doesn't just claim my mouth...

He conquers it.

CHAPTER 40
CASEY

I slide my tongue into her mouth, owning her because I've finally figured it out.

She's mine.

Fuck, that felt good to say.

When she pulls back for air, she stares at me like she still can't believe it, so I give her a pointed look and growl the word "Mine" before planting one more firm kiss on her lips, then taking her hand and pulling her away from school.

She trots after me, struggling to keep up with my quick feet as I practically drag her down the path.

"Where are we going?"

"I just need to be with you," I murmur.

She doesn't seem to mind that answer, a smile curling her lips as I hurry us right around to the back of the hockey arena.

"Where are you taking me?"

"My secret spot." I wink at her.

Thankfully, she follows me without question as I lead

her to a fence that borders the edge of the school. Beyond it is a wooded area, thick with trees and foliage. No one really comes around this way because of the high fence, but I found a chink in its armor and duck low, holding the fence for Caroline so she can scramble through the gap.

"How have you not told me about this?" She slips her hand in mine again, and we take big steps over the bushes and roots.

"Asher and I found it last year and decided to stay quiet about it. Figured it's nice to have a place to go where no one can find you. I hardly ever come here, but it's closer than Hockey House, and I don't want to bump into anyone going to your dorm."

"Wow," she murmurs. "I thought you'd never want to talk to me again."

"I didn't." I turn to give her a sad smile. "That lasted for about a minute, and then I was fucking miserable without you."

She bites her lip, looking like she's trying not to cry again. Her eyes glow with a glassy smile, and I brush my thumb over her lips.

"I'm sorry it took me so long to figure it out. I was being a stubborn prick and felt like it'd make me weak not to punish you with a decent cold-shouldering, you know?"

"I deserved it."

"No." I hate that look on her face right now. Cupping her cheek, I bend down so she can look me right in the eye. "I appreciate your apology, but...I get it. Yeah, you lied to me, and that sucked... but I understand why you did. And I could have handled it better." I lick my lips, my gut twisting as I finally admit one of my biggest regrets. "I should have called like I said I would. None of this would have happened if I'd just fuckin' called you."

Her eyes continue to glisten despite my efforts to avoid any tears. The way her lips curl up at the corners tells me I'm forgiven, but then she blinks and sniffs like another thought has just occurred to her. "Since we're apologizing, I...I'm sorry you got ejected from that game."

"Fuck," I mutter, shaking my head. "You weren't there to see that shit, were you?"

"No, I just heard about it. Felt kind of bad because it's my fault you were in such a foul mood."

"My mood is not your responsibility." I pull her against me, cupping the back of her head as I kiss her gorgeous curls.

Letting her go just as fast, I hurry us to the secret glade.

There's a small stream that runs near it, so you can hear the water bubbling. The birds flit among the trees, and the way the light falls through the branches gives this place a magical vibe. I swear, if fairies existed, they'd be born here.

And I will never admit to anyone that I think that.

Plunking onto the ground, I nestle my back against the tree trunk before pulling her down to straddle me.

Her smile still has a watery quality to it, like she's on the verge of tears.

"Please don't cry," I whisper, smoothing the hair back off her face.

"I'll try not to." She sniffs. "But if I do, they're happy tears. I've missed you so much, and I've been trying so hard to resign myself to the fact that we're over."

"We're not over." I shake my head, my insides tensing as I know what I want to say... but it'll take me down a path I've never gone before.

Fuck it. I'm doing it anyway.

"You're my woman. I don't want anyone else. Just you."

"Just me?" Her lips look like they're fighting a smile, but her eyes are filling with tears.

Happy tears, remember?

I swallow, holding her face and trying to be gentle when what I really want to do is growl the words and claim her right here. Show her how much I mean this shit.

"Just you." Pulling her close, I kiss her again, slow and tender, taking my sweet time to explore her mouth before peeling back the layers that are keeping us apart. I wasn't actually planning on doing this out here, but it's naturally happening, like our bodies need to experience everything our hearts are saying.

She's soon topless, her head lifted to the sky as I kiss my way from her neck to her luscious tits. They're big and beautiful, her nipples like beer-scented grapes—my favorite drink and my favorite fruit all rolled into one.

My fingers crawl their way beneath her skirt, finding her ready and waiting for me.

I start to play while she fumbles with my zipper, yanking my pants open and greeting Mr. Jones with a smile.

"I've missed you." She bends down and kisses his tip, sending him to heaven with a sucking action that makes me see stars.

I fist her hair and groan, nearly spurting right into her

mouth, but I don't want to come that way. I need her to see. To know.

"Stop," I whisper.

She pulls back, her pink lips wet and glistening.

"C'mere." I guide her back up my body, pulling her to settle over me.

Grabbing my pulsing dick, I part her folds and line us up. Then she sinks onto me with this slow, languid move that's pure pleasure.

My hands round her ass, and I pull her all the way down, stopping her from riding me.

She rests her hands on my shoulders, looking at me for answers. Emotions are coursing through me so thick and fast, I can't find the words I want to say.

But man, I feel it.

I feel this thing for her that is so huge and foreign, I barely know what to do with it. No matter what fucked-up situations we're facing right now. No matter the complications...

Fuck, I think I love her.

I should probably tell her that, but I've never said it to a girl before. And I've just done the whole "I don't want anyone else" thing, which is pretty fucking big. The L-word's gonna tip me over the edge, and—

Her fingers skim down my cheek, resting against my jawline. Her glistening smile is beautiful, and I know without a doubt that this thing between us is something else. Something precious we have to protect.

The second her lips touch mine, I release my hold on her and she starts to ride me—slow, smooth motions that are deep and soulful.

It's like we're making love for the first time.

Because maybe we are.

All those other times were mind-blowing, amazing, and I want that ravenous sex again. But this is something else.

This is more than a twelve.

This is infinity times infinity.

CHAPTER 41
CAROLINE

So, after a sex-filled weekend in bed, I'm feeling pretty amazing.

And it wasn't all sex.

There was a lot of holding and talking and figuring out the future.

I told him about my parents visiting and everything they said to me. I apologized again for how I handled things. He apologized again for how he handled things and then told me we had to stop beating ourselves up and move on. We couldn't keep hanging out with past regrets when we had this other massive thing looming in our future.

"So, we're keeping the baby, then?"

I bit my lip and studied his face for any signs of dread or fear. But I couldn't find it. I mean, it's not like he was stoked with the decision, but he was accepting.

We're doing this. Although I still couldn't bring myself to say the words out loud, so sufficed with a short nod and then changed the subject.

I need to let my parents know my decision, though. We've got a lot of figuring out to do. Will they still be willing to upend their lives for me if Casey's in the picture too? It'd be great to still have their help. But can I honestly ask them to walk away from their jobs, all their friends and comfy routines? I'd be asking them to do the parenting thing all over again, but with two people in their early twenties still trying to do this adulting thing and start their lives.

When I think about logistics and how this will all pan out, the headaches kick in again.

"So, just stop thinking about it!" I whisper-bark, rubbing my forehead as I walk toward the Humanities building.

I'm barely inside the door when I hear my name being shouted.

I look around me, confused, as I don't recognize the voice.

But then I spot the tall, angry person charging toward me, and I let out a strangled gasp before backing up against the wall.

Ben doesn't seem affected by my fear. In fact, he seems oblivious to it, and that's probably because he's too mad to notice anything but what he wants to say.

"You're pregnant? When were you going to tell me!"

Everyone around us goes still, eyes bulging our way before a flurry of whispers whips down the hall.

"Ben, I... I... how did you find out?"

"Someone overhead a conversation, and it got back to me. Apparently there's a chance it's mine. I can't believe you wouldn't come to me about this. What, were you just gonna hide it? Like I don't have a right to know about my own kid?"

He looks so cut up. So angry and distressed and...

And now I have to make it a million times worse.

"But I don't know if it's your kid," I whisper, my jaw trembling as his face mottles with this hurt-filled rage that has me looking to the floor.

"Yeah, so I heard," he grits out. "I mean, what the hell, Caroline? What if it is mine? You don't think I have a right to know?"

Shit, I should have told him. I should have been honest from the start.

I close my eyes, struggling to figure out how I can explain myself.

"Who's the other guy? Is it Casey Pierce? Or are there like a bunch of us who you're going to have to work your way through?"

My lips part, not even sure how to respond to that insult.

"Was it the same night? The same party? Or do you spread us all out like a lineup of guys—one per day."

"S-Stop." I squeeze my eyes shut. "It wasn't like that. I... I—"

"You have to find out," he cuts me off, his tone unapologetic.

I peek my eyes open, daring to look at him. "I... I know. I was going to come see you and—"

"Were you?" His glare is enough to crush my insides to dust.

I look away from him and have to admit, "I was, but then I wasn't sure."

He leans his hand on the wall behind me, bending

low so he's right in my face. "If it's mine, I have a right to know." His voice has dropped from a roar to a stony whisper, and I can't decide which is worse.

"I'm sorry, Ben. I—"

"Don't," he spits, obviously disgusted with me. "You were going to hide this, and if I hadn't found out, I never would have known."

"Well, everyone's gonna know soon enough." I rub my belly, and he stares down at it. His crestfallen expression is heartbreaking, and I feel awful.

Like seriously awful.

"Hey!" someone barks behind Ben, and seconds later, an irate Casey appears beside me. "What the fuck are you doing yelling at my woman?"

Someone must have run to get Casey.

I don't know who it was, but I'm grateful for the support. I think.

Ben's sad face is turning angry again. He looks between us, his dark eyes sparking. "He's the other guy?"

"Yes," I whisper.

"And it's just him? No other players in this mix?"

"Shut your fucking mouth, man," Casey warns him.

Ben gives him a derisive snort before shaking his head and staring daggers at me.

Casey's arm comes around me. It's both a protective move and an obvious staking of his claim. I feel like I'm standing between two cavemen for a second.

One's ready to defend my honor, while the other wants to drag me to trial where I can be punished for my reckless behavior.

"I can't fucking believe this." Ben grips the strap of his

bag, the muscles in his jaw clenching as he stares down at me.

My chin bunches as I find a spot to stare at on the floor.

"You shoving your tongue in my mouth and telling me I was hot was just all bullshit. All those sweet words while you fucked me. While I made you come—"

"That's enough!" Casey barks, fisting Ben's shirt and shoving him away.

The guy might tower over my boyfriend, but Casey's shifting into pit-bull mode, and I don't doubt the damage he could inflict.

"It's fine." I touch his arm. "Just leave it. He has a right to be mad."

"He doesn't have a right to yell in your face and humiliate you." Casey's voice is low, his eyes trained on Ben with a steely warning. "He needs to back the fuck off."

With a little growl, Ben shoves Casey's hand off him before pointing a finger at my face. "I'll be expecting to hear from you. I want to know who the kid belongs to. I need to know if it's mine." He turns and stalks away, shouting over his shoulder when he reaches the door, "Find out!"

Every head in the hall turns to watch Ben leave, then swivels back to stare at me.

I slump against the wall, my body aching from the searing headache to the tips of my toes. I want to disappear into a dark room and beg the universe to swallow me whole.

"Hey." Casey's voice is a soft lilt, his knuckles grazing

my jawline as he moves in front of me, creating a wall from the prying gazes.

The tender touch is so sweet, I want to hide within his shell.

But another part of me can't even look at him right now.

This is such a fucking mess, and I want it to be over.

No amount of hugs or comfort is going to change the fact that the baby growing inside me might not belong to the man I love.

And if it belongs to Ben... who the hell knows how that's going to unfold.

"You look pale." Casey touches my forehead.

"I don't feel great," I admit.

"Here, let me walk you back to your dorm. Why don't you sleep it off, and you can catch up on your coursework later."

"No, you're not skipping any more classes for me."

"I don't care."

"I do!" I snap, brushing his hand off my face. "I'm fine. Please, just go." He looks kind of hurt by my dismissal, and I try to soften it with a smile. "I'll call you later, okay?"

He sighs, reluctantly stepping away from me.

"I promise I'll call."

He nods, giving me one last frown before walking away like a dejected puppy.

Great. Now I've managed to hurt two guys. Perfect.

But I need a minute on my own.

I feel like shit—mentally, emotionally... physically.

With a frown, I rub at the pain in my stomach. It's new. Maybe the ache in my head is extending throughout my body. Casey's probably right, I should go back to my dorm and rest. It'll get me away from curious glances and gossipy whispers.

But I already missed a bunch of classes last week, and I don't want to fall too far behind.

Rubbing at my aching temples, I try to ignore the throbbing throughout my body and shuffle toward my next class. I'm too caught up in my regret to stop and think about why my body's acting weird until I feel a spurt of something wet in my underwear.

I jolt to a stop, the ache in my stomach contorting into a sharp pain that nearly buckles my knees.

My lips part like I want to wail, but nothing comes out. I feel like someone's fisting my insides and squeezing the life out of me.

The life.

Out of me.

"Oh shit." With a soft gasp, I start running for the bathroom.

Shouldering the door open, I make a beeline for the end stall, but before I can even reach it, another gush of liquid floods my underwear. It's warm, and when I look down, I spot the red soaking into my pants, painting a trail toward my knee. I gape at this bloody warning, struggling to comprehend it fully. But as another sharp pain tears through me, I finally let out a wail and drop to the floor.

CHAPTER 42
CASEY

I'm kind of thrown by Caroline's dismissal. I was trying to make her feel better, protect her after she'd been shouted at by the asswipe. But she didn't want me around.

It's hard not to feel the sting of her rejection. She looked so pasty after that crapweasel shouted at her. I wanted to shut him up so badly. It's hard to scream in someone's face when you don't have any teeth, and I would have happily extracted every one of them for him. Free of charge, even.

It would give me the greatest fucking pleasure!

But that would have only made Caroline feel worse.

She obviously regrets sleeping with him. He obviously doesn't. Although he might now.

Fuck! Why didn't I just call her after she gave me her number?

She stayed with me. I've got the tattoo to prove it, but my stubborn ass just didn't want to fall in love. If it wasn't for the baby, I'd still be out there sleeping my way through life and never knowing this... this feeling.

This feeling that only Caroline can give me.

I don't get how a fuckup like me ever got so lucky.

The truth is, Ben's probably the better match, you know?

Sure, he shouted at Caroline today, but he was in shock. Sure, I still want to punch him in the balls and turn him into a toothless wonder, but I've heard good things about the guy.

Yeah, I asked around when I was at a low point, sat there glaring at the wall while a few different people told me what a great guy he is—studious, hardworking, kind, caring, comes from money but isn't an asshole about it. Blah, blah, blah.

He's definitely got his shit together. Probably doesn't feel like it after today, though.

Shit. His face.

He was fuming, but he was also hurt. I know how he feels. Caroline's handled this thing pretty badly. But I get why, and maybe he would, too, if he took the time to listen.

In saying that, he doesn't get to walk away with the girl he wants... so why would he even want to listen?

This is such an epic clusterfuck.

He'd probably make a great dad, though, bring with him decent folks and family to help the kid manage life.

What do I bring?

A checked-out mother, an absent father, and me. Oh, and like fifty bucks to my name.

That's it. I don't got shit.

Well, maybe the Hockey House bros. Man, they'll make the best uncles. The thought makes me grin, and by the time I reach the building that my next class is in, I'm actually feeling better about things.

Caroline just needs some space. She'll call me when she's ready, and I'll show up and be the guy she needs. Ben will deal with this, and somehow we'll figure it out. Even if he is the dad, we're gonna make this work... for her. For my sweet Caroline.

"Hey." Asher raises his chin at me.

I slap his hand in greeting, then pound my knuckles against Ethan's.

"What's the haps?" I ask, trying to remember what classes they have now.

"I'm heading to econ." Asher points over his shoulder, walking backward and raising his hand in farewell.

I look to Ethan. "I'll probably go park it in the library while I wait for my tutoring session. What about you?"

"I'm—" My phone starts playing "Sweet Caroline," and I grin. "I'm taking a phone call."

Ethan chuckles, slapping me on the shoulder and starting to walk off.

"Hey, Cherry Girl. You need me?" I'm only joking. After the way she looked, sex is probably the last thing she wants, but anything to get a smile out of her, right?

She sniffs, and her voice is barely audible when she answers me. "I need you."

"Hey, are you okay?" Alarm bells start ringing out of nowhere, and it must come through in my voice, because Ethan jerks to a stop and spins around to check on me.

"Something's wrong." Her voice catches. "There's so much blood, Casey."

She can barely get out the words, and I sway on my

feet, wondering what the fuck she could mean. Ethan's walking back toward me, asking what's wrong as I struggle to form a thought. "Where are you?" My voice is ragged as images of her lying on the floor in a pool of blood try to decimate me. Who did that to her? Was she shot? Beaten?

Did Ben come back for some kind of retribution?

Are all the things I heard about him total bullshit?

Will I be killing a man for hurting my woman?

My mind is going so wild with a frenzy of questions that I nearly miss her answer.

"Bathroom," she whimpers. "In the Humanities building."

And just like that, my brain clicks into action mode.

I start running. "I'm coming, baby."

CHAPTER 43
CAROLINE

I drop my phone as another blinding pain wraps around my lower back and abdomen. A splurge of liquid fires out between my legs, and I whimper, scrambling to unbutton my pants and check my underwear. I nearly pass out when I notice a huge clot, my stomach revolting as I close my eyes and try to breathe through the pain.

It's so intense, I don't know what to do with myself.

Blood is flowing down my leg now, coating my clothing and making me cry.

Curling onto my side, I lie down on the floor, pressing my face against the cold tiles. The cold, disgusting, germ-filled tiles. Leilani would be horrified.

I close my eyes, not giving a shit about germs.

I'm freaking out right now.

Something's wrong. I think I'm losing the baby.

But I don't really have time to process that, because another pain is building, growing to a blinding ache that's pulsing through my upper thighs now too.

I need this to stop. I cradle my belly, pulling my legs to my chest and groaning.

The bathroom door swings open, and I register the gasp. My eyes pop open and I spot a girl, frozen in the doorway, gaping at me.

She looks like she's struggling not to hurl as she mutters, "Oh gross," and covers her mouth.

"Get out," I whisper at first, but then she doesn't move, and I end up screaming at her, "Get! Out!"

She flinches like I slapped her, then spins and darts out of the bathroom, leaving me all alone in my misery. I close my eyes again, the tears building behind my eyelids, burning and stinging while my body rejects this baby.

This little life that I wasn't sure I wanted.

But now that I'm losing it... I kind of feel like my heart is breaking.

CHAPTER 44
CASEY

"Move. Move!" I shout at the people crowding around outside the women's bathroom. I didn't know which bathroom Caroline was talking about, and when I tried to call her back, she didn't pick up.

That fucking freaked me out, and I raced through the Humanities building like a crazy man. Ethan's been right on my tail the whole time, and it was him who whacked me on the shoulder and drew my attention to the crowd forming.

I muscle my way through them.

"...then she screamed at me to get out," a girl is saying.

"I tried to go in there as well, and she screamed at me too. I'm not sure what to do."

"This is ridiculous. Someone needs to be in there with her."

"She won't let us."

"I'm calling 9-1-1."

I growl, fear making me act like an angry bear.

Shoving past the last two people blocking my way, I shoulder the bathroom door open and jerk to a stop when I spot Caroline on the floor. Her eyes are closed like she's passed out. Blood is coating her pants as terror tries to choke and blind me at the same time.

"She needs to get to a hospital," Ethan murmurs.

"An ambulance should be coming soon," a woman says over his shoulder. "The operator is telling me they're delayed with another emergency, but she's on the list. They'll get here as soon as they can."

"Fuck that, she needs a hospital now." Ethan frowns at the woman. "I'm getting a car. Case, meet us outside." He starts muscling his way back through the crowd, and I barely acknowledge him as I slowly walk toward Caroline.

"Hey," I softly whisper, crouching down beside her.

Wiping the hair off her sweating forehead, I bend down and kiss her hairline.

She whimpers, "Something's wrong."

"I know, baby." It's hard to talk, to try to hide my shock at what I'm seeing right now.

I've never been great with blood, but seeing her like this is fucking debilitating. She's in pain, and I can't make it stop.

A low groan comes out of her, and not the good kind, her expression buckling as she pulls her knees up, writhing against whatever is happening to her body.

"It hurts." Her voice is barely audible, her skin paling as she grips her legs and deals with what looks like a wave of agony.

I swear my heart is cracking right open and bleeding

along with her. I can't handle this shit. Watching her suffer is killing me.

I want to tell her it's okay, but it's not. I won't be the fucking moron making empty promises when I have no idea how to stop this. How to help her.

Yes, you do! Get her to a hospital!

"I can do that," I whisper under my breath.

The pain that was torturing her a second ago seems to be passing, the grip on her legs relaxing, and I take my chance.

"I'm gonna pick you up, okay? I'm gonna take you to the hospital."

She nods, sort of, and I scramble forward, gently wriggling my fingers beneath her legs and ignoring the wet moisture soaking into my arm when I stand. Her body flops against me, her red hair splayed over my shoulder as I back up toward the door.

Blood is smeared on the tiles where she was lying, and I spin away from it, trying not to freak out as I carry her into the crowded hallway.

"Move!" I yell to the nosy, useless people who are only after the gossip and drama. I should smile at the few who have been helpful, like the woman still talking to the operator on the phone, but then Caroline lets out a pitiful-sounding whine, her hand landing on her stomach as she squirms in my arms. She's getting another wave of pain.

"I've got you, baby. It's okay. I've got you," I murmur against her forehead as I turn sideways and navigate my way through the crowd.

They're shuffling aside for me but all wanting a look at the same time.

Fuck. I should have tried to cover Caroline up with my jacket or something. I hate to think what people are gonna say. The rumors will balloon into some huge story that she doesn't need right now.

The main doors to the Humanities building fly open, and two guys from campus security charge in. The second they spot me, their eyes round with surprise.

"She's pregnant and bleeding! I need to get her to the hospital!" I'm yelling for the whole fucking world to hear right now, but it gets me the results I want.

One of them opens the door wide for me to pass through while the other starts talking into his radio.

I don't really register what he's saying, because the second we're outside, I spot Asher's truck pulling up along the curb, and I make a beeline for the back seat. Ethan jumps out the passenger door and yanks it open for me.

The horrified look on his face tells me how bad Caroline must look right now.

Fuck!

The thought that I might lose her rockets through me for a second.

Maybe it's overly dramatic, I don't fucking know, but I'm feeling it, and I can't breathe as I slide into the back seat of Asher's car and bark, "Go! Fucking floor it!"

CHAPTER 45
CAROLINE

The car jolts, then takes off, and I'm pushed into Casey's chest.

He's freaking out right now, his breaths punchy, his hand shaking as he smooths it down my face and checks on me. The fear in his eyes makes them shine brighter than I've ever seen them, and I want to tell him that everything will be okay, but I seriously don't know if it will be.

I have never felt this awful before.

I've never been in this much pain.

Another whimper builds in my chest, and I feel my face bunching.

"Just hold on, baby. Hold on. I've got you." Casey's whispering the words on repeat.

"I want my mom." The request makes me sound like a five-year-old, but I don't care.

I need her. She's always been the one who soothed me when I was sick, and as much as I appreciate Casey and all he's doing for me right now, I want my mom.

"I'll call your parents as soon as we reach the hospital, okay?" Casey's voice is hard to hear, it's shaking so badly. I've never seen him like this before.

"Hand me her phone. I can make the call now." Ethan reaches into the back while Asher takes a corner too fast.

"Would you slow the fuck down!" Casey barks. "You're gonna kill us before we even get there."

"I'm sorry!" Asher shouts back. "That's a lot of blood, okay."

"What, you worried about staining the leather?" Casey bites back.

"Fuck you, man! I'm trying to get her help as fast as I can."

I close my eyes against the shouting, burying my face in Casey's chest while he barks something and gets a quick retort. They keep snapping at each other until Ethan shouts above them both.

"Would you two quit it! Asher ran out of his class as soon as he heard you needed help, so shut the fuck up, Casey," he huffs. "And Asher, just fucking drive in silence so I can make this phone call."

Everyone shuts their mouths, the tension in the car like a thick fog as Ethan gently asks me what my passcode is so he can unlock my phone.

I murmur the numbers to him, and a few seconds later, he's talking with a calm that seems to take the sting out of the air around me.

"Yeah, hi, Mrs. Mason? My name's Ethan. I'm a friend of your daughter's."

I want to hear the rest, but another pain snatches me and I gasp, tensing in Casey's arms as the talons clutching my abdomen dig in deep and sharp. Another splurge of liquid fires out between my legs. This one feels big and horrific, and it makes me fist his shirt with a whimper.

Casey's frantically looking at me, asking me what he can do, but I just shake my head and burrow further into him, hoping to God this isn't enough to put him off me for good.

It's probably a crazy thing to think, but I'm feeling weak and vulnerable right now, and I'm currently bleeding all over my boyfriend. If that's not enough to put a guy off, then I don't know what is.

Asher's tires screech, my body jerking forward when he brakes outside the emergency room. Ethan's still talking to my parents as Asher bolts out of the truck and runs around to open the door for me and Casey.

It's awkward for Casey to slide out with me still in his arms, but Asher pulls on his jacket sleeve and soon he's standing, hoisting me up and charging into the emergency room, yelling for help like he's gonna lose his mind if seven doctors and the head of gynecology don't drop everything immediately to assist his girlfriend.

CHAPTER 46
CASEY

They took Caroline away from me.

Put her on one of those beds with the wheels and made me come back out to the waiting room.

I sat with her and held her hand during the initial examination, which took forever to actually happen. Nurses kept fluttering in and out to check on her, but we sat behind a curtain in a small cubicle for an age before a doctor who knew what they were talking about finally showed up. I listened to the woman talk in what felt like a foreign language. Apparently this isn't a standard miscarriage, and Caroline had to go in for some procedure. D&C—whatever the fuck that means.

I had to let her go while she cried. All I could do was kiss her on the forehead and watch her get wheeled off down the sterile hallway.

"You're welcome to get a coffee or drink in the waiting room. Someone will be out with news as soon as they can." The nurse had a nice voice, and I followed her pointing finger, shuffling out to the waiting room like a lost man.

Fuck. They better not be causing my girl more pain. I feel limbless without her.

When did this happen?

How did I go from Mr. One-Night Stand, Mr. Independent, to feeling like I can't breathe if I lose her?

You're not going to lose her.

She was in pain, and I couldn't help her! I couldn't make it stop!

My chest hurts. My head is pounding.

"Casey?" Asher grabs my attention, beckoning me across the room. "What did they say? What's happening?"

"She'd had to go in for some procedure. I don't know." I shake my head, feeling sick. "I didn't understand everything the doctor said, but she needs it, and it'll keep her safe or stop infection or... I don't know. I don't know." I sink into the seat opposite Ethan, burying my hands in my hair and dipping my chin so I don't have to look at anybody. "Shit."

Mikayla moves to sit beside me, resting her hand on my back. I have no idea when she showed up, but I let her comfort me because I feel like I'm gonna lose my mind if she doesn't. Her calm, steady circles on my back are stopping me from tearing my hair out and wailing at the speckled linoleum floor.

Watching Caroline in pain was a suck-fest of mammoth proportions. I've never felt so helpless in my life.

"It's gonna be okay, man," Asher murmurs. "She'll be okay."

"Yeah." I grit out the word. It's all I can manage right now.

And then everything just gets worse.

"Hi, we're looking for our daughter, Caroline Mason."

My head pops up, the air leaving my lungs in a whole different way as I stare at their backs. Her father is tall, wears a sports jacket that denotes his age. He looks like he must be in his fifties already. Shit, they're probably closer to my grandparents' age than my mother's.

His hair is speckled gray while hers is a short bob that frames her round face. Caroline said people couldn't tell she's adopted, but I can. I can see the differences, see how she has a uniqueness about her that doesn't belong to them.

But there's her mom—just the woman she wanted to see.

So, I stand.

I hitch my pants and feel my chest constrict as I step around Mikayla and approach them.

"Mr. and Mrs. Mason?"

They spin at the sound of my voice, both surprised for a moment, trying to figure out who I am. His gaze feels critical as he eyes my tattooed arms, then looks at me like maybe he knows me. But then he spots the blood on my shirt and pants—Caroline's blood—and the color drains from his face.

"Are you the one who brought my daughter to the hospital?" Mr. Mason croaks.

"Yes, sir."

"You called us." Mrs. Mason's voice is soft and wispy, her hand fluttering as she holds it against her chest, her eyes darting from my bloody shirt to my face.

"Actually, that was my friend Ethan." I point behind me, and Ethan stands, giving them an awkward wave.

They nod, then turn their attention back to me. The worry on their faces is pretty painful, so I quickly fill them in as best I can. I do a shit job and end up wincing, my words petering out to a pathetic finish.

"I know what a D&C is," her mother murmurs. "I've had a few in my time." Her expression buckles, and she starts blinking like she's gonna cry. Her husband touches the back of her neck, giving it a gentle squeeze. "I hate that she has to go through this, Ronnie. Our little girl."

"I know, sweetie." He pulls her close, kissing her forehead as she tucks herself against his chest. "She'll get through this just fine. She's a fighter."

Mrs. Mason sniffs and nods, sucking in a shaky breath. She can obviously feel her daughter's pain in a way no one else can. Is that why Caroline wanted her here?

"So, are you the hockey man? Or do you play basketball?" Mr. Mason's gruff voice pulls my gaze toward him, and I notice the sharp dip of his eyebrows when he asks. I can't help feeling like he already recognizes me. Caroline said he watches the college games, but there's something dangerous in his glare that warns me of the facts. I'm not just a Nolan U Cougar anymore. I'm one of the guys who slept with his baby girl.

Oh fuck, she really did tell them everything, didn't she?

My lips part as I try to process this shit.

"I'm, uh..." I lick my lips and finally sputter, "Hockey. I'm the hockey man."

Her father's eyes take on an even harder edge.

Shit.

I look away from him, wondering how I can explain all of this. Wondering what exactly she said.

"You're the one she wants," her mother murmurs. "So, I'm glad you're the one who's here."

Her smile is weak, and I try to smile back, but my lips are too heavy.

"Well, she was asking for you, so she'll be stoked you made the trip."

"Of course we did." Her dad's still glaring at me. "We're her parents. What I'm trying to figure out is who you are and what you're going to be once she comes through this."

My mouth goes dry.

And his voice drops a few more degrees. "There's no baby anymore. Not that you necessarily had any responsibility, but you definitely have none now."

"I—"

"You gonna break my girl's heart?"

"No, sir." The words pop out of me fast and sure. In fact, I only just swallow the ones that want to naturally follow—*I love her.*

Wow. I've never thought that about a girl before.

I mean, I did after my first time—that Japanese goddess made me kinda ga-ga—and there have been a couple girls who have piqued my interest. I've got the tattoos to prove it. But this... whatever the fuck is happening in my chest right now... this is different.

Oh fuck.

I'm in love with Caroline Mason. Like legit.

My lips part, and I'm struggling to put words in my mouth when a doctor strides into the room.

It's the one from before!

The one who took Caroline!

I dart around her parents, rushing up to her and looking around her head, as if Caroline is going to magically appear behind her.

"She's fine." The doctor smiles at me. "It was a quick procedure. Everything has been cleared, and she's resting now."

"Can I see her?" My voice pitches with urgency.

"Yes, but she's exhausted, and I don't want her crowded out." She raises her eyebrows, and I glance behind me and spot all my support plus Caroline's parents anxiously looking at the doctor. "Only one or two people at a time, okay?"

As much as I want that one to be me, I fight my selfish desperation and glance at her parents. Taking a small step back, I raise my chin toward the doctor. "It should be you two. She wants to see you."

They don't fight me on it, too distracted by the thought of checking on their daughter to give me a second glance.

I stay rooted to the spot, watching them walk away and shaking my head at what just happened. I gave up what I wanted. I put Caroline's needs above my own.

It kinda sucks, but it also solidifies this whole revelation.

I love her.

I fucking love her.

———

Caroline's parents take forever with their visit. I pace the waiting room like a caged animal. The afternoon turns into evening, and I tell everyone to get going. With hockey season over, we don't have any practices until next week, though we're still expected to keep up on our skills and workouts during this short break.

Even so, there are assignments to be done. The summer's not here just yet, but finals will be happening before we know it. I won't let them hang out in this torturous waiting room longer than they need to. After some whispered arguments, they finally leave, but Asher insists on coming back with takeout. I try to eat the burger he bought me, but it sits like a rock in my stomach, and I end up throwing half of it away.

Finally, Caroline's parents return.

"They're going to keep her overnight," her mother tells me. "Just as a precaution."

"Okay." I look past them, anxious to get back to that room.

"We're going to stay in a motel for a few days, help her get settled back in her dorm." Her father's got the glaring thing going on again, and I let out a short huff before facing him square on.

"I'm not going to hurt your daughter, sir. I care about her... *a lot.*" I can't say the L-word to him before I've even told her. *Care* will have to do. But it's so much more than that. "You can stop glaring at me. I may have fu—screwed up in the past, but I'm not doing that to her again."

His jaw clenches, his nostrils flaring before he gives me a stiff nod. "She's asking for you."

"Thanks." I wonder if I should shake his hand or some shit, but he's already guiding his wife away, and I take my chance to hustle past them and find Caroline's room.

She's lying on her side, her arm tucked under her pillow and staring at the wall when I pad into the room.

"Hey." I smile down at her, brushing the hair off her face.

She gives me a weak smile. She looks so pale and exhausted.

"Are you still in pain?"

"Just a little uncomfortable." She sniffs. "They've given me meds."

I go to reach for a chair to sit beside her, but the sadness washing over her face right now is killing me, so I move around the bed and gently get onto it.

The plan was to spoon her, but she rolls over, resting her head on my chest and clinging to my waist. I hold her close, pressing my lips against her forehead and wondering what I can say to make this better.

"It's weird, you know... I... I can't decide how to feel." Her voice starts to wobble, and I resign myself to the fact that there will be tears. I will myself to handle them, because she needs to cry right now, and that's okay. "Part of me is relieved that I don't have to deal with pregnancy and motherhood right now, but then that just makes me feel guilty and sad because... I lost my baby." She starts to cry against me, her body shuddering. "I'd finally decided to keep it, to go through with this whole thing. No matter who the father was, I was going to do this. I was gonna be a good mom and do right by this kid."

"I know," I croak, cupping the back of her head and kissing her wet cheek. "You would have been great."

"So, why did I lose it, then?" she whispers.

"Because it wasn't meant to be." My voice is soft and

gravelly. Emotion is clogging my windpipe, making it hard to speak. "Not this one. Not this time."

Her head bobs, so I know she's heard me, but her response is a pitiful cry. I hold her tight, surprised by the sting in my own eyes. Am I fighting tears because I hate seeing her hurting? Or is a small part of me feeling the loss for myself?

Because maybe just for a moment, I had pictured it. Pictured a baby in my arms—how small and delicate it would have been with a fuzz of orange curls and bright blue eyes. Maybe I'd imagined tying skates on their little feet when they were old enough and teaching them how to glide across the ice. Maybe I had dreamed about looking up from the ice and seeing Caroline and our kid waving at me from the corporate box while I got ready to play a heated game of hockey for my pro team.

Maybe I'd dreamed those things.

And maybe they hadn't been as scary as I'd first imagined they would be.

Maybe they'd actually been kinda cool.

CHAPTER 47
CAROLINE

It's been three days since I lost the baby, and I'm now back in my dorm. My parents left last night, and I've spent my day attending classes and finding out everything I have to catch up on. My professors have been very kind and concerned, which makes me think my dad must have contacted each and every one of them to explain the situation. I even got a free pass in one class, so that's been a bit of a relief. I have some major catch-up reading to do this weekend, but that's okay. I don't feel like going out and partying hard.

Everything about my body still feels tender.

Can a heart be bruised?

I shake my head, sitting down on my bed and tucking my feet beneath me. Leilani should be back soon, and Casey said he'd pop over after his workout. He's been the most attentive boyfriend in the world. It's super sweet— and, okay, just a touch smothering, maybe? He's treating me like fractured glass, but I guess I did bleed all over him. That whole incident shook him up big-time, and he's desperate for me to be okay.

Which I am.

I will be.

Once I can get my emotions under control. I'm still swinging from sadness that I lost a baby to pure relief that I can continue down this college path I had planned for myself. I guess it's made me realize that I do want kids one day, though.

I just hope the next one is planned and it sticks. My poor mom had ten miscarriages before finally resigning herself to the fact that she'd never have children of her own. But then she got me. And as much as I'll always think about the fact that I was given away... at least I was given to the most amazing couple on the planet.

Filled with gratitude, I reach for my phone, about to text a check-in with my mom when there's a knock at my door.

Assuming it's Casey, I walk over with a smile that drops the second I open the door.

"Ben." I whisper, my insides clutching until I notice a bouquet of flowers and the apologetic look on his face.

Now my insides are clutching in a different way. Oh crap, he's not trying to woo me or something, is he? The guy's relentless.

"Hi." He lifts the bouquet awkwardly. It's a pretty rainbow of flowers... I don't really know which ones are in there, but it's bright and colorful, and my lips twitch with a grin as I take it.

"Thanks." I look up at him, not really sure what's going to happen next.

This is so awkward.

He fidgets with the zipper of his jacket for a second, then points behind me. "Do you mind if I come in?"

"Oh, uh… yeah, I guess so." I step aside so he can pass me, then turn to face him, leaving the door open.

I'm not sure why.

I'm not afraid of the guy. I don't think he'd hurt me… and he did just bring me flowers for some reason… but if he gets agitated and starts yelling at me again, I want easy access to backup.

Crossing my arms, I cradle the bouquet in the crook of my elbow while clinging to Casey's sweater with my other hand. It's the one I haven't taken off since he gave it to me a couple nights ago. It's huge and soft and smells like him, so yeah… my new favorite piece of clothing.

"How are you feeling?"

"Okay." I nod.

"I heard what happened." He winces. "I'm really sorry you had to go through that."

I shake my head, putting on a brave smile and begging my eyes not to water. He looks so sincere right now. Leilani's right about him being sweet. His eyes are kind—when he's not super pissed at me.

He had a right to be, though. I handled things pretty badly.

His lips curve into a gentle grin as he stares down at me. It's obvious that he thinks I'm pretty, that he still likes me, even after what I did.

Oh crap, he's not going to try and tell me that, is he? Because that would be super awkward.

"I won't stay long. I just wanted to say—"

His words are cut off by a sharp bark from the hallway.

"What the fuck are you doing here?"

Casey thunders down the hallway, barging into my room and coming to stand beside me. He notices the flowers in my hand, and his entire face bunches into a sharp frown before he throws a lethal glare at Ben.

"Get out!" Casey points at the door.

"Fuck off, she said I could come in."

Casey's head jolts back like that's the craziest thing he's ever heard. I open my mouth to explain, but he turns back to Ben with growl.

"We don't want you here."

"One, stop speaking for her." Ben gives him a pointed look. "And two, I don't give a shit what *you* want. I came here to talk to Caroline, and unless she asks me to leave, I'm staying until I've said what I came here to say."

Casey shifts in front of me like a protective wall, actually pushing me behind him.

Ben tips his head back with a groan. "Stop being so fucking protective. I'm not here to hurt her!"

"Last time you saw her, you yelled in her face and made her cry, so if you think for one fucking second that I'm just going to step aside and let you do that again, you are out of your damn mind! You need to leave. Now. Before I put my foot so far up your ass, you'll be choking on your shoelaces."

Ben's eyes narrow as he leans down to get in Casey's face. "Go ahead. Give it a try."

"Okay!" I raise my voice, grabbing Casey's arm and stepping around him. "That is *enough!*" I'm not about to have World War Three erupt in my dorm room. "Just, both of you... stop." I huff, casting a quick glance at Casey before looking up at Ben and lowering my voice. "I appreciate the flowers, and I do actually want to hear what you have to say, so if you can both stop growling at each other and act like civilized human beings, we can get through this."

Casey clenches his jaw, but at least he keeps his mouth shut.

I turn to give Ben my full attention. Casey's hand lands on my lower back, curling around my waist and making it clear who I belong to in this situation.

It's almost funny that my boyfriend is jealous right now. I've never had feelings for Ben. This tall basketball player is a zero threat, yet Casey's acting like he's about to steal me away.

Not wanting to embarrass Ben, I keep the thoughts to myself and look up at him.

The second his eyes meet mine, his expression crumples. "I'm so sorry I yelled at you. I felt like shit as soon as I walked away, but I didn't have the guts to come back and apologize. And then I heard about the miscarriage, and I..." His eyes take on a look of pure agony. "I didn't cause it, did I?"

"What?" I blink, horrified that he would even think that. "No. No, of course not."

My answer doesn't seem to give him much relief. He scrapes his fingers through his hair, his expression drenched in guilt. "I didn't mean to yell at you. I was angry and in shock. I'd only just found out you were pregnant and that it might be mine, but it also might not be... and... I kinda snapped." He winces. "I was hurt and jealous, and... I like you so much, you know? I just wanted you to like me back."

My mouth goes dry for a second, and I have to

swallow before I can find my voice. "It's okay. You had every right to be annoyed. The baby might have been yours, and I should have told you."

He nods.

"I'm sorry." I give him a sad frown. "I handled everything so badly. I never wanted to hurt you."

His mouth twitches like he's trying to give me an understanding smile, but he looks so damn sad right now.

I feel awful.

His crestfallen face is so dejected... and I'm making him feel that way!

He keeps his eyes on me, but raises his chin at Casey. "I guess you've made your choice then, huh?"

Glancing over my shoulder, I gaze at my boyfriend for a second before turning back to Ben. "It's always been him. I should never have slept with you at that party. I was upset that he hadn't called me, and I got drunk and used you to make myself feel better." I cringe. "That is inexcusable, and I am so sorry."

I turn onto the sides of my feet, staring at the flowers, counting colors and petal shapes while I wait for his response.

After a thick, painful beat, he finally sighs. "I'll get over it."

He's so obviously trying to hide how much this all hurts, and I want to wrap him in a hug and comfort him, but I'm not sure how that's gonna fly, so I stay put, glancing at his flowers again before trying to smile at him as kindly as I possibly can.

He really is a sweetheart.

After a glum smile, the poor guy shuffles toward my

door, gripping the edge and turning around one last time. He fires an intense look at Casey. "Treat her right."

My boyfriend pulls me a little closer to his side and nods at the tall basketball player. "I will."

And then Ben slips out of my dorm, and I get this sad sense that I might see him again, but I'm not sure we'll ever talk or do anything more than share the odd, awkward smile.

I don't know why that makes me feel sad.

Maybe it's because I know I hurt him.

Resting my head on Casey's shoulder, I grip the colorful bouquet in my hand, wishing it had the power to take all of this shit away and cheer me up.

CHAPTER 48
CASEY

The air in the room is thick with something... tension or sadness, maybe. Whatever it is, I'm not loving it.

Fucking Ben. Why'd he have to show up and make my girlfriend all sad?

I want to be pissed with him, but a small part of me actually pitied him as he walked out the door. He looked like a dejected giraffe.

"You okay?" I rub my hand up Caroline's back and give her neck a gentle squeeze.

"Yeah, I just feel... bad for him, guilty that I used him like that." She winces and shakes her head. "I was horrible to him." Then she turns and looks at me with those big blue eyes. "I was horrible to *you*. I just screwed this whole thing up so monumentally, and I hate that I hurt people."

She looks about ready to cry, so I pull her closer, squishing the flowers between us.

"Oh." She steps back with a little gasp, then mumbles something about water.

I rest against the edge of her bed while she finds a glass in the bathroom and fills it. She takes her time arranging the flowers and then sets them on the edge of her desk.

I glare at them, hating that Ben thought of something so sweet and romantic. Flowers didn't even occur to me. Shit, he probably is a better choice for her. But she went and chose me. I still don't get why, but I'm pretty determined to be the man she needs right now.

"How's your body feeling today?" I reach out and take her wrist, gently tugging her toward me.

She comes with a sad smile, perching on my lap and looking down at me.

"I'm okay. Still feeling kind of bruised on the inside. Still swinging from relief to guilt to sadness." Her eyes start to glisten as she shrugs, like she's trying not to make a big deal of this.

I kiss her cheek before resting our foreheads together and whispering, "You lost your baby. You're allowed to feel whatever the fuck you want right now."

She lets out a soft, watery laugh, then sniffs.

I lean back to look at her. "So, you'd really decided to keep it, huh?"

"Yeah, my parents were making it sound like a good idea, and then as soon as you told me it was yours no matter what, I had to." She leans back, holding my face and forcing me to look at her. "I couldn't deny the world a boy or girl with your DNA running through their veins. They'd be so talented and good-looking."

I grin, cupping the back of her head and kissing her. "They'd be funny and sweet and smart. So fucking smart."

My answer pleases her, and she drapes her arms over my shoulders, playing with the ends of my hair as she smiles at me. "I know you don't believe this, but you're going to make an amazing father. I just know you are. You'll be funny and adoring and invested." She gives me a smile—the kind that says I love you—and I have to kiss her again. I need her to know the truth now.

Pressing our lips together, I hold her close, desperate for her to feel what's going through me.

I don't deepen the kiss or try to make it anything more than what it is.

Caroline's not allowed to have sex while her body recovers from the miscarriage, but even if that wasn't the case, I wouldn't be pulling those moves right now. I need this kiss to be only that, because I need her to know that she's so much more than my sex buddy.

She's become everything.

Pulling back, I look into her eyes and murmur something I never thought I'd say. "Next time, it'll be ours. There'll be no doubt, because you're mine and I'm yours, and there's no sleeping with random people anymore."

Her beautiful lips pull into a grin. "You want to have a baby with me one day?"

I smile up at her. "Baby, I want to make a family with you. I want to have a whole bunch of kids. They can have your red hair and big blue eyes and those cherry lips." I kiss them again, then pull back to drink in her pretty face before kissing her once more.

She starts to laugh against my lips, and I swipe my tongue inside her mouth for a deeper taste. She's addictive and delicious, so I pull back before my sex-crazed body does something stupid.

She's too hot. That's the problem.

I nearly say that to her, wanting to hear her laughter, but there's something else I gotta say first.

Nerves rattle through me as I move back on the bed, bringing her with me. She straddles my lap, her expression creasing with worry.

"Are you okay?" She runs her fingers through my hair. "You look about ready to pass out." Her lips pull into a resigned smile as she shakes her head. "Hey, it's okay. I know you're just trying to make me feel better with talk of a future family and stuff. We don't have to go there. I know you're not a 'plan ahead' kinda guy. I know the idea of a serious relationship freaks you out. We can take it slow. No stress, okay? For now, I'm yours, and you're mine. We can just leave it at that."

She's giving me an out.

Fuck, that free pass is dangling right in front of me, but...

I swallow, kinda hating that she's summing me up this way, but I've never given her any reason to think otherwise.

I lick my lips and cling to my floundering courage.

"I love you." The words come out deep and gravelly, like I didn't really want to say them.

Shit, I suck at this!

Her lips part, her eyes bulging. This was the last thing she was expecting me to say.

Holding her face, I suck in a breath and say it again. "I love you."

She's still gaping at me, and now she's doing a thick swallow of her own, and I'm starting to worry that she doesn't want me saying this to her. That maybe *she's* not ready.

She told you she loves you, dude.

Yeah, she shouted it at me in desperation. How much did she actually mean it?

My heart's in my throat by the time she finally finds her voice. "Have you ever said that to anyone before?"

"Not like that," I rasp. "You know, all romantic and shit."

Laughter bubbles out of her. It's a soft sound, but her shoulders are shaking as she dips her head.

"What? Why is me loving you funny all of a sudden?"

"It's not." She looks up, her eyes sparkling as she touches my face. "It's wonderful." She looks about ready to cry on me, and I nearly beg her not to, but then she starts to explain before I can. "When I lost the baby, I was worried for a minute that you might not want me anymore. There's nothing tying us together. You don't have any responsibilities. It'd be so easy for you to walk away right now."

The tension in my chest pops, this release flooding through me. Holding her face, I thread my fingers behind her neck and rest my thumbs against her earlobes. "I'm not going anywhere. I want to be with you. No matter what, you're mine. And I love you."

She grins, biting her lip and looking so fucking happy that I want to punch the air with a whoop. "You like me saying that, don't you?"

"I love it." Her lips stretch even wider. "I love *you*."

Fuck, that feels good to hear. I always thought those words came attached with a ball and chain, but right now I'm drinking them in like I'm guzzling a cold beer. I want to hear her say it again, but asking would be so fucking lame, so I go for playful instead.

"That works out well, because... you know..."

"You love me?"

"I do, baby. I really do." Pulling her close, I kiss her again, slow and gentle, taking my sweet time to explore her mouth. Oh man, I'd love to peel back the layers keeping us apart and show her just how much she means to me, but the doctor said no. She needs time to heal, and I'll respect that. Kissing will have to do. Talking, hanging out, just being together... it's enough.

I pull away, swiping my thumb over her glistening lips and drinking her in. "Shit, I really love you." My voice is filled with awe, and I know I've already said it a stupid number of times, but each time the words come out of my mouth, they seem to hold more meaning. The emotion expands inside me even more, and she can see it.

Her eyes start glittering all over again, and she smiles at me like she gets what I'm going through right now.

"I really love you too," she whispers against my mouth, and the buzz in my chest vibrates to a glow that spreads throughout my entire body.

It's happening. I'm turning into a romantic sap like Ethan and Liam.

I'm whipped.

I'm owned.

And fuck if it's not the best feeling in the world.

CHAPTER 49
CAROLINE

My eyes are just drifting shut when the door pops open and Leilani appears. She dumps her bag on her bed and turns to spot me snuggled up beside Casey. He fell asleep about twenty minutes ago, and I'm kind of hoping he stays the whole night. My head resting on his shoulder, his strong arm cradling me against him—it's my happy place.

"Hey," I whisper, waving at her.

She frowns down at us. "I thought you weren't supposed to have sex for another week or so."

I perch up on my elbow, a little put out by her grumpy attitude. What's her problem now? Why is she still upset with me?

"We didn't have sex. We just fell asleep together." I try to keep my voice low so I don't disturb Casey. He admitted that he hasn't been sleeping well this week. School pressure is getting to him, plus he's been really worried about me. Which is so freaking sweet!

I want to tell Lani all that, make her see that I may

have screwed up when it came to the Ben situation, but I've made the right choice.

She crosses her arms, looking small and agitated as she mutters, "Oh. I figured he wouldn't be able to keep his hands off you. Sex seems to be the thing you guys are best at."

I frown at her, nearly snapping, *"What the hell is your problem?"*

But I don't want to get into an argument and risk waking up my boyfriend.

Instead, I take a breath and try to think, *Calm. Just be calm. Go for happy.*

"He told me he loves me." I'm looking at Casey's face when I tell her, because I don't want to see her upper lip curl with disgust or something. But when I risk a glance, she's actually smiling. She has this slightly lost look on her face, and her smile is touched with sadness.

"What? You still don't believe him? Do you think he just said it to make me feel better? Because if you'd been here... if you'd seen his face... you'd know he meant it. He really meant it, Lani."

She nods, her smile growing wider, but I can see how much effort it's taking on her part.

"Why don't you like him? Why don't you want me to be with the guy I love?"

"I do." She holds up her hands like two white flags. "I'm happy for you. Really, I am."

"You don't look it." I don't bother hiding my disappointment. I so want her support on this. Casey's going to be around a lot more now, and it'll suck if she's being icy every time he walks into the room.

"I am happy for you, Cinny. I promise."

"Then what's the matter?" I study her face, desperate for any clue she can give me.

But her expression shuts down, her face going blank as she looks at the floor and mutters, "Nothing. I'm fine."

"You don't sound fine."

"I am." She gives me a pointed look, like she's daring me to question her.

"Lani." I soften my voice. "I'm your best friend. You can tell me anything."

She shakes her head, closing her eyes and looking sick. "I'm okay. I... I don't want to talk. I just..." She clears her throat, pulling her shoulders back and lifting her chin. "I'm fine."

"You're not fine," I softly argue. "And I want to help."

Her eyes are glistening when she finally lets me catch her eye. "You can't help me with this."

"But—"

"Please don't ask me." She smiles, but it's so forced and bright, it looks deranged. "I have to do this on my own, and you forcing me to talk about it will only make it worse."

"But I want to help you. I'm worried."

"Don't be." The spark in her eyes is fierce. "I'm strong, and nothing can beat me. Come on, you know that."

"I do." I nod, happy to see her old spark back for a moment.

Unfortunately, it's only a moment. The second she thinks I'm not looking, her lips dip into a frown once more and she's shuffling toward the door.

"I forgot my..." She points over her shoulder. "I'll see you later."

"But—"

The door clicks shut, and with an unhappy sigh, I nestle back down against Casey, worry coursing through me.

Replaying the conversation in my head, I try to figure out what might be eating at Leilani and wishing she'd let me in. But I know her. She doesn't share stuff until she's ready, and even then, she's a very private person. She always wants to deal with her shit in her own way and in her own time.

But whatever's got the better of her now seems too big for her to handle on her own.

Closing my eyes, I whisper a prayer, hoping she'll let me in before she digs herself into a hole so deep, she can't get out of it.

CHAPTER 50
CASEY

It's been two weeks since I told Caroline I love her. I still reel a little every time I think it, but it's becoming more natural and easier to say. I find I mean it just as much as I did the day before, and no ball and chain has appeared in my life. Every morning I wake up, my ankle is shackle-free whether Caroline's lying next to me or not.

We've spent as many nights as we can together, including a wicked weekend in Denver where a whole bunch of us crashed at Ethan's dad's place for two nights. We went into town, danced our asses off, and enjoyed some liquor. Ethan's dad played Mr. Uber, and it was the best.

Oh, except for the fact that Asher drew short straw and had to drive Leilani back one night early because she was adamant that she had a test she had to study for. Caroline wasn't sure if she believed her or not, but the fact that we got her to come at all was a miracle, so she didn't want to push it.

Caroline's been trying to get the truth out of Lani, but

all she's managed so far is getting her tight-lipped friend to join in on a few things. She's really hoping that will help, but the fact that she bailed early on the Denver trip was a total bummer.

We thought she'd been having fun. She joined in a few laughs with us, did some line dancing at the club we went to, and even beat our asses in a game of poker. But a few minutes after the girls came back from their spa session, Lani started packing her things and saying she needed to go.

In the end, Asher gave me the darkest look known to man while he opened the door for Leilani. She sat in the back seat like he was her chauffeur or something. As he stalked around the car, he muttered, "You owe me so fucking big, man."

I thanked him with a kiss on the cheek, which he made a big show of wiping off before giving us all the finger and getting behind the wheel.

The rest of us spent the night imagining just how painful the car ride must have been and cracking up over Asher and Leilani's misery.

Caroline felt really bad about it in the morning, though, and has been working overtime trying to make it up to her best friend. Leilani told her it was fine and to stop working so hard. Actually, she kind of yelled it.

"I'm good, okay? Just leave me alone!"

So yeah, things aren't going great in that department.

As for Asher, he's still giving me the icy stare-downs when I see him, and he hasn't told me shit about the drive, so I'm guessing it sucked.

Oh yeah, and he's also super pissed with me over a surprise I've arranged for Caroline. Yes, I probably should have asked him about it first since it's happening in his uncle's house, but I knew he'd say no, and it's easier to ask for forgiveness than permission, right?

My belly jumps and pinches as I walk up our front steps.

Caroline's already here. She texted me a few minutes ago, and I told her to wait in the living room.

"Did you get it?" Rachel meets me in the entryway, her face alight with excitement.

I hold up the box and grin.

She lets out a soft squeal, and I have to shush her. "Don't give it away."

"I won't, but just give it to her right now because I have to see her face."

"Okay, okay," I whisper, holding up my hand to calm her down.

Walking into the living room, I spot Mikayla and Caroline playing *Just Dance* and have to pause for a minute to watch her, because she's so fucking gorgeous and she's all mine. Her red curls bounce as she jumps and spins, her laughter filling the space as she beats Mikayla.

"Ugh!" Mikayla tips her head back. "We have to go again."

"Nope, she's mine." I step into the room. "I need to talk to her; you guys can dance later."

"Okay, fine." Mikayla gives me a pointed look, but once her back is turned to Caroline, her smile grows huge, her eyes sparkling just as brightly as Rachel's did.

I tip my head, ushering her away while Caroline looks at me like she knows I'm up to something.

Crossing her arms, she tips her head with narrowed eyes. "What's going on?"

"I have a surprise for you."

"O-kay."

"Sit." I point at the couch, resting the box next to it.

Taking a seat opposite her, I take her hands and study her expression closely. Hopefully I've done the right thing. Hopefully she wants to have this as much as I want to give it to her.

"I bought you something."

"Aw." She squeezes my hand. "Why do you look so nervous about giving it to me?"

"Because I really want you to want it."

Rachel makes a little squeak from the doorway, and I whip around to bulge my eyes at her.

"Sorry," she whispers, raising her hand and moving out of the room.

Caroline starts to laugh. "Casey, you're starting to freak me out. What'd you get me?"

"Okay." I sigh. "Look, I know it's a big commitment, and if you're really not ready, you can say no."

Her eyebrows dip together. "Are you about to propose or something?"

"No." I laugh out the word. "Baby, come on..."

"Well, what, then?"

Biting my bottom lip, I check her expression one last time before reaching back for the box and carefully opening the lid. "I bought us a puppy."

She gasps, quickly checking the box like I might be bullshitting her.

But nope, there, nestled in a fluffy blanket, is a sleeping ball of fur.

"You bought us a puppy?" Her voice is so high and squeaky, it wakes the dog.

The little guy jumps to his feet, letting out a squawk before trying to climb out of the box.

"It's a shih tzu something. They're not really sure exactly what he's made of, but there's definitely shih tzu in there. I picked him up from the pound. A whole litter was left there six weeks ago, and they've been adopting them out. I saw this little dude and couldn't resist."

"Aw, hello, little one." Caroline reaches for him, her eyes alight and beautiful as she greets him, kissing his face and letting him lick the tip of her nose. "I love him." She gives me a swooning smile and holds him close, kissing the top of his head. "Does he have a name?"

"I figured that could be your job."

She holds him out, studying his face and the little patch of white on his forehead while he wiggles and squirms. "How about Goliath?"

"He's tiny." I laugh.

"I know, that's what makes it funny."

Damn, I love this woman.

"I mean, it doesn't have to be Goliath, but it'd be hilarious to pick a name of a really huge character, like..." She pulls him close, nestling him against her chest. "Who's the giant from *The Princess Bride*?"

"Fezzik." I used to watch that movie all the time when I was a kid. I grin, scratching between the dog's ears. "I like it. Let's go with Fezzik."

She gives me a loving smile before holding the puppy out. "Hey, Fezzik. Welcome to the family, kiddo."

"Yay!" Rachel can no longer contain herself and rushes into the room, taking a seat beside Caroline so they can swoon over the puppy together. Mikayla soon gets in on the action, and I'm shunted out of the way so the girls can fawn over the new man in their lives.

I stand back with a frown, crossing my arms and watching them until Ethan and Liam flank me.

"Dude, what did you do?" Ethan shakes his head.

"Come on." I nudge him with my elbow. "Look how happy she is."

"Puppies are a lot of work," Liam murmurs.

I turn to him with a grin. "That's okay. All of you guys are here to help me."

"I didn't sign up for that." He shakes his head.

"Looks like your woman doesn't mind." I grin. "I'm guessing she'll be over here a lot more wanting to hang with the new man in this house."

"So, that's why you bought it? As a chick magnet?" Ethan raises his eyebrows at me.

"I don't need a chick magnet. I've got myself a woman. A woman who is now very happy because I bought her a damn puppy."

"Hey, don't say 'damn' in front of the kid." Caroline frowns at me.

A loud laugh bursts out of Ethan as he slaps my shoulder. "Oh, you have no idea what you've gotten yourself into, dude."

I watch him walk into the kitchen, still cracking up, before turning back to the couch. Caroline is grinning at me, and I tip my head toward the stairs. "Wanna see his setup? I've got him a bed and everything."

"Okay." She jumps up, taking the dog from Rachel and carrying him upstairs. He's making these cute little squeaks, and I'm pretty sure my heart is turning to putty on the spot.

Caroline is so fucking happy right now, and our little guy is all kinds of adorable.

I don't care what the guys say, we're gonna be great doggy parents.

People might call me stupid for launching into something like this so quickly, but I know without a doubt that Caroline's my woman for life. I might not be proposing to her right now, but I'm showing her that I'm not afraid to be a one-woman guy anymore, that we can handle raising a dog together, and one day... maybe we can raise some kids too.

Fuck, I never thought I'd be the kind of guy to think that way, but she's given me the courage to believe it's possible.

The day she told me she was pregnant, I thought my life was over.

I didn't realize it was only just beginning.

CHAPTER 51
ASHER

A shih tzu mutt. A fucking shih tzu mutt in my house!

Well, my uncle's house, which only makes it worse. Casey hasn't even given me a chance to ask for permission, and I have no idea if Uncle Hayes and Aunt Carla are good with pets in their rental properties. I hope to God they are, because Casey ain't giving that puppy up without a fight, and as much as that inconsiderate fuck pisses me off, I don't want to lose him from Hockey House.

And we can't lose Hockey House. Not that my aunt and uncle would kick us out, but still. This place is sweet. The fact that we get to live here for free is insanely nice of them, and I don't want to do anything to fracture the awesome deal we've got going here.

Stalking into my office, I flick the door shut behind me with a growl. Caroline and Casey are probably in their room by now, settling the puppy into his new bed and no doubt getting it on. Casey was giddy last night because Caroline can finally do it again.

I roll my eyes, shaking my head at my sex-obsessed friend. I never thought he'd get serious with anyone, but she caught him hook, line, and sinker. And now they have a puppy together.

What the fuck is the world coming to?

Flopping onto the couch, I stare at my shelves of comic books, all neatly packaged in case I ever want to sell or trade them one day. Everything about this space is neat. It's the only place in the house that is. Oh, and my bedroom, of course. They're the two rooms I have full control over, and I guard that shit with my life. I love my hockey bros, but they can be total slobs. At least in this space, I'm safe, you know?

My eyes land on the cardboard coaster on the coffee table, and suddenly that safe feeling goes away, replaced with an intense gnawing that I don't know what to do with. Snatching it, I rub my thumb over the beer stain along the edge, wondering why the hell I even kept this.

You know why.

"Fuck," I mutter, dipping my head and trying not to think about last weekend.

Trying and failing.

———————

Last weekend...

"Please, man. Please." Casey gripped my shirt, glancing over his shoulder to eye up his girlfriend. "She's having such a good time, and I want to give her one more night. You've seen how happy she's been." His desperate expression made my resolve crumble, and I hated myself in that moment.

"I can't believe you're asking me to do this," I groused.

"You're taking one for the team, and we all love you for it."

I glared at him, then tried to turn my expression to neutral as Leilani walked out of Mr. Galloway's house with her brown leather tote. She spotted me waiting by the car, and her expression turned instantly icy. I gave her a pointed eye bulge, and she looked about ready to snarl at me.

Stalking over to Caroline, she started up a snippy-looking conversation. It looked like the female version of what Casey and I were doing, and I gritted my teeth, about ready to punch Casey if he opened his mouth and tried to say anything else to me.

Like I hadn't been having a good time in Denver too?

Like I wanted to leave early?

But Leilani was determined to get back to Nolan U, and when everyone refused her a ride and she said she'd take the bus, I just couldn't let that happen. The look on her face... the way her lip wobbled... my stupid mouth opened before I could stop it. "I'll take you back."

I'm such a fucking idiot.

She basically refused on the spot, until Caroline and Rachel went to bat for me. Even Mikayla told me I was sweet for helping her out. She also went on her tiptoes and whispered in my ear, "You're doing us all a favor."

And maybe that was another reason I stepped up, because I wanted my friends to enjoy the rest of their time away. Caroline had dragged Leilani along, and the Hawaiian beauty had done nothing but bitch and moan or sit there with a sulky frown. I mean, yeah, she smiled a little during poker, and I guess she laughed once or twice throughout the weekend, but it was so fucking rare, you can barely count it. I seriously have no idea how she can be best friends with such an effervescent person like Caroline. They don't fit at all... although I did hear Caroline telling Casey that something was really wrong with Leilani, and she wished she could figure it out.

"She's changed, Case, and I'm really worried about her. I've tried to get her to open up, but it seems to be driving her further into her shell. I don't know what to do. I thought this weekend might lighten her up a bit, but she seems worse than ever."

The introvert in me understood how being around a bunch of people could drive Leilani a little loopy, and I wondered if she was like that too... and maybe even more extra than me.

Which is possibly another reason why I agreed to drive her home a day early.

And after a heated debate that insulted me on myriad levels, she finally gave in with a huff. "Okay, fine! He can drive me!" And she stormed out of the room to get her stuff.

Stopping by my car, she looked up at me with a pointed glare and zero appreciation. Then her eyes darted to my hand on the car door, and she suddenly looked nervous as hell.

I rolled my eyes. What did she think I was going to do? Kidnap her? Drive her off to some undisclosed location to have my way with her?

She might be stunningly beautiful, but I was pretty sure she had titanium claws that would appear without warning and rip me to shreds. Plus, she'd drive any captor to the brink of insanity with her snarky little quips.

I wasn't a complete idiot. I was driving the woman to her dorm, then bailing as fast as I could.

Her eyes darted to the passenger door, and she swallowed before lifting her chin with this haughty bravado and curling her upper lip, like sitting next to me for the entire ride home would be pure purgatory.

I rolled my eyes again and moved to the back door. "If the idea of sitting next to me is so repulsive, then park your ass in the backseat." I yanked the door open, and she fucking took me up on my offer.

I gave her an incredulous look, which she stared down with the iciest glare ever given to anyone ever before slamming the door shut.

As I walked around the car, I growled in Casey's face, "You owe me so fucking big, man."

He thanked me with a kiss on the cheek, which I wiped off before giving every one of them the finger and jumping behind the wheel.

I could hear Casey laughing just before I slammed the door shut.

Gripping the wheel, I looked in the rearview mirror and stared at Leilani huddled against the door, her seat belt on and her arms crossed tightly over her chest. There was a deep scowl on her pretty face, and I started the engine with a sense of dread.

Let the nightmare begin.

At least I thought it would be a nightmare, but then it wasn't. It was everything I didn't expect...

I shake my head, reliving that out-of-control kiss and then the aftermath.

With a wince, I shake my head, still trying to figure her out. I wish I knew what the fuck was going on with her and why I can't stop thinking about that infuriating, stunning, intelligent, mercurial woman. Seriously, she's gonna be the death of me. And there's no way I can just avoid her and forget the whole thing, because she's Caroline's best friend. I'm gonna see her again. It's inevitable.

And then what the fuck am I gonna do?

Find out exactly what happened during Asher and Leilani's trip home from Denver and how these two enemies are destined to become lovers... no matter how hard they want to fight it.

THE LOVE PENALTY is releasing in May 2024. Keep an eye on Katy's social media for the release announcement.

Thank you so much for reading *The Game Changer*. Casey has been a favorite of mine from the outset, and I knew Caroline would be his perfect partner. I can already picture their life together, and it's going to be chaotic, crazy, loud, and fun. You'll get a little snapshot in the Nolan U Hockey Epilogue (coming out Sept/Oct 2024)

They're a totally different couple to what Asher and Leilani will be, but bring on a little enemies-to-lovers, right? There's nothing like a steamy-hot couple who think they hate each other but can't resist their attraction either. Can Asher break through Leilani's walls and find out what's eating at her? And can she find the courage to trust him with the truth about what happened?

If you're after a book that will make you laugh, swoon, cry, and sizzle, then *THE LOVE PENALTY* is just for you.

———

Now, there's one more scene I couldn't fit into the book, so I thought I'd give you a little bonus. Keep reading to discover the story behind Caroline's tattoo...

BONUS EPILOGUE

The flow and pace of a story is really important and sometimes you can't fit everything in. When you have to edit out, or can't find the right space, for all the stuff you want, it can hurt the heart a little. So, I thought I'd give you a little extra scene.

If you're anything like me, you can't get enough of Casey and his sweet Caroline, so enjoy just a touch more.

Happy reading!

xoxo
Katy

CASEY

This dog is going to drive me fucking nuts. Yeah, sure, he's adorable and everything but he pees everywhere, whines and snores in his sleep and yesterday, I don't know what the fuck was in his food, but he went psycho, running around the house and barking like he'd just been streamlining cocaine.

Thankfully Asher wasn't home and Baxter and me managed to catch the little speedster and take him for a walk.

Just quietly, I think Baxter's more in love with Fezzik than I am. Our weird-ass goalie with his quiet looks and hermit behavior is a closet animal lover. It's hilarious. He's allergic to people, but when it comes to this little Shih Tzu, he can't get enough. And Fezzik knows it. He's got the guy wrapped around his little paw.

Kind of works out well for me, actually, because Fezzik is currently napping in the Bax-Man's cave, which means I can go down on my woman without interruption.

She lets out a soft gasp as I lick her wet folds, then suck on her clit.

"That feels so good," she groans, scraping her fingers through my hair.

I curl my hands around her legs, licking my personal wet dream like an ice cream cone and loving every second of her pleasure-filled writhing.

I've been with her enough times now to sense the orgasm rising within her. My lips twitch with a grin as I lay my tongue flat over her clit then tickle her folds with my fingers.

"Oh shit," she gasps, her voice all breathy as she lets

out a series of sweet moans, then starts to splinter in my arms.

Her hips arch and I rise with her, holding her ass cheeks while she buries her head in my pillow and moans.

Damn, she's so fucking beautiful.

Mr. Jones is ready for action, forcing my hips forward as she starts to recover.

"Can I, baby?" I quickly ask, already reaching for a condom.

"That'd be a *fuck yeah*!" Her voice is muffled by the pillow and I laugh, rolling the condom on and double-checking it's secure.

Her body flops back to the bed and she finally turns to grin up at me.

"How'd you want your Casey lovin', cherry girl?"

She bites her lips, making my dick twitch with antici-pation, then with a soft giggle turns on her side, lifting her left leg up to her chest.

I kneel down behind her, rubbing my hand over the perfect curve of her hip, before lining Mr. Jones up. Her slippery wet folds entice him in, making it impossible not to start this off with a deep, firm thrust.

"Ahhh." She lets out that cry I love so much. It's excited ecstasy and fuck if I'm not feeling the same. Her hot core wraps me like a glove and then she goes and lowers her leg, tightening her grip on me and heightening this already cosmic sensation.

"Baby, I love you so fucking much," I rasp, using her hip as an anchor and setting a pace that suits us both.

I get lost in it, floating out of time and place while this heady rush sends me over the edge. Gripping her hip, I go even faster, plunging deep and hard, the way she likes it.

Halfway through, she turns onto her stomach and soon I'm kneeling behind her, gripping those luscious ass cheeks and coming home with a blinding orgasm.

"Fuck. Fuck, baby, I'm coming."

"Yes," she purrs, thrusting her ass back further until I'm balls deep in my woman and the happiest guy on the planet. Mr. Jones twitches and jerks, releasing cum with celebratory fireworks. I can hear them popping in the back of my brain and let out a deep laugh. It rumbles in my chest as Caroline's hips drop, so she's lying flat.

I go with her, still tucked up tight in her pussy while she sighs happily in the pillow. Taking the weight on my elbows, I try not to squash her as I nuzzle her cheek, then brush my nose across her face and lightly kiss her ear. "You're the best. A solid twelve, every time."

"I'm working my way up to a thirteen." Her eyes pop open and she grins at me.

CAROLINE

Casey's laughter is the best sound in the world. I so needed to hear it this afternoon. I so needed to be with him in this way.

Exams are just around the corner and it's stressing me out. Not to mention all the other stuff going on at Hockey House. Asher and Lani's dramas have certainly affected us all.

But in two weeks, exams will be over and it'll be

summer break. A chance to spend some time with my family and Casey. I think I've managed to convince him to come with us to the lake house for a long weekend. Dad is definitely warming to him, although it takes time to defrost an Arctic blast.

Fezzik is a nice ice-breaker, though. Mom is so in love with the little cutie and that makes Dad happy.

Casey pulls out of me and I let out a little whimper. I always hate it when he leaves. Yes, I know how impractical it would be to go around with him permanently living in my v-jay, but it feels so damn good every time he comes to visit.

"Thanks for coming." I roll over with a playful wink and he grins over his shoulder at me.

After a quick clean up, he's resting on his side, gazing down at my body while I study his various tattoos. I brush my finger over the red heart on his wrist while he circles the mirror image on my hip.

"You ever going to tell me the story behind this?" He bends down and kisses it.

I sit up on my elbows, my boobs swaying as I peer at the tattoo on my skin. That's right. The last time he asked, I was kinda pissed off with him and he hasn't asked again.

Turning to him with a soft grin, I kiss his lips, then finally give in. He loves me now, right? I'm his and he's mine.

"Well..." I clear my throat and nestle my head back on his pillow. "About four years ago, I got hit with this serious sense of abandonment and suddenly became obsessed with finding my birth parents. I wanted to know where I came from and why they didn't want me." I wrinkle my nose, the old pain firing through me. "I didn't tell anyone. I was sixteen by then and I didn't want to hurt my parents' feelings, so I did my best to find out what I could. It took months, but eventually I managed to track down someone who was willing to tell me what they could. It was through the adoption agency, I think." I shake my head, fuzzy on the exact details. All I can really remember are the feelings associated with it. That deep sense of rejection when the lady sat across the desk and gave me a sad smile...

"I'm sorry, honey. She doesn't want to be contacted. And I can't find your father." She placed an envelope on the desk. *"I'm not technically supposed to do this, but here is a little history about her. No names or anything, but her age when she had you, her height, weight, hair color."*

"She was a redhead?" I had to ask.

The woman shook her head. "Blonde."

"Oh." I swallowed, lamenting the fact that I couldn't even share that. I had no connections to where I'd come from.

It killed me in ways I didn't expect, but I ran out of that office, leaving the envelope behind.

"Anyway, it didn't work out how I'd hoped." I skim the memory, getting to the good part. "Dad found me in a Denny's." I let out a humorless laugh. "I'd been due home hours before and he was worried sick about me. But I couldn't go back until I'd stopped crying and every time I went to leave, the tears would start all over again. So, I just sat playing Solitaire on my phone and ignoring their texts and calls." I sniff, my mind jumping back there with a clarity that surprises me. "When I saw him, I thought he was going to yell at me for being so inconsiderate, but he just took a seat beside me, wrapped his arm around my shoulders and asked if I needed to talk.

"I didn't want to, but the words spilled right out of me. I blubbered away, never taking my eyes of the game I was playing. Never stopping. When I was done he let out this soft sigh and kissed the side of my head."

"Those two may not have wanted you, baby girl. But your mom and me... we couldn't wait to meet you and hold you and bring you home. You were only two weeks old when we met you. The hospital had been taking care of you until we could get there. The second we saw you through the glass..." He grinned, his eyes starting to shimmer. "That little tuft of red hair..." His voice wobbled and he kissed my forehead again. "I knew you were going to own my heart forever. You're my little Queen of Hearts, Cinnamon. And you always will be."

He squeezed me tight and I finally found the courage to inch my way out of the booth and go home.

I wrap up the story with a soft sniff while Casey brushes his thumb over the tattoo. "I thought I didn't belong to anyone, but I've always belonged to them."

"And now you belong to me." His eyes are glassy as he gifts me a tender smile, then moves his wrist so our tattoos are kissing each other.

A soft silence settles between us until his eyebrows pucker and he gives me a freaked out frown. "It's not weird that your dad and I both think you're the Queen of Hearts, right?"

"Ew." I shove his shoulder. "Don't make it gross."

"I'm just checking."

I tip my head back with a groan and quickly clarify.

"I'm my daddy's queen of hearts in that cute, lovable, puppy dog kind of way." I push him onto his back and straddle him. Resting my hands on either side of his head, I give him a playful smirk. "And I'm your queen of hearts in that red rose, saucy, romantic kind of way."

"I can deal with that." He grins, running his hand up my neck and cupping the back of my head. Pulling me down, he brushes our lips together, then whispers, "You own my heart, cherry girl. My sweet Caroline."

I start humming the tune into his mouth, laughing when he pulls away to sing, "Dun-dun-dah!" then rolls me onto my back and starts nibbling his way down my body until he's kissing that red heart on my hip and telling me that I'll own his heart forever too.

I hope you enjoyed that 🩶

I'll be back with more goodies from Hockey House very soon!

NOTE FROM KATY

Dear reader,

Thank you for reading Caroline and Casey's romance. I had SO much fun with this one. I knew Casey had to go through something huge in order to change his trajectory in life, and Caroline was the perfect girl to do this for him.

I stressed a little that readers might be mad with me over how things played out with the miscarriage, but the story needed me to take that path. And I know for a fact that Caroline and Casey are going to have a big family one day. You'll see a little snapshot of this in the epilogue novel that's coming out later this year. Watching Casey be a dad, melts my heart like ice cream on a summer's day.

Next up is Leilani and Asher's enemies-to-lovers romance. It's fiery and passionate and heartbreaking and beautiful. It deals with some heavier topics, the way *The*

Heart Stealer did, but there will still be moments of lightness and laughter. Plus, there so many swoon-worthy acts of bravery from Asher and so much found family goodness, that I can't wait for you to read it!

If you enjoyed *The Game Changer*, I would so appreciate you leaving an honest review on Goodreads. Even just a star rating is helpful. You don't have to write anything if you don't want to. But star ratings and even short reviews really help validate the book, letting readers know it's worth a shot. It also tells Goodreads that this book is worth shining a spotlight on. I know there are a bunch of readers out there who love college sports romance just as much as we do. If you can help me reach them, then that would be freaking fantastic. Thanks for the assist!

I'd also like to thank a few key people who have been instrumental in helping me prepare and release this book —Megan, Kristin, Beth, Rachael, Meredith, Melissa. Working with you guys is so freaking cool. I'm honored and privileged to have your support. You're so loyal and helpful and wonderful to be around. I love you guys.

My review team—I love interacting with you and so appreciate your love for these books. I couldn't do this without you!

My readers—wow! Like seriously, wow! You are the bestest! Thank you for reading these books. Thank you for gushing over them. Thank you for the lovely emails which seriously make my day. I keep them all and cherish every kind work. Thanks for blowing me away with your generosity.

My first love—thank you for seeing me. Thank you for wanting me. Thank you for loving me always. I am yours and you are mine. Forever.

xoxo
Katy

BOOKS BY KATY ARCHER

NOLAN U HOCKEY

Hockey House V-cards (prequel)
The Forbidden Freshman
The Heart Stealer
The Game Changer

...Also coming out in 2024...
The Love Penalty
Baxter's V-Card story (Title TBC)
Hockey House Epilogue Novel (Title TBC)

NOLAN U FOOTBALL

In development

NOLAN U BASKETBALL

In development

CONTACT KATY

I love to hear from my readers, so feel free to email me anytime. You can also find out more on my website.

EMAIL: katy@katyarcher.com

WEBSITE: www.katyarcher.com

And if you want to connect with me on social and see pretty reels and teasers from the books, you can find me Addicted to College Sports Romance on...

INSTAGRAM
@addictedtocollegesportsromance

FACEBOOK
@collegesportsromancebooks

TIKTOK
@katyarcherauthor

Made in the USA
Monee, IL
20 July 2024

62383233R00236